TILT A WHIRL

CHRIS GRABENSTEIN

CARROLL & GRAF PUBLISHERS

NEW YORK

Carroll & Graf Publishers
An Imprint of Avalon Publishing Group, Inc.
245 West 17th Street, 11th floor
New York, NY 10011

AVALON
publishing group incorporated

Library of Congress Cataloging-in-Publication Data is available.

ISBN-13: 978-0-78671-781-1
ISBN-10: 0-78671-781-5

9 8 7 6 5 4 3 2 1

Printed in the United States of America
Interior design by Jamie McNeely
Distributed by Publishers Group West

For Jennifer

Because of Dave, Dylan,
and all the guys who rush in when
everyone else is rushing out.

Acknowledgments

I want to thank Eric Myers for his faith and encouragement, Don Weise for making this real, Michele Slung for making it better, and Bruce Springsteen for lending me his words.

I am eternally grateful to all my "First Readers" and cheerleaders: J. J. (the first of the first), Kathy & David, Tami, Sue L., Hugh & Susan, Jen S., Betsy & Dan, Beth & John, Brian McC, Charlene & K, Elyssa & Billy, Ronny & Lianne, Buffy & Dawg, Jennifer G, Mom, and Scout. I also appreciate the early criticism and guidance given by Grace F. Edwards and all the members of the Fiction Workshop at the Writing Center of Marymount Manhattan College.

I would be remiss if I forgot to thank Buster, my faithful companion of thirteen years, who always gives me time to dream up stories while he takes me for a walk. And Jeanette. She sat on my lap purring through most of the typing.

ONE

Some guys have a code they live by, some guys don't.

John Ceepak? He has a code.

Me? No code. Not unless you count my ZIP code or something.

I took this job because I'm twenty-four and Sea Haven is, as you might've guessed, a sunny haven situated by the side of the sea—an eighteen-mile-long barrier island crammed with motels and beach houses and bait shacks and ice cream shops called stuff like "Do Me A Flavor" and the "Scoop Sloop."

Tourists come here to soak up the sun, lick down orange-and-white swirl cones, and bury each other neck-deep in hot sand. My hometown is best pictured on one of those perky placemat maps dotted with squiggly cartoons of buildings like The Shore Store, Santa's Sea Shanty, and King Putt Golf.

It's Saturday in Sea Haven.

I pull into the parking lot outside The Pancake Palace at 7:30 A.M. When I was in high school, I worked here as a busboy. Now I'm what they call a summer cop. I help out during the muggy months when the population of Sea Haven, New Jersey, quadruples and then quintuples

1

and then you need a plastic pass pinned to your swim trunks to even think about walking on the beach.

I swing the customized Ford Explorer into a parking spot near the newspaper dispensers at the side door. The Ford is white with tropical turquoise and hot pink lettering to let everybody know we're cops with a beachy kind of 'tude.

Inside, the restaurant isn't very crowded. Saturday is changeover day. People who rented last week are leaving, people renting this week will show up later, after the maid brigades have vacuumed the sandy floors and tossed out the abandoned seashell collections. This morning, I see mostly locals eating sensible stuff like eggs and toast, cereal and muffins. It's the tourists and day-trippers who go for the specials—chocolate chip French toast, Coco-Loco Pancakes, and a little something I like to call The Heart Stopper: a waffle, with crispy bits of bacon baked right into the batter, topped with two scoops of butter and a fluffy igloo of whipped cream.

Like the T-shirt says: "My diet's on vacation, too!"

Ceepak meets me here at The Pancake Palace every morning at 0730. He likes to use that Army clock lingo. We've met here every morning since he joined the force back in May.

John Ceepak doesn't like to drive.

Apparently, something happened while he was soldiering with the 101st Airborne over in Iraq that put him off driving for good. I'm not sure what, because he's never told me about "the sandbox." Usually he just tells me where to turn left, where to park, stuff like that.

Sometimes, we talk Springsteen. Ceepak digs The Boss and knows all the lyrics to all his songs, even the ones nobody else listens to like that "Ghost of Tom Joad" song. Ceepak can quote "Tom Joad."

We hook up here in The Pancake Palace because it's close to Ceepak's apartment—a one-bedroom job situated over The Bagel Lagoon, a block up the street at 102 Ocean Avenue. Ceepak never orders bagels for breakfast. Guess he sees enough at home. He usually orders bran flakes and, if he's feeling frisky, some kind of fruit to plop on top. I'm not sure, but I think bran is part of The Code.

I've only known Ceepak a couple months, but I know one thing for sure: He's basically been a "good guy" all his life.

He just finished a thirteen-year stint with the Army, ending with Operation Iraqi Freedom. He was Military Police, the guys with the MP patches on their shoulders. That's where Ceepak met our boss, Chief Cosgrove. They served together in Germany seven or eight years back and that's how Ceepak swung this cushy "no-driving" deal. His old army buddy gave him a new job *and* a personal chauffeur. Me. I may be part-time, but I know which side of the Ford the gas tank is on.

Before the Army, Ceepak told me he studied criminology. Before that, he was an Eagle Scout. Before that? I'm not sure, but I'll bet he was one helluva hall monitor in kindergarten. This is his first civilian cop job. He told the local newspaper "he loves being on the job in Sea Haven" because he can "help visiting children safely enjoy wholesome family fun."

Okay. Fine.

I like working here too. Mostly because we get to wear cargo shorts and baseball caps and a polo shirt with the police patch sewn on the chest. Ceepak carries a gun; I don't, which is fine by me—as long as I get the baseball cap. Chicks dig the cop cap.

Don't get me wrong—I want kids to have fun, too, but I'm more interested in the college kids who hang out on the boardwalk and the young babes I meet over oysters and brewskis down at The Sand Bar.

Ceepak is a cop 24/7. He spends his spare time reading about forensics and what he calls "interesting cases." I know he has cable TV because he's always telling me about these shows he watches where blood-splatter patterns and grass clippings and DNA solve crimes. Last weekend, some friends and me were heading down to The Sand Bar and I invited Ceepak to come along.

"Can't," he said.

Turns out, *The FBI Files* comes on the Discovery Channel Saturdays at 9 P.M.

"It's an episode called 'Shattered Shield,'" Ceepak said. "Sure, it's a summer rerun, but I'd like to catch it again. I missed a few details the first time. . . ."

I don't think I'll be asking Ceepak out for a bucket of beers again any time soon.

Ceepak is sitting in a booth near the big glass windows up front in The Pancake Palace. He likes to feel the sun warm his face while he eats breakfast and that's where the sun likes to sit at 7:30.

He waves at me, like I don't know it's him or where he might be sitting. He sits at the same table every morning.

Ceepak is hard to miss. He's big—about six-two. I figure he must be thirty or thirty-five, but he has this baby face and a big boyish grin. He even has dimples. When he's not on duty or watching the tube, he's down at the gym. I don't think he's taking yoga or Pilates classes. He's probably flinging hundred-pound dumbbells up over his head— pumping up his biceps and triceps and all those other "cep" muscles I don't even know if I have. The police shirt clings and bulges on his chest. It just sort of hangs on me.

Ceepak keeps his hair looking pretty military. It's razor-tight around the ears, but he lets it go hog-wild on top: it's at least an inch or two long up there with a cowlick flip in the front that adds to his whole Baby Huey look.

He doesn't wear the uniform shorts, prefers the cargo pants. More pockets to carry stuff in. And he likes the official navy blue windbreaker: it has SEA HAVEN POLICE stenciled across the back in big yellow letters, just like the FBI or the DEA or the cops on *Cops*.

"Morning, Danny," he says, as sunny as the booth he's sitting in. "How's it going this fine day?"

"Fine."

"Awesome. I ordered your coffee. Black, per usual."

"Thanks."

I don't have much besides coffee at breakfast. I'm usually lugging around the chicken wings or mozzarella sticks or raw oysters I ate the night before.

Most of the booths and tables near us are filled with local shopkeepers fueling up for another day of selling trinkets and taffy. But there are a few tourist families scattered here and there — the ones with hyper kids who'd never let mom and dad sleep in on a Saturday, changeover day or not. The ones who fling their forks at each other and topple sippy cups and steal their sister's crayons so they can color in the maze on the Kidz Menu and help Princess Griddlecakes escape from Margarine Mountain.

At least that's who's sitting in the booth next to ours.

Behind Ceepak's head, I see two monsters bouncing up and down on the banquette, a boy and girl standing so they can pour syrup out of sticky bottles and soak their plates three feet below. I think they're playing airplane.

I anticipate a sugar-rush hurricane will hit the table in under five.

"Someone stole a tricycle this morning," Ceepak says.

"Really?"

He checks his notebook, I guzzle coffee. He's raring to go; my engine isn't even primed.

"From a residence over on Rosewood," he says. "Chrome-colored three-wheeler. Valued at $350."

"Three hundred and fifty dollars? For a tricycle?"

"Roger that. It was stolen right off the folks' front porch. Call came in at 0630."

Did I mention — Ceepak has a police scanner in his apartment?

"We might want to swing by and see what we can see," Ceepak says, pulling a white-bellied strawberry off his bran mound.

Now, I'm sure the guys on duty at 6:30 A.M. have already swung by and taken everybody's statement. But Ceepak wants to go "see what he can see," which means he wants to hunt for footprints or dandelions that came from some lawn on the other side of town or skid marks and tire treads on the driveway. See what kind of forensic evidence we can dig up. See if it's enough to get our own show on the Discovery Channel.

"Sure," I say, getting in a second gulp of coffee, wishing I hadn't drunk all five of those beers last night. "We ought to swing by. Check it out."

"Have a good one!" The shopkeeper at the table across from us gets up to leave. He does one of those salute-waves in our direction and drops eight quarters on the table to cover his tip. He hikes up his khakis and strolls to the cash register where they have so many brochures, you could spend your whole vacation reading about stuff you ought to be doing.

I'm not the only one who sees the loose change lying unprotected on the table. One of the monsters sees it too. The boy, about eight or nine, in a surfer tank top soaked with syrup. The shark on front looks like it's bleeding purple because the kid went heavy on the blueberry during his recent bombing run.

His parents are reading the newspaper. Actually, they're hiding behind big sheets of newsprint, trying to forget that the hellions jumping up and down in the booth belong to them. Mom's behind "World Business," Dad's under "Sports." If the kids won't let them sleep in, they can at least tune the kids out for however long it takes to eat breakfast.

I make eye contact with the kid.

He sees my arm patch and baseball cap with the humongous word POLICE stitched across the front. Neither seems to faze him. Maybe he can't read.

He saunters over to the table and scoops up the quarters.

I focus on my coffee, stir it some, and pray Ceepak hasn't seen the little brat stealing a waitress's hard-earned tip.

But of course he has.

Ceepak stands.

Like I said, he's six-two, so the midget tough guy stuffing loose change into his pockets has to pay attention when suddenly a giant towers over him, hands on hips, smiling.

"What'ya doin' there, son?"

"Nothin'." The kid uses the oldest line in the book.

"Nothing?" Ceepak's smile gets broader. There go the dimples. "Looks to me like you were taking something that doesn't really belong to you. . . ."

"Is there some problem?"

It's the mother. She flutters shut her newspaper and sighs, like Ceepak is ruining her day. I figure she's a lawyer or money manager or some kind of corporate ballbuster up in the city.

"No, ma'am. It's all good," Ceepak says. "Assuming, of course, your son puts it back."

"Puts what back?" Down come the baseball scores. Papa Bear is interested too.

"Nothin'." The kid needs to work on his vocabulary. He only seems to know the one word, and it sure isn't working with Ceepak.

"Is there some problem?" The mother is repeating herself, for dramatic effect or maybe to scare us.

Ceepak doesn't scare easy.

"I believe your son took some quarters that a customer left on the table as a tip. . . ."

"Did not!"

The kid is stupid. While denying the theft, he pulls the quarters out of his shorts and tosses them back onto the table next to an empty glass.

"I just needed change," the kid says. "For the gumball machine."

Oh. He wasn't stealing, he was making change! Like the nice ladies in the cages down in Ocean Town do when they take your twenty and give you a cup of quarters for the slot machines.

"He needed quarters," the mother says. "That's all. Sit down, Trevor. Finish your breakfast."

Trevor sneers at Ceepak and returns triumphantly to his table.

"Let's see your dollar bills," Ceepak says.

"What?"

The mother is mortified.

"Officer," she says, *"we are on vacation."* She's spreading out her words and not using contractions and that means she means business, buster.

"If this is how you people down here treat your visitors. . . ."

"Let's see the greenbacks and it's all good."

The kid has a look on his face: *busted!*

He doesn't have two dollar bills in his pocket. He doesn't have diddly except lint or a wad of snotty Kleenex.

"That's it," the father says. "What's your badge number? I'm going to have a word with your supervisor. . . ."

Ceepak smiles.

"I will not lie, steal, or cheat, nor tolerate those who do," he says.

"What?" The father is confused.

So's the mom—she's scrunching up her nose and forehead, exhaling loudly, doing an excellent job looking "flabbergasted."

Me? I've heard it a hundred times. It's *The Code*. The Honor Code from West Point or something.

"If your son shows me the dollar bills he was attempting to change, albeit in a rather unorthodox fashion, I will apologize immediately. In fact, I will turn in my badge and leave town in disgrace. . . ."

Ceepak is laying it on thick. Yanking their cranks. I love it when he busts some ballbuster's balls.

The kid starts to sweat.

"Show him your money, Trevor," the father says.

The kid sweats some more.

I'm sweating too, but mine is because Ceepak insists on sitting here in the booth near the untinted windows. I squint through the glare to see if there is some merciful cloud about to scoot across the sky and save me.

That's when I see her.

A blonde girl. About twelve. Maybe thirteen.

She's stumbling up Ocean Avenue toward The Pancake Palace.

When she gets closer, I see her dress is covered with blood.

So's her face.

The girl is screaming.

TWO

T he little thief got lucky.

Ceepak forgets all about Trevor and races out the front door. I run after him.

The girl is screaming in the middle of the street, staring down at her dress. I think it used to be white. Her face is freckled with blood, too.

"My faaaa. . . ." She's wailing now.

Cars slam on their brakes, fishtail to stops.

"My faaaa. . . ."

"Traffic!" Ceepak roars. "Lock it down. Now."

I throw up both of my hands. A line of cars starts backing up down Ocean Avenue. Like I said, this is changeover day and people are in a hurry to get the hell out of town before everybody else gets the hell out ahead of them.

"Help me, please God, help me God, please. . . ."

The girl is hysterical; stretching her arms open wide, turning around in circles. She looks like she's sweating blood. Her whole body is trembling.

Ceepak takes off his windbreaker and drapes it over her shoulders like a cape.

"Easy, sweetie," he says. I can tell he's trying to keep her warm so she doesn't go into shock. You learn that kind of stuff in the Boy Scouts.

"My fa . . . fa . . . fa . . . ther!"

"Easy. . . ."

"He killed my father!"

"Who?"

"The crazy man. The crazy man! The crazy man!"

She's screaming again.

"He has a gun! Make him stop! Please make him stop. . . ."

"Okay." Ceepak stays calm. "Where is he?"

She points.

Across the street, up the block.

Sunnyside Playland.

It's a small (by Disney standards) amusement park tucked into four square blocks along the beach side of the avenue. They've got carnival rides, a video game arcade, an ice cream parlor, putt-putt golf—everything a kid needs when he's on vacation at the shore for a week and starts to get tired of swallowing salt water.

"Danny?"

"Yeah?"

"Focus!"

"Yes, sir."

"Stay with the girl." Ceepak flips her hands over, and I see deep gouges where her palms are cut.

"Clean her wounds."

"Right. Come on, kid."

"Where?" She looks at me but can't seem to focus.

"You're going to come with me . . . okay?"

I move her out of the street, and two dozen cars immediately start honking their horns at me for blocking traffic. I'd flip them all the finger, but I'm kind of busy.

Ceepak crosses the road and pulls out his Smith & Wesson. I can see he's unlocking the safety, checking his ammo clip. I hope Trevor sees this from his window seat and thinks Ceepak's coming back inside The Pancake Palace to ice him.

Ceepak works his way up the sidewalk, tight against the painted fence that lets you know "Sunnyside Playland Is The Most Fun Under The Sun." The girl with blood all over her dress might disagree.

"The Tilt-A-Whirl!" the girl suddenly yells to Ceepak. "We were on the Tilt-A-Whirl!"

Ceepak nods and makes his way toward the entrance. It's an asphalt pathway under an arching rainbow that's part of the whole sunshine motif they've got going inside Playland.

But the park doesn't open until ten or eleven, and a locked chain-link fence is there blocking the way in. The girl must have scaled the gate and ripped her hands coming over the top.

Ceepak sidles right and does one of those patented Starsky and Hutch moves where he sweeps the horizon with his gun held out in front of his face with both hands. The coast must be clear: He tucks the pistol back into his belt and hauls himself up over the fence. He's on the other side in less than ten seconds. Like I said, the guy spends a lot of time at the gym. The gun comes back out when he hits the pavement on the other side. He runs inside Playland, stopping to use a cotton-candy kiosk for cover.

Now I can't see him any more.

I hope he's as good a cop as I think he is.

"My father and I snuck in," the girl says, and she's shivering like she just stepped out of an icy cold shower and can't find a towel. I wrap my arm around her shoulder and gently guide her up the sidewalk.

"You snuck in, hunh?" I repeat what she said because I'm trying to get my bearings, figure out what I do next.

"Yeah. . . ."

She's fading on me.

"Hey, everything's going to be okay. Okay?" I say this crap because I don't know what else to say to a strange young girl soaked in blood. I'm no forensics freak like Ceepak; but I figure if she has this much red stuff splashed down the front of her dress and up on her cheeks, she was pretty close when somebody shot her father.

"It's going to be okay."

I know I'm repeating myself, but I'm a summer cop and they teach us how to write parking tickets and help old people shuffle across the street, not how to deal with traumatized murder witnesses who may not even be teenagers yet.

"My faaa. . . ."

She's trembling again, shaking up a storm. She sniffles back some tears and wipes her eyes with her bare forearm. She has a stack of those surfer bracelets wrapped around her wrist. Colorful strings and beads. She's a kid. She shouldn't have seen what I think she just saw.

"Why don't we wait inside here, okay?"

We're right in front of Pudgy's Fudgery. I can smell burning chocolate.

I figure it's probably smart to move indoors, find a place to sit, get some ice water or something, clean up her hands and face. The shop isn't open, but I see someone inside working a big wooden spatula against a ten-pound slab of butter. It's Amy Decosimo. We went to high school together. I bang on the front door.

Amy just about loses it when she sees the bloody kid.

"Ohmygod!"

"We need to sit down, okay?"

"Ohmygod!"

"Amy?" I shake my head to let Amy know she can't keep "Ohmy-godding" or she'll freak the kid out even worse.

I usher my charge into the shop.

"Back there, okay?" I say, guiding her to a small cluster of tables in the back. "Is this all right, Amy?"

"Unh-hunh," is all Amy can say and it comes out sounding more like a choked-back gag because her mouth is covered by both of her hands.

"Amy? Work with me here, okay?"

"Unh-hunh."

I get the kid seated. "Could we have some water?" I ask. "Maybe a wet towel?"

"Unh-hunh," Amy says, but she just stands there.

"Amy?"

The little girl rolls her wrists across the table and stares at her open palms. The gouges are deep.

"Ohmygod," Amy gasps and chokes some more.

The girl looks up, right at Amy.

"Do you have something to. . . ."

She can't finish, so I fill in the blanks.

"You got a first-aid kit, Amy?"

"Unh-hunh. . . ."

"Could you maybe go get it? Grab some peroxide? Gauze?"

It's like Amy finally wakes up. She runs up front to grab the first-aid stuff.

I see a towel hanging near a sink back where they make the fudge. I go grab it and run some warm water to make it soppy.

When I get back to the little table, the girl is staring blankly at the menu board on the wall behind the fudge counter, like she's trying to decide whether she wants the almond-coconut or the pecan-marble.

I wipe her face. Then her hands.

"We go there to talk," she says.

"You go where?"

"The Tilt-A-Whirl." She sounds like she's narrating somebody else's dull home video, like she's not really here. "Even when it's not running, we go to the Tilt-A-Whirl. The cars look like big sea turtles."

"Yeah. I know."

"Big green sea turtles."

"Yeah."

"They call it the Turtle-Twirl Tilt-A-Whirl."

"I know. It's my favorite ride in the whole park."

Not really, but it seems to work.

The girl smiles faintly, flashing braces. She's a pretty kid. Long blond hair framing an open, eager face. Bright blue eyes, the kind that sparkle.

"We share secrets. . . ."

Her voice fades, the smile vanishes, her head drops. I can see tears tumbling into her lap.

"Here you go." Amy has the first-aid kit and a paper cup of cold water.

The girl takes a big gulping sip.

When she's done, I pour peroxide on her wounds. She sucks in the sting between her teeth.

"Easy," I say. "I know it burns. We need to clean you up." I mop up her palms with the wet towel. She helps, taking the towel and rubbing it all over her hands.

"The sting going away?" I ask.

"Yes," she says. "Thank you."

"No problem."

I show her my smile. Then I finish cleaning up her hands. Amy's got another wet towel. The girl takes that one and pats her face with it. The white towel soaks up the brownish blood. She's looking more like a kid again.

"We'll wrap your hands with the gauze now, okay?"

She nods.

I start unwrapping the roll of Johnson and Johnson around her mitts.

"We snuck in from the beach," she whispers. Maybe she thinks whatever happened to her father happened because they were trespassing.

"Really?" Let her talk, I figure. Let her get it out.

"We've been sneaking in like that ever since I was a little kid. . . ."

She stops talking again.

I think she just realized she and Daddy won't be sneaking in anywhere any more.

The walkie-talkie clipped to my belt squawks. It's got to be Ceepak. I push the talkback button.

"Yes, sir?"

"I'm at the scene," Ceepak says, "and have made a preliminary identification of the victim."

There's a real long pause.

"It appears to be Reginald Hart."

I turn to the girl.

"Is your father Reginald Hart?"

The girl nods.

Oh, man.

"Danny?" Ceepak's filtered voice comes through loud and clear in The Fudgery. "Need your help here. Did the girl see who did this? Can she ID the perpetrator?"

She nods again.

"10-4," I say into the walkie-talkie.

"Okay. Danny?"

"Yes, sir?"

"This is important. Focus."

"Yes, sir . . . ,"

"You need to take her someplace safe."

I wonder if Pudgy's Fudgery works for Ceepak.

"10-4."

"Stick with her. Call the house for backup and secure your position. The bad guy's still at large and must be considered armed and dangerous. Alert the chief. I'll secure and preserve the crime scene."

I look at my companion. She's too scared to be frightened any more. Not me. My knees now start shaking.

Amy, having heard all of this, rechecks to make sure the Fudgery's front door is locked and deadbolted. Then she lowers the blinds. This morning, no one's going to get to check out the fresh fudge in the window.

There's a bad guy on the streets, someone crazy whom Ceepak says

is "armed and dangerous" and who's probably looking for the one witness who can pin a huge homicide on him.

Then there's me.

A summer cop.

The guy without a gun.

THREE

Reginald Hart is kind of like Donald Trump, only richer and without the gravity-defying comb-over.

Plus, now he's dead.

If you grew up around Sea Haven, you've heard about Hart all your life. He owns half the skyscrapers up in the city and more than half the casinos further down the shore in Ocean Town. He also owns a bunch of restaurants, an NFL franchise, some oil tankers, and an airline. I think he used to own a mansion here on the ritzy south end of the island, but his third wife scored it in their divorce.

There are all sorts of stories about how Reginald Hart got his start and earned his nickname—Reginald "Hartless." Apparently, when he was a young tycoon-in-training, Hart bought up cheap buildings in neighborhoods he figured were ripe for gentrification. But before he could renovate them, class them up for yuppies—or whatever they called professional people with money to burn back before Starbucks— Hart had to convince the old folks already living in his newly acquired tenements to move out.

Many of these longtime tenants didn't wish to accommodate Mr.

Hart's desires. They had rent-controlled apartments and fixed incomes and wanted to stay where they were, thank you very much.

Hart energetically encouraged them to reconsider their real estate options.

He hired hookers and drug dealers and junkies to move into the buildings, even made some of the scuzzballs his resident superintendents.

Some people say Hart bought rats and turned them loose in the hallways. I don't know where you buy rats. Petco? Some eye-shadow factory that's laying off lab workers? I don't know, but I guess Hart did.

People fled his pigsties. Mostly senior citizens. Grandmothers and grandfathers. Hart was named "Slumlord of the Year," but he got what he wanted—empty apartment buildings he could gut, gussy, fumigate, and flip. He did it a couple hundred times and made a ton of money. Then he started shopping for casinos and malls and high-end hotels. Hart was playing Monopoly on a really big board.

Mr. Hart is, correction, *was*, your basic bazillionaire.

And his daughter watched him die.

I did like Ceepak said. I radioed the base and in about thirty seconds every cop car on the island came screaming down Ocean Avenue to back me up.

Chief Cosgrove was first on the scene.

He's a big, burly 300-pound bear and when he starts growling orders, everybody hops to it. I don't even know Cosgrove's first name. I think it might be Bob, or Robert, but everybody calls him "Chief."

"Lock down the causeway," he says to Mark Malloy, this muscle-bound cop with a year-round tan.

"Right, chief!"

"Roadblock!"

Malloy jumps into his cruiser, but not fast enough for the chief.

"Move it! Hustle. Go!"

Cosgrove is like a junior-high gym teacher. He's always yelling at you to move it or lose it, haul ass, get the lead out—effective motivational stuff like that.

Malloy does a quick whoop with his siren, swirls his roof lights, and races off to blockade the bridge.

Those people who honked at me when I stopped them on Ocean Avenue? Man, are they going to be bummed with they bump into Malloy. The causeway is the only way on or off the eighteen-mile strip of sand we call Sea Haven Township. Unless, of course, you've got a boat. Lots of boats down here. There's even a pirate ship, but it's mostly a theme restaurant so it really wouldn't make a very good getaway vessel.

As I'm standing on the sidewalk in front of Pudgy's Fudgery watching a half-dozen cops running around, I realize that this is probably the worst crime this town has ever seen. Usually we deal with smaller stuff. Like stolen tricycles.

The chief marches up and sticks his face into mine.

"Where the hell is Ceepak?"

"Securing the crime scene, sir."

"Good."

Cosgrove walks away and retrieves a big blanket from the back of his Chief Car—a hulking Ford Expedition. It's way bigger than my Explorer and has the black-tinted privacy glass. There's not much turquoise and pink on the chief's vehicle. His police car is more Darth Vader death star, less friendly flamingo.

The chief galumphs into Pudgy's to get Hart's daughter, who's still inside with a couple cops. Guys with guns.

I look down the street at Sunnyside Playland and wonder what kind of gruesome stuff Ceepak is looking at right now.

All I see is Sunnyside Clyde's big beaming face on a billboard near the entrance. Clyde is Playland's mascot—a baggy-panted surfer dude with a big ray-rimmed sun for a head. He's always wearing dark sunglasses; but I never understood this, because if his head is the sun, how come he needs sunglasses?

"Cover me!" I hear the chief bark.

He has the girl bundled up in the blanket and is hustling her out the front door. Two cops with pistols flank him. When the girl's strapped into the back seat, she sees me and waves goodbye.

I wave back.

I see that Amy Decosimo insisted the girl take home some free fudge. She's clutching the clean white box against her bloody dress.

Cosgrove slams the door shut.

"Kid?" Cosgrove is in my face again. Apparently, he doesn't know my first or last name.

"Yes, sir?"

"What's your 10-38?"

He's using cop code. Something I should have studied more or maybe even memorized.

"What's your destination?"

"I, uh . . . I. . . ."

"Go help Ceepak," the chief says, checking his watch. "Tell him I've contacted State. The cavalry's on its way."

"Yes, sir," I say.

"Move it!" Cosgrove barks. "Get the lead out, son."

I do as I'm told.

Just like in junior high gym class.

FOUR

've never seen a dead body before.

Well, I saw my grandfather's at his funeral, but he was all dressed up in a suit and tie and lying in his coffin. He even had on make-up, something he wouldn't have been caught dead doing when he was alive.

The weirdest part was his hair.

Grandpa always had a crewcut flattop, a holdover from World War II. The funeral director didn't know my grandfather, so he slicked his bristly hair over to the side and grandpa didn't look like grandpa any more.

I'm thinking about this stuff because I don't want to think about what's waiting for me down at the Tilt-A-Whirl.

Reginald Hart's dead body.

One of our guys, Sergeant Dominic Santucci, had snapped off the padlock on Playland's front gate with this humongous wire-cutter tool, so I didn't have to scale the fence. He's stationed at the gate to wait for the state police and the medical examiner and "the meat wagon," as he called it. Santucci's a hardass and wants everybody to know it.

I walk down the pathway. Past the Sunnyside Clyde garbage cans where you stuff your trash into Mr. Sunbeam's wide-open mouth. Past Pirate Pete's Pretzels. Past the Sea Dragon, past the Water Balloon Pistols, past the Knock 'Em Down.

Down to the Tilt-A-Whirl and my first dead body.

I've heard stories about how cops love to initiate rookies; love to bust a gut laughing while they watch the new guy lose his cookies when he sees his first fresh corpse. Santucci was cracking gum and smirking when he let me in the gate.

"What'd you eat for breakfast, kid?" he asked. "Never mind. Don't tell me. We'll see soon enough."

Then he laughed his Dominic-the-Donkey laugh and cracked his gum some more.

I come to the entrance to the Tilt-A-Whirl, wishing there was a long line ahead of me.

There isn't. And I'm tall enough to ride this ride.

"Ceepak?"

"In here," he says. "Careful where you step, Danny."

I'm sweating. My mouth is dry but sticky.

Ceepak meets me on the pathway.

"Danny?"

"Yes, sir?"

"I know you've never done this before. Never seen a dead body. But you don't have to act brave. Not for me, okay?"

"Yes, sir."

He steps aside.

Behind him, I can see a blue-faced man slumped in a green plastic seat. His eyes are wide open. His mouth, too. His shirt is splotched with red paintballs, only they aren't paintballs—they're bursts of blood.

"This way," Ceepak says.

He grabs my elbow and hustles me back up the path, over to these bushes on the other side of the main walkway, over near an ice cream cart.

I puke.

Ceepak props me up when my knees go wobbly.

If he wasn't there, I think I would fall face-first into my own vomit.

"Her name is Ashley."

Five minutes later, I'm doing like Ceepak suggested. I'm staying "emotionally detached." This isn't a dead guy, this is evidence. I'll save my emotions for later, for when we're hunting down the rat bastard who did this.

"Ashley?" I say, my voice cracking a little.

"Roger that."

Ceepak holds up his clue: a letter-block ID bracelet.

"It was snagged on a bolt." He points inside the Tilt-A-Whirl car.

"Great," I croak. "Good." My voice sounds steadier.

"You're doing fine, Danny."

I nod.

My thighs aren't quivering any more, so I step back and study the Turtle-Twirl Tilt-A-Whirl.

I think Sunnyside Clyde had this ride custom-made. Either that, or he bought it second-hand from Sea World. The seven cars are molded to look like giant green turtles sitting up on their haunches. Rounded fiberglass shells form the car backs; funny-face turtle heads jut out up top, making a little canopy.

"She sat on the right-hand side," Ceepak says. I nod. I think Ceepak just needs to say what he's thinking out loud so he'll remember it later.

He's wearing lint-free gloves so he won't contaminate any evidence. He keeps the gloves tucked into the upper-right hip pocket of his cargo pants. Ceepak brought a box of these gloves to the station back in June and suggested that everybody "keep a pair handy."

Yeah. Right. Like any of the guys were going to wear sweaty gloves in the middle of the summer. I took a pair just because I knew Ceepak was watching. I think they're still in my sock drawer.

Ceepak paces around the turtle. He starts mumbling.

"'That tilt-a-whirl down on the south beach drag, I got on it last night and my shirt got caught. . . .'"

He's sort of half-singing, half-muttering a snippet from Bruce Springsteen's *4th of July, Asbury Park*. Today's the tenth of July, but I think the karaoke routine helps Ceepak think.

"Interesting." He's looking at the safety bar on the car. It's up.

"What?"

"Blood spray."

I look at the metal bar. I see red dots clustered in the area in front of Reginald Hart's slumped body like somebody flicked a wet paintbrush at it. The guy's body is riddled with bullets. I count five, six before I'm almost ready to run to the bushes again.

Ceepak is sniffing the air.

"Checking for transient evidence," he says. "Smells don't last."

"When do you think . . . you know?"

"Half an hour. Forty-five minutes. Of course, I'm merely speculating based on observable rigor mortis. . . ."

Ceepak leans inside the car and sniffs again, about six inches from the dead guy's head. I look the other way.

"Vanilla, patchouli, sandalwood," he says. "Fascinating."

"What?"

"Young Ashley purchases her perfume from Victoria's Secret. Or. . . ."

"Someone else was out here?" I catch on quick.

"We need the yellow tape. Digital camera. My crime-scene kit."

I stand there nodding, assuming that's what I'm supposed to do.

"They're in the Explorer. Cargo hold?"

"Great. I'll go get 'em." Like I said, I catch on quick.

"Danny?"

"Yes, sir?"

"See if Cosgrove can cut loose some troops. We need to seal the site, cordon off the area. Streetside. Beachside."

"Right."

"And Danny?"

"Yeah."

"Don't walk there. Could be latent evidence underfoot." He points to the center of the asphalt trail winding from the Tilt-A-Whirl back to the main pedestrian pathway. "We go out the way we came in."

"Yes, sir."

I look down to see if we left any footprints on our earlier run for the shrubs. We didn't, so I improvise, gingerly lifting my legs and tip-toeing like I'm some kind of sneaky stork.

While I hustle up to our vehicle, I remember how the Tilt-A-Whirl used to be my favorite ride—back before I discovered the fried food group and swore off any ride that involved stomach-churning centrifugal force.

But when I was a kid, I loved how the Tilt-A-Whirl could surprise you. How it spun you around one way and the next time you hit the exact same spot, it spun you around some way completely different. Sometimes the cars would stutter between moves; sometimes they'd start swinging in one direction, then shift to another. You never knew what to expect next.

I remember this day in math class.

We'd all seen *Jurassic Park* hundreds of times and were asking for an explanation of the "Chaos Theory" Jeff Goldblum's mathematician character kept yammering about when he really should have been keeping an eye peeled for dinosaurs. Our teacher quoted this article by a guy named Ivars Peterson and told us about the Tilt-A-Whirl and its geometry of a circular platform with cars that pivot freely along a track of hills and how, if the operator keeps the whole thing going at the proper speed of 6.5 revolutions per minute, it's practically impossible to predict what will happen next as you spin around and around and around.

The teacher called it "mind-jangling unpredictability." Chaos Theory in action, for two tickets a ride.

When I return with the gear and a couple rolls of "Police Line Do Not Cross" tape, Ceepak points at a wallet lying on the Tilt-A-Whirl platform.

"It's Hart's."

He takes the digital camera and starts snapping pictures. Tons of them. Like our Reginald is the cover boy for *Grisly Crime Scene Magazine.*

The wind starts kicking up.

"Wind might contaminate the evidence," Ceepak says. He retrieves a pair of surgical-looking tweezers from his crime-scene attaché case and bends down to pick up the wallet. There's a driver's license lying near it. He picks that up too.

He places them separately into small paper bags he's taken out of his upper left cargo-pants pocket. He keeps a miniature magnifying glass in another pocket near his knee. He must need to reload his pants first thing every morning.

"I thought police used baggies for evidence," I say, trying to talk about anything other than the dead guy in front of us riddled with holes where his life leaked out.

"Plastic sweats, and the moisture could contaminate the evidence. Paper is better."

"Unh-hunh."

"The perpetrator didn't take the credit cards, but he thought about it."

Ceepak points to a scruffy bush across from the footpath, about six feet from where he found the wallet. I think it must have been some shade of evergreen before the sun bleached out all the color. There's an Amex and two Visas stuck in the branches.

"We can speculate, from the discarded driver's license and credit cards, that the perpetrator discovered his victim's identity."

Yeah. Reggie Hart. One of the richest men in the world.

Ceepak tells me to tape off the area around the Tilt-A-Whirl.

"We want to keep it clean for the State Boys."

The "State Boys" are the guys from the State Police Major Crime Unit. A town like Sea Haven, which I don't think has ever hosted a murder before, doesn't have all the people necessary to run a proper crime-scene investigation, so the state police send in the MCU when something major goes down.

I try to figure out how to unroll and string the yellow tape without ruining evidence. I keep my eyes down on the dirt but look up now and then to see if Ceepak's watching, see if he's okay with my crime-scene tape-rolling technique.

"Make sure you seal off down there."

Ceepak points to the chain-link fence where Playland meets the beach. Some kids and an old dude with a metal detector are up in the dune grass watching us. It's about 8 A.M. The kids carry bright red buckets and were probably looking for seashells. The old guy? Hunting for nickels, dimes, and Rolexes.

"We'll want to canvass the beach," Ceepak says. "Check for witnesses."

"Right."

I can see a little tunnel burrowed out of the sand under the fence. Must be where the Harts snuck in. I find it kind of funny.

I mean, if Reginald Hart liked having early morning chitchats with his daughter in a Tilt-A-Whirl car shaped like a giant sea turtle, why didn't he just buy the damn ride and set it up in his back yard, like Michael Jackson?

But I guess Hart got a buzz out of breaking the rules, doing things people said he shouldn't do.

I step across the hole, sideways. It's pretty deep. I can see rocks and pebbles in the manmade gulley. On the other side of the fence, the hole ends under a sand-covered square of plywood. About two feet by two feet. It's a tunnel door—like in one of those prison escape movies.

I turn to tell Ceepak what I see.

He's on the pathway, holding a bright red beach bag with that big-mouthed monkey on the front like they sell at the fancy-schmancy shops on Ocean Avenue. I think the monkey's name is Julius. Anyway, the beach bag doesn't match Ceepak's shoes, so I figure it must be Ashley's.

"It's Ashley's," Ceepak says, confirming my hunch and holding up the bag's straps with a ballpoint pen. "She must've dropped it."

Can you blame the kid?

Your father starts spewing blood like a berserk lawn sprinkler, you'd drop your beach bag too.

Ceepak puts the bag back where he found it and looks toward the ocean.

"Did they rake the beach this morning?"

I turn to check the sand on the other side of the fence. It's all smooth, with furrows running in parallel lines.

"Yeah. Looks like."

Sea Haven is very proud of its pristine beaches. That's how I know they call them "pristine"—it's the word they use on the back of every postcard.

A few years ago, the town fathers bought a Surf Rake 600, a tractor-towed contraption that actually vacuums up the trash people dump on the beach and leaves the sand behind it smooth and silky. I know all this because my buddy Joe Thalken drives the tractor. Poor guy has to crawl out of bed around 5:30 so the early-morning joggers will have pristine sand to run on as advertised. I don't know when Joey T. sweeps this particular section of the beach, but I'm sure we'll find out. I see Ceepak making a note, and I know it says something like "Possible Witness: Beach Sweeper."

He looks down at the asphalt walkway ringing the ride and spots something. He gets down on his hands and knees and pulls out his magnifying glass. I don't think he's going to torture ants.

Meanwhile, I need to find a place to pee.

I'm not proud of this, but I need to take a leak.

Now.

I had grabbed a big tub of coffee at Dunkin' Donuts on my way to the police station to pick up the car this morning. Then I poured myself a thick half-cup from the stale pot the late shift must have brewed twelve hours earlier—it had been sitting so long, the glass bottom was kind of glued to the warmer plate. Plus, I had that coffee at The Pancake Palace.

Like I said, I need to pee.

I check Ceepak one more time.

He's still on all fours, moving away, heading toward the Tilt-A-Whirl.

Lucky for me, Sunnyside Clyde put up this big plywood portrait of himself behind the bushes across from the ride. I think it's there so you don't see whatever's hiding behind it.

I crouch low and find a hole through the hedges.

If I'm quick about it, I can relieve myself and Ceepak will never know.

Now I see why they put the cartoon wall up: to block the dumpster. It's one of those rolling trapezoidal trash bins. You know—it's not square. Got that slanty part up front for tipping the load, like the big Rubbermaid tubs hotels use for rolling around dirty towels. This one's filled with black plastic trash bags, but the park porters must've been short on twist-ties: the bags are all hanging open.

Flies are buzzing everywhere, dive-bombing the Hefties, searching for half-squeezed ketchup packs and sticky cotton-candy cones. I'm too busy swatting flies to unzip my shorts. I'm fanning the air around my head and looking down at the ground.

I see boot prints.

They look like the prints I make when I go to the mountains every winter.

When I'm wearing my Timberlands.

Who wears Timberlands in July? On the beach?

"Ceepak?"

There are broken syringes near the boot prints.

I think I might've found something for Ceepak to look at with his magnifying glass.

FIVE

D r. Sandra McDaniels is the Chief Crime Scene Investigator for the state's Major Crimes Unit. She's also a genius. At least that's what Ceepak says.

"The lady wrote the book."

He means it.

Ceepak studied her textbooks in criminology college and keeps one of her field manuals tucked into the little map pocket on his side of the Ford. Sandra McDaniels solved the famous Ocean Town Slasher case that almost closed down the casinos eight years back. She figured it all out with carpet fibers and fruit flies.

"Forensic entomology," Ceepak told me.

McDaniels studied temperature readings to calculate the hatch time for fruit fly eggs found on a corpse, and that helped her pinpoint the time of death, and that sealed the Slasher's fate by blowing his alibi.

Don't ask me how. McDaniels is the one who wrote the book, not me.

Unfortunately, Dr. McDaniels is at her annual family reunion in Arizona, which is like three or four thousand miles away on the wrong side of the country to do us any good.

So we pull somebody else.

Somebody we can hear stomping around on the Tilt-A-Whirl platform.

"Hello?" a voice hollers. "Hello?" Then the guy hocks a loogie. "Where the fuck are you guys?"

We're busy back in the bushes, examining the needles and boot prints. You know how pine trees drop a carpet of brown needles in the fall? There's a tree back here that sheds hypodermics. They're everywhere.

Ceepak told me the Timberland imprints I found back here match some muddy prints he noticed up on the platform. It hasn't rained in a couple days, but there's a puddle where they roll the trash bin in and out. The water comes from a broken lawn-sprinkler head that doesn't flick around like it's supposed to (otherwise the bushes ringing the walkway wouldn't look so dead): It just dribbles and makes a nice big puddle for mosquito eggs and bootprints.

We hear a radio squawk on the other side of the shrubs. "Sea Haven? Come in. This is MCU. Who the fuck did you idiots post out here?"

"At the crime scene?"

I recognize our dispatcher's voice coming out of the guy's radio. It's the only way I do recognize her voice—squeezed through a tinny speaker.

"Yes, the fucking crime scene. Jesus. I told you I'm with MCU."

"Officer Ceepak should be there now," the dispatcher says.

"Well, guess what? He isn't!"

"Back here!" Ceepak calls out. "Just a second."

"Take your fucking time," the guy says sarcastically. "I got all fucking day." We hear the thud of metal hitting plastic, like he just tossed his walkie-talkie into one of the twirling turtles.

Ceepak picks up one last dirty syringe with his tweezers. There's blood in it, like a junkie pulled out on the plunger right after he pushed in. I didn't write the book, but I gotta figure a tube with somebody's blood sample in it should give you some mighty fine DNA.

"Officer Ceepak?" Grumpy is yelling now. "What the fuck are you doing in the bushes? Taking a fucking dump?"

"On my way," Ceepak says. He gestures for me to take one more digital photograph of the drug den. I do.

"Good work, Danny," he whispers. I can tell he means it. He'd probably rub my hair like a proud papa if I wasn't wearing my cap.

We walk out from behind the big plywood Clyde.

There's this fat guy with a droopy moustache sitting up in a Tilt-A-Whirl car, the one next to the one with Hart's body in it. He's chowing down on some kind of breakfast sandwich wrapped in bright yellow tissue paper—our first clue about what made him an overweight walrus.

"You Ceepak?" he says to me.

"No."

"I'm Ceepak. John Ceepak."

"Lieutenant Saul Slominsky, Major Crime Unit. Can you believe my shitty luck? I just pulled into Burger King when I caught this call."

He takes another jumbo bite and orange stuff squishes out both sides of the bread. I think it's a sausage, egg and cheese Crois-san'wich, because he keeps wiping his greasy paws on his belly and there's some spongy egg stuff snagged in the whiskers under his nose.

"I can't sit down inside and eat a civilized breakfast, I gotta hit the goddam drive-thru and there's this total asshole in front of me who acts like he doesn't know what the fuck Burger King serves for break-fast. Like it's some kind of complicated menu and he needs to study it and take his fucking time. So I hop out of my car, show him my shield, and tell him to make up his fucking mind and move along. Asshole."

Slominsky takes a triumphant whopper of a bite, snaring half of what's left of the sandwich.

He gestures over his shoulder with the thumb that's not busy with breakfast.

"The rest of my crew is hauling their shit out of their vans." I guess Saul Slominsky's mother never told him not to swear with a mouth full of food. "Thanks for hanging the tape. We'll take it from here."

Slominsky. The name finally rings a bell.

I've heard stories about this guy.

Ceepak hasn't, because he's new on the job and Slominsky never wrote a book.

In fact, Slobbinsky (which is what everybody calls him when he's not around) had the book *thrown* at him a few years back on account of his bad table manners. He blew the State's whole case in a major murder trial by dribbling sauerkraut from a Reuben sandwich all over a fingerprint card.

"Hey, you're the guys who made me work on my fucking lunch hour," was his defense. But his uncle or cousin or best friend from grade school or something was a big shot in the governor's office so, instead of canning him, they gave Slobbinsky a slap on the wrist and an air-conditioned job pushing papers around his desk. Judging by his gut, the papers don't weigh enough to give him much of a workout.

The state police only let Slobbinsky loose in the field when everybody else is on vacation and things should be slow.

Like the second week of July.

"Lieutenant," Ceepak says, "you might want to finish your meal outside the primary area of evidentiary value."

Slominsky snorts at Ceepak.

"What?"

"Maybe you should finish your sandwich somewhere else?"

"You're the new guy, hunh?"

He wipes his hands on his pant legs. Burger King must've been short on napkins this morning.

"They call you Dudley Do-Right. You're the fucking Boy Scout . . . just back from Iraq? Dudley Fucking Do-Right?"

"I wouldn't know what people call me, sir."

"Well, what kind of fucking cop are you? You need to keep your ear to the ground, son—cultivate your snitches, know what's going down, who's saying what behind your back."

Slominsky crumbles up his BK wrapper and tosses it at one of those sun-faced garbage cans a few feet from the Tilt-A-Whirl ticket booth. It's a long shot and, of course, he misses. He stands up and flicks the crumbs off the front of his shirt. I swear to God, one flake flies off his chest and lands on Reginald Hart's face—right on the tip of the dead guy's nose. It gets stuck there in the drying blood.

Ceepak is seething. I can see his ear tips turning red.

"Lieutenant, I must protest . . ."

"No. The only thing you must do is get your ass off my crime scene."

The rest of the Crime Scene Investigation team is proceeding single-file down the Tilt-A-Whirl pathway, trying to step where the guy in front of them stepped, just like Ceepak told me to do. There's about six of them. They all have on gloves (like Ceepak's) and hairnets and surgical masks and white Tyvek jumpsuits that make them look like walking FedEx envelopes. You can tell the State Boys are pros, even if their boss for the day isn't. They shoot looks to Ceepak and me that say they have to work with this bozo if they want to pick up their paychecks come Friday.

"What the fuck are you guys doing? Single file, Indian-style? Jesus, we'll be here all fucking day. Spread out. Get to work. I told Fox I'd have something for them by noon."

Great. Slominsky alerted the media. The circus is coming to town. Ceepak pulls on a fresh pair of gloves.

"If you don't mind, Lieutenant, I'd like to examine a few more—"

"Buzz off, Boy Scout. This is the State's crime scene now."

"I understand, but—"

"You were in the Army, right?"

"Right."

"You know about obeying orders? Chain of command? Shit like that?"

"Yes, sir."

"Good. Return to fucking base, soldier."

Slominsky wipes the last bit of egg off his chin with his sleeve. He sees the wallet lying open on the platform and bends over to pick it up.

"Somebody drop this?"

His greasy paw prints smear all over the leather, covering up any fingerprints that might be on the dead man's wallet—like, oh, I don't know, the shooter's?

Ceepak looks like somebody just kneed him in the nuts.

"You might want to put that down, sir," says one of the CSI guys from behind his white mask. "Could be evidence."

"Jesus, fellas—relax. We've got an eyewitness! The little girl saw everything. All we need to crack this case is a halfway decent sketch artist."

"Shelly's with the girl now," says another techie, a guy on his hands and knees studying the same boot prints Ceepak studied earlier.

"See?" Slominsky smiles at Ceepak and me. "The big boys are in town. This case is almost closed. We'll flash the sketch all over TV and have this thing wrapped up before lunch. Hey, goody-two-shoes?"

I think he's talking to Ceepak.

"Is there any decent clam chowder down here? I like the Manhattan stuff better than the white stuff. . . ."

"Yes," Ceepak says calmly. I can see he's mastering his emotions like he's taught himself to do instead of telling the blowhard to go fuck himself, which is, basically, what I've taught myself to do. "I am given to understand there are numerous chowder options available on the island."

"Good. Because two fucking Croissan'wiches won't hold me for long."

Slominsky struts over to the dead body.

"So this is Reginald Hart, hunh? Stayed at one of his casinos down in Ocean Town once. The Fantasia? Place had class. Real class. Marble tile in the toilets. Shit like that."

Slominsky raises Hart's left arm, and lets it drop.

"Yep," he says, "I'd say this guy is officially, one-hundred-percent dead. Where's the goddamn Medical Examiner?"

"On his way," somebody says.

"Guess we better figure out a time of death. I'd say it was sometime this morning. How about you guys?"

None of the CSI team says anything. They're busy, trying to do their jobs fast—before Slominsky screws things up even worse.

"Okay. Good. This morning. That's what I'll say until we come up with something better."

He sees Ceepak staring at him.

"You still here? Jesus—go home. You did your good deed for the day. You told me about the chowder."

Ceepak is quiet for a second. Then he starts unsnapping his cargo-pants pockets.

"We found some items earlier," he says, handing his paper evidence envelopes over to one of the white suits. "Wind started blowing. . . ."

"Recalibrating the crime scene," the CSI guy says, letting Ceepak know he did the right thing.

"You picked shit up?" Slominsky yells. "Jesus H. Christ! Fucking local yokels. . . ."

"We recorded original conditions and positions," Ceepak says. He slips the data card out of our digital camera and hands that over, too.

"You might want to check back there," Ceepak points to the big Sunnyside Clyde sign. "Danny?"

He snaps his head to the side to let me know it's time to go. We walk out, watching where we step, as if it still matters.

Like I said, John Ceepak plays by the rules.

Even when the rules suck.

SIX

finally get to hit the head when we hike back to The Pancake
Palace to pick up the Ford Explorer.

This is a family place, but the bathroom? Whoo. It's all kinds of
stinky. Not dirty, just kind of grungy, like it's uncleanable and always
damp on account of all the humidity. There's these metal half-walls
between urinals (so guys won't look at each other's willies, I guess)
and they're splashed with rust.

"Gross," I say to myself, imagining the worst possible rust-creation
scenario. I shudder because I realize: I'm starting to see the world like
Ceepak sees it, analyzing splatter patterns while I pee.

Ceepak is in the restaurant, settling up with the cashier.

"Sorry we had to run out like that," he says as he pays six bucks
for the breakfast we skipped out on so we could rescue the bloody kid
out in the street.

Next, Ceepak flags down the waitress who brought him his cereal
and me my coffee. He hands her a three-buck tip on our six-buck tab.
And he apologizes for "any inconvenience we caused by making her
wait."

I'm sure this is all part of The Code.

"We're good to go," he says when he's paid off all his debts. "Let's roll."

We head out into the parking lot. It's still only 9 A.M. but the sun's already starting to steam things up. Ceepak is lugging his aluminum crime-scene attaché case. I've got the camera and what's left of the "Police" tape rolls. We head to the rear of the Explorer to pop open the cargo door.

All of a sudden, there's this loud "ka-boom!"

"Get down!"

Ceepak shoves me to the ground.

"Grenade!" he yells. "Down!"

I'm covering my head and thinking: *No way! Maybe an M-80 left over from the Fourth of July. . . .*

"Stay down!" Ceepak screams.

I look up and Ceepak's running, crouched low, using parked cars for cover like he's expecting incoming rounds from a rocket-propelled grenade launcher. There's this stockade fence behind the restaurant's kitchen and I can see a puff of smoke come out from behind it.

The dumpster.

I see three boys, about ten years old. They look scared shitless and start high-tailing it out of the parking lot, into the trees. They'll probably run all the way across the bay to the mainland.

I was right. Leftover firecrackers. An M-80, which is basically a quarter stick of dynamite, tossed by some kids into an open dumpster. *Ka-boom. Ka-bang.* Happy 10th of July!

Ceepak stands, watching the boys flee.

All I can see is his back. But I have a funny feeling he might have been momentarily blown back to Bagh-nasty-dad, where his buddies probably got blown up more times than he'd care to remember.

I grab hold of the rear bumper on the Ford and haul my ass off the asphalt, brushing stones and pebbles out of my naked knees. Maybe tomorrow I'll go with the cargo pants instead of the shorts. I see Ceepak's shoulders heave up and down like he's taking in a long, deep breath.

He turns to face me, smiling.

"Kids."

"Yeah," I say.

"Fourth of July fireworks."

"Yeah."

"Let's hit the house."

"Right."

The house, the Sea Haven Police Station, is only five blocks up Ocean Avenue, but traffic is all kinds of backed up. We may never make it.

"From the roadblock," I guess.

"Yeah," Ceepak says. He's looking out his window like he's still thinking about grenades, still seeing stuff in the rearview mirror of his mind, so to speak. I have a feeling those objects might appear closer than they actually are.

I see a TV satellite truck rumbling down the avenue, heading back to where we came from. Word spreads fast.

We're still not moving. In fact, we're stuck behind an ice-cream truck. Not the cute, ringy-dingy kind that cruises up and down the side streets selling Good Humor bars. This is a Ben and Jerry's delivery truck with black cows painted on the back panel and it's crawling its way up to the supermarket, hoping to get there before all the Chubby Hubby and Cherry Garcia melts. I can't see what's in front of it. Probably a beer truck. Or a Frito-Lay step van. Ice cream, beer, and potato chips. Come summer, these are the three basic food groups in my hometown.

In the lane to the right of us is a convertible with the top down. They want to turn left, crawl in front of me and the trucks, hit the causeway, and leave the island behind. Their vacation is obviously over.

Mom and Pops are up front, fuming, craning their necks, trying to see what the heck the holdup is, looking like their whole week of rest and relaxation evaporated the second they hit this gridlock. Two boys, about six and seven, are sitting in the back seat, all buckled in. They're bored stiff and start waving at us like kids will do when they see cops. One's wearing a diving mask. The other has on some kind of pirate hat. I'm not driving anywhere any time soon, so, when the kids catch my eye, I wave back. The scuba-faced boy gives me a big military salute and I salute back.

Ceepak is still staring out his window. He sees the convertible, too. "Danny?" he says. "We need to expedite our exit."

"10-4."

I hit the lights and siren, pull around the ice-cream truck, and scream up the avenue in the wrong lane.

"That'll work," Ceepak mumbles.

He never did salute the cute kids.

Guess he's done playing Army for today.

Police headquarters kind of looks like a house. We've got a nice wrap-around porch, a white picket fence, and a tidy little lawn. This being the beach, our lawn is made out of marble chips and red pea-pebbles instead of grass, but we keep it raked and weeded.

We're on Cherry Lane, a street that cuts across Ocean Avenue, and heads from the bay on one side of the island to the beach on the other. In this part of town, the east–west streets are named after trees and are arranged in alphabetical order, north to south. Beech Street is north of us. Dogwood is south.

Ocean Avenue is to the west of us, Shore drive to the east. One block past Shore is Beach Lane, not to be confused with Beech Street, but, as you might guess, it often is, especially by out-of-towners looking for the beach, which is on Beach. Not Beech.

State police cars and vans are parked in our lot and up and down the street out front. Two hours after it went down, the Hart homicide is already big. By noon, it'll be huge.

"Let's see where the CO needs us," Ceepak says, climbing out of the car. He's talking military talk again, saying "CO" for Commanding Officer, sounding more like the old Ceepak.

We move inside and feel the 68-degree AC smack us in the face. It feels good.

"What a freaking day, hunh?"

It's Gus Davis, the desk sergeant. He's about sixty years old and completely out of shape. His regulation police pants don't fit any more and sort of droop off his bony hips. Gus is about two months away from retirement and has been a Sea Haven cop for close to thirty years. He used to ride up and down Ocean Avenue in a pink-and-turquoise cruiser, but now he works behind the front desk answering phones, taking messages, dealing with walk-in civilians.

I think Ceepak took Gus's street job, but Gus isn't bitter. Not about that, anyway—just everything else. Life in general.

"This freaking day!"

"What's up?" Ceepak asks. He and Gus get along. Maybe because Gus did time in the Army, too. Korea. Vietnam. One of those. "Switchboard busy?"

"Busy? It's a freaking funhouse in here. First, we get a call at 6:28."

"The tricycle?"

"You heard?"

"I was up anyhow. . . ."

"Normally, I'd blow the caller off. You know, tell her to come in at a decent hour and file a report. I mean, come on—it's a freaking tricycle! Who spends three hundred and fifty bucks on a tricycle? But guess who the caller is?"

"Who?"

"The mayor's sister. You ever meet her?"

"No. Not that I'm aware of."

"Consider yourself lucky." Gus shivers to help paint the picture. "She's like a piranha that's had plastic surgery. A real man-eater."

"Check."

"So I radio Kiger. Pull him off beach sweep, send him over to write up the missing bike."

"Who's Kiger?"

"Adam Kiger. Young kid. Works the graveyard shift. Rides his scooter up and down the beach, looking for riff-raff."

"Scooter?"

"ATV," I say. "All Terrain Vehicle? Good on the beach. . . ."

"It's a freaking scooter! He looks like a mailman!"

I can tell Ceepak's gonna want to talk to Kiger. Find out what kind of riff-raff's been spotted near the Tilt-A-Whirl playing with hypodermic needles.

"Then you two . . ." Gus gestures at Ceepak and me like he's disgusted. "Seven something—you get a body! Now, I got the press calling. The mayor? He's bitching about the roadblock, how it's ticking off the tourists. I gotta track down the kid's mom, find Hart's lawyer, his corporate people, the works. I'm never freaking going home."

"What's the problem? You don't like it here, Gus?"

It's the chief.

He's a big ol' bear, but he has this quiet way of slipping up behind you right when you're bellyaching about him.

"No, chief. I was just saying—"

"Sketch artist needs coffee," the chief says.

"Do I look like freaking Starbucks?"

"Go rustle her up a cup. Move it. Shake a leg."

Even old-timers like Gus jump when Chief Cosgrove pulls his gym-teacher act.

"So," the chief says to Ceepak, "how badly did Slobbinsky screw things up?"

"Royally."

"Damn. Sorry he caught the call. Good thing we have the eyewitness. . . ."

"Yeah," Ceepak says. "How's she doing?"

"Not bad. Considering."

"Yeah."

"Her name is Ashley. Ashley Hart. She's been asking for you."

"Me?" Ceepak seems surprised.

"Apparently you're her new hero. Says you flew over a fence or something?"

"Playland's main gate was locked. I gained access by alternate means."

"She said you looked like Batman." The chief turns to me. "Guess that makes you Robin, hunh, kid?"

"Yes, sir," I say.

"Sorry McDaniels was out of town," he says to Ceepak.

"I think we'll survive. The CSI crew is boots-on-the-ground. They're all pros."

The chief nods. "I'd like you to go in and talk to the kid. We're getting nowhere on the perp sketch. It's like she can't remember what happened, what the guy looked like. Either that or she doesn't want to remember."

"Post-traumatic stress?"

"Maybe. I dunno. Seeing you might help."

"Where is she?"

"Interrogation Room."

"Seems kind of severe. . . ."

"The windows in the other rooms spooked her. She thought the bad guy might be outside."

"Check. I'll see what I can do."

"Jane and the artist are with her."

"Yes, sir."

Ceepak heads up the hall to the windowless cinderblock room with the one-way mirror. The Interrogation Room.

"How's he holding up?" the chief asks when Ceepak's out of earshot.

"Fine, sir." I see no need to mention the M-80 incident behind The Pancake Palace. "Just fine."

"He hates to see kids in trouble."

"Yes, sir."

The chief leans up against the front counter and crosses his hamhock arms across his chest. He looks like a contemplative moose resting against a stump. I've never had a heart-to-heart with Chief Cosgrove, but I think he's about to unload a monologue on me. I'm right.

"We were stationed in Germany together," he starts, his eyes narrowing like he can actually see what he's remembering. "There was this chaplain. Baptist minister, I think. Short guy. Little moustache.

Had this soft southern twang when he spoke. Anyhow, he was accused of molesting kids at his church down in Texas, so they got rid of him by shipping him overseas with us. A year later, he starts messing around with some of the kids on base. Soldiers' boys. Nine-, ten-, eleven-year-olds. Their moms and dads are over there serving their country, and he's . . . you know. . . ."

"Yes, sir."

"Ceepak led the investigation. I was tactical support."

"Did you guys stop him? The chaplain?"

"Of course. John Ceepak? He always gets his man."

SEVEN

slip into the dark room next to the Interrogation Room. It's dark because otherwise, everybody in the IR would be able to see me through the one-way mirror.

This is one of the few times our IR has actually been used for questioning. Usually, it's where stuff like Christmas decorations gets stored or where we cut somebody's birthday cake. In fact, I can see a wrinkled red balloon lying on the floor near Ashley Hart's new shoes.

She's also wearing a new dress with Hawaiian flowers and hula dancers on it. I figure somebody picked it up on Ocean Avenue so Ashley wouldn't have to sit around all day in a blood-soaked sundress. Her hair is damp. She probably took a shower in the women's locker room. She looks like a young girl who just finished swimming in a motel pool and went back to her room to get dressed for dinner. Her cheeks are clean and ruddy; her blond hair is pulled back in a ponytail. It's only her eyes that look terrified, like she found some horrible monster stuck to the floor drain in the deep end of that swimming pool.

Ceepak is sitting at the head of the long table. Ashley is to his left. Next to her is Jane Bright, the closest thing to a child welfare officer we have on the Sea Haven Police Force—Jane has her masters degree in Social Work. Across from them both is the state police sketch artist.

"I like your new dress," Ceepak says, trying to break the ice.

"Thank you," Ashley says. "Mrs. Bright picked it out for me."

"She did good."

"Yeah."

"We keep the old dress?" Ceepak kind of whispers it to Jane.

"No. But we photographed it."

"Good."

"It's in the trash if—"

"No. That's okay."

Ceepak smiles at Ashley, like he's apologizing for talking shop with another cop.

"I'm sorry I can't remember more," Ashley says.

"Maybe we could make it like a game?"

"A game?"

"You ever play Twenty Questions?"

"Sure."

"Okay. Was it a man or a woman?"

"Man."

"Skinny or fat?"

"Skinny."

The artist starts moving her pencil, swooping it around the sketch paper.

"Okay. That's good. Was he black or white?"

"White."

"Hispanic?"

"You mean like a Puerto Rican?"

"Or a Mexican."

"No. He was white-white."

"Handsome or ugly?"

Ashley actually giggles.

"Ugly. He had this, you know . . . dragon on his neck."

"A tattoo?"

"Yeah. Like Ozzy Osborne?"

"And it was a dragon?"

"I think so. There were flames coming out the mouth. It stuck out from under his T-shirt."

"He was wearing a T-shirt?"

"Yes, sir. With colors all over it."

"Was it orange?"

"No."

"Pink? Purple?"

"No. It was all kinds of colors. Like rainbow sherbet?"

"Tie-dye?"

"Yes! It was a tie-dyed shirt!"

"What about his pants?"

"Dirty blue jeans. With holes in the knees. I could smell him."

"How'd he smell?"

"Like pee-pee."

"Urine?"

"Yes, sir. Urine."

I peek at the sketch. The guy is starting to look like a bum.

"What kind of shoes? Did you see his shoes?"

"Yes. He had on boots. Hiking boots."

"Unh-hunh."

Nobody in the room with Ceepak knows why this is so incredibly huge. I do. The Timberland prints.

"Were they tan hiking boots?"

"Yeah. Kind of light brownish."

The chief slips into the Interrogation Room.

"Don't mind me, Miss Hart," he says. "You and Ceepak keep going."

"Is that your name?" she says. "Ceepak?"

"Yes, ma'am. It's my last name but it's what everybody calls me."

"You can call me Ashley."

"I know. We found your bracelet."

"Is it broken?"

"No. It's fine."

"Will I get it back?"

"Sure you will, honey," Jane says, patting Ashley's hand.

"My boyfriend gave it to me."

Ceepak smiles.

"You have a boyfriend?"

"Kind of. Yeah. I mean, sort of. He gave me the bracelet."

Ah, the ID bracelet. The gift choice of cheap boyfriends for decades. Right up there with the J.C. Penney's heart locket. Major bling-bling when you're twelve, thirteen. I can remember handing out a few such baubles in my day.

"Nice gift," Ceepak says. "What's your boyfriend's name?"

"Ben. Ben Sinclair? His father is the mayor."

So now the mayor's son is dragged into this deal. I see the chief's big jaw popping in and out around his ears, like he's grinding his teeth, sanding them down nice and smooth, wondering how much more bad news he's going to get this morning.

"We were supposed to hook up tonight . . . Ben and I. . . ."

"A date?"

"No. Dad won't . . . I mean . . . he wouldn't let me date, even though I'm almost thirteen. So Ben and me just sort of hang out with everybody else. . . ."

"Let's get back to the sketch," the chief says, not interested in the whole Tiger Beat Teen Romance report.

"Yes, sir," Ashley says.

Ceepak sort of sighs in a way that says, "I wish you hadn't cut her off, chief."

"Remember this morning when you told me about a crazy man with a gun?" Ceepak gently asks the girl.

"Yes, sir."

"Why'd you say he was crazy?"

"I dunno. The way he looked, I guess."

"How'd he look?"

"Freaky. Big eyes. Like a bug or something. Like they were going to pop out of his head."

"Did he have a beard?" The chief lobs in another lead balloon.

"Yes, sir."

"What kind?"

"I forget."

Ceepak tries to help.

"Was it a big, bushy beard—like Santa Claus?"

"No." Ashley closes her eyes, trying to remember.

"A goatee?" the chief asks.

"Yes, sir. Like a goat! It was white."

"Was his hair white, too?" Ceepak asks.

"Black and white. Like he was older? You know?"

"Sure," Ceepak says. "Was it short? Like mine?" He playfully scratches the stubble around his ears.

"No. It was way long. And greasy. He looked like a hippie."

"A hippie?" Ceepak leans back in mock surprise. "What's a hippie?"

"I dressed up like one for Halloween this one time. You know— long hair with a bandanna, beads, flower-power sunglasses."

"Did the crazy man have on flower-power sunglasses?"

"No."

"What about beads?" The chief seems to want to turn this into a tag-team interview.

"No . . . I don't think so . . . maybe. . . ."

Ashley's getting confused.

"Maybe. He could've had beads. . . ." She now looks about to cry. "I can't remember."

"That's okay," Ceepak says.

Jane pats the girl's hand again.

"I want to see my mom. . . ."

"Of course," Jane says and turns to Ceepak. "We reached her on her cell. She's on the way."

"She was in the city," the chief adds and looks at his watch. "Should be here soon."

"Hey," Ceepak says to Ashley, "are you hungry?"

"Kind of."

"Maybe we should take a little break. We've got some Pop-Tarts and stuff in the kitchen here."

"Okay." Sounds like Pop-Tarts don't really cut it, though.

"Or," Ceepak tries again, "we could send a car over to The Pancake Palace. Pick up their chocolate-chip special. With marshmallow sauce if you want. Does that work?"

She nods.

"You want to wait in here while we send someone out? Maybe help Shelly work on the picture some more?"

"Sure."

Ceepak stands up from the table. "One order of chocolate chip pancakes, coming right up."

"Thank you, Mr. Ceepak."

"You're welcome, Ashley."

Ceepak and the chief head out the door. I meet them in the hall.

"Sorry about barging in like that," the chief says to Ceepak.

"We survived."

"Yeah. I'll find someone to run out to the restaurant." The chief looks at me.

"I could do it," I volunteer.

"You need Danny in the back room?"

"He's my partner. Second set of ears."

"10-4. Stick with Ceepak, kid. And John? I want you to, you know, basically head this thing up."

"I'm sure the State boys—"

"I don't give a damn about the state police. I want you on point. We need to wrap this thing up quick or Mayor Sinclair's going to have another heart attack."

Ceepak nods. I guess you're not breaking any rules if your boss writes new ones.

"After she eats something," he says, "I want her to walk us through what she saw. Then, we need to talk to her mother. Find out if Mr. Hart had enemies."

"It'll be a long list," the chief says

"We'll try to narrow the field."

"Check."

"We should work out a security detail with State," Ceepak suggests. "24-hour coverage. . . ."

"Done and done."

It's like they're back in the Army, protecting another innocent kid, hunting down another bad guy.

Only this time, it isn't a chaplain.

It's a crazy guy with googly eyes, a goatee, and a gun.

EIGHT

The pancakes delivered to Ashley look good. I can see the chocolate chips melting inside the soft, spongy flapjacks.

The sketch artist is gone.

They finished the composite of the killer about fifteen minutes ago and are taking a little break before moving on to the rough stuff, the "tell-us-what-you-saw" stuff.

Meanwhile, my stomach is rumbling. It's almost noon and all I've eaten today is about six cups of black coffee. No sugar. No cream. Nada. I'd do some Oreos from the vending machine but I'm all out of loose change and the dollar slot never works, just spits your crinkled bills back at you.

I saw the sketch before the artist hustled it out the door. Our suspect resembles a roadie for the Grateful Dead who hit rock bottom sometime around 1974. A crazy, aging hippie. A beach bum junkie.

There's a TV mounted on the wall behind me that's usually tuned to ESPN or one of the other sports channels. Since there are few interrogations, this viewing room is mostly used for catching whatever game is on. Today, however, the set is tuned to Fox, the first network to have "live" coverage of the "Murder Down The Shore," as they call it.

The TV guys always like to give disasters snappy titles. I'm surprised this one isn't called "Beach Blanket Bang-o," seeing how many bullets were used.

They cut to State Crime Scene Investigator Saul Slominsky.

This I have to hear.

I turn up the TV.

The mayor of Sea Haven, a youngish guy named Hugh Sinclair who owns a bunch of motels, car washes, and ice cream shops up and down the island, is standing next to Slobbinsky.

I wonder if Hizzoner knows his son is dating the victim's daughter.

Maybe. He sure looks glum, like people are checking out of his motels in droves now that there's a long-haired, bug-eyed, smack-junkie killer running amok on our pristine sandy beaches. This is bad for business, worse than riptide or pink jellyfish—even worse than that shark in *Jaws* because, face it, to avoid the damn shark, all you really had to do was stay out of the water.

Slominsky has about two dozen microphones stacked in front of him. I can tell he finally dragged a comb through his greasy hair and brushed up his moustache. At the moment, no egg is visible anywhere on his face.

"At approximately 7:15 this morning," Slominsky starts, trying to sound solemn and serious by lowering his otherwise whiny voice, "Mr. Reginald Hart was the victim of an armed robbery here at the Sunnyside Playland Amusement Park. He was shot seven times at point-blank range in the chest."

I'm glad Ceepak's not in here listening to Slobbinsky blow it.

I'm only a summer cop, but even I know you don't give away *all* the gory details of a crime when your suspect is still at large. It helps you eliminate the weirdos who'd confess to anything. Doesn't Slominsky watch any cop shows at all?

"Mr. Hart was pronounced dead at the scene by the Ocean County

Medical Examiner. Fortunately, Mr. Hart's thirteen-year-old daughter, who was with him at the time of the murder, escaped and has helped us put together this composite sketch. . . ."

Oh, great. Now Slobbinsky's telling the perp he needs to find Ashley and gun her down, the sooner the better.

The kid can ID you, mister.

Slominsky should hire one of those airplanes to buzz the beach dragging a long banner off its tail: "Hey—Don't Forget To Kill Ashley Too!"

He holds up the charcoal sketch. The artist did a good job. The guy looks completely scary. Eyes popping out of sockets, long scraggly hair, a stringy goatee, and a dragon tattoo crawling up his neck.

"Who is this asshole?"

A woman in a very short skirt has entered my room.

"The hippie?"

"The asshole holding up the sketch."

"Saul Slominsky," I tell her. "State Police Crime Scene Investigator."

"Jesus. What an idiot. You a cop?" She's looking at my shorts and baseball cap. She's only a year or two older than me, but she's a grownup wearing a short-skirted business suit and I'm sitting here in my playclothes.

"Are you with the police?" she asks again, with that don't-make-me-ask-again-dummy tone underlining every word.

"Yeah. Sort of. Part time. Yeah. Cop."

What is it about women with long tan legs and tiny skirts that turns me into a mushmouth? If I knew, I couldn't tell you right now, because my mouth is full of mush.

She's got very strong calf muscles, the kind that could crack walnuts, and this light blue tribal tattoo wrapping around her ankle that lets every man who sees it know that beneath her all-business exterior, she can be a naughty girl, too.

"I'm Cynthia Stone. Mr. Hart's attorney?"

"Unh-hunh."

"They told me to wait in here. Is that right?"

"Uh—"

I don't know why I open my mouth. She's not waiting for me to answer anything.

"Jesus fucking Christ."

She looks good when she swears like that. She puts her hands on her hips and sticks out her chest, all huffy. She has a big chest and one of those miraculous bras that pushes everything up and makes it all look even bigger.

"I can't believe this shit. We were down here on business—"

"You and Mr. Hart?"

"Yes. Real estate transaction."

The way she says it? She's warning me not to even think impure thoughts about the nature of her relationship with her boss, a guy at least thirty or forty years older than her. But then again, Mr. Hart was a billionaire and, hey, what's thirty or forty years between friends when one of them's worth thirty or forty billion dollars?

"Why the hell didn't they call me? I was at the beach house."

"Unh-hunh."

"I'm using the guest cottage."

"Sure."

"What the hell happened?"

"Can't really say."

"Because you don't really know?"

"Something like that."

Ms. Stone sits down and crosses her legs, obscuring my view of them. She's shifted her attention to Ashley and Jane and Ceepak on the other side of our window.

I take in a deep breath. It's been a tough morning.

Vanilla, patchouli, sandalwood.

I only know that's what I'm smelling because that's what Ceepak said it was back at the Tilt-A-Whirl when he wondered whether young Ashley purchased perfume at Victoria's Secret.

Maybe Ashley doesn't.
But I bet Ms. Stone does.

NINE

Malloy's roadblock, we hear, is moving more smoothly.

Now that they kind of know who they're looking for, they don't need to stop every car on the causeway, just the ones with hippie burnouts riding inside. I figure all VW bugs and microbuses are considered totally suspicious.

So far, the guys canvassing the beach and streets around Playland have come up with diddly-squat. No witnesses, no one who heard the nine pops go off. Seven bullets hit Hart, two hit the turtle shell behind him. Ceepak told me he got a good look at all nine holes before the State boys showed up. He sounded like he was describing the front end of a golf course.

The only jogger on the beach at 7:15 A.M. was this guy with his iPod earbuds stuffed in so deep, the music was melting his earwax. He didn't hear a thing. Neither did my buddy Joey T., the beach sweeper. His tractor makes all kinds of noise when he's out there waking up the gulls.

Here at the house, Ashley's mother showed up and that means our eyewitness stopped talking.

"My poor baby!" she said, understandably upset. "I think it might be best for all concerned if I took Ashley home."

My visitor, the lawyer, decided—"Hey, if the ex can barge in, so can I." She just about knocked the IR door off its hinges when she sent it swinging.

Ashley's mother smiled frostily when Ms. Stone made her entrance.

"Betty," the lawyer said, clipping the two syllables with a sharp bite.

"Ladies?" Ceepak stood up. "We need to ask Ashley a few more questions. . . ."

"They're just doing their jobs, mommy," Ashley said.

"Of course they are, dear," her mother agreed. "I just think it might be better if we did this at home. . . ."

"With a lawyer present." Ms. Stone tossed in her two cents.

"A lawyer? Heavens. Do you officers think Ashley needs a lawyer?" She smiled again. I'll bet she uses a lot of those Crest whitening strips.

"It's up to you, ma'am." Ceepak turned to Ashley. "Would you be more comfortable at home?"

"Yes, sir. If that's all right with you." The way the kid said it? Broke my heart.

Ceepak's too.

So the ex-Mrs. Hart took her daughter's hand and led her outside to their Mercedes. Two state police cars escorted them home. Ms. Stone told us she was checking into a B&B and would be remaining in Sea Haven "for the rest of the weekend."

Ceepak said that was swell, or words to that effect.

Then he and I climbed back into the Ford Explorer and headed south to Ashley's house.

We still had diddly-squat.

"Mrs. Hart doesn't seem too upset by the murder," Ceepak says.

"Because she hated his guts."

A few years back, "The Broken Harts" bumped the Martians and Elvis off the front covers of all the supermarket tabloids. I never buy the gossip rags, I just read them while I wait in the express line behind people who can't count to fifteen.

I know Hart's ex-wife (she was his third) scored the Sea Haven beach house in the divorce settlement but she didn't score much else. She had signed an "ironclad pre-nup" and all she got as a parting gift was the house and a small monthly allowance (which I'm sure is more money than Ceepak and me make all year—combined).

The house is about six miles south of town in Beach Crest Heights, a gated community on the golden tip of the island, where even the sea shanties cost two or three million dollars and come with private pristine beaches.

We pass the Beach Crest gatehouse and drive down to 1500 Rodeo Drive. The guy who developed Beach Crest? He named all his streets after the ones in Beverly Hills.

There's a state police car parked out front of the mansion and two troopers standing guard. They wave us into the big circular driveway.

Flowers that shouldn't grow anywhere near the beach blossom alongside the paved walkway to the front door. The shrubs are trimmed to look like pompons on a stick or a frou-frou poodle's tail.

The house could be a modern art museum or something, all sharp angles and stone and glass. It almost disappears into the dunes, except, of course, that it's huge and there's no way not to see it.

I see six matching suitcases of various sizes and shapes sitting near the manicured flowerbeds. I figure they belong to Ms. Stone and came from the guesthouse. *If* that was where she was really bunking. I see her legs, I have my doubts.

"Mrs. Hart is in the solarium," this old guy at the front door tells us. I guess he's the butler, like that guy with the accent who used to be on *Joe Millionaire*. I bet there's a scullery maid, too. I don't know what a scullery is, but rich people always have a maid for it.

"This way, if you please."

He sounds like he studied Snooty Attitude 101 at the Butler Institute of Technology.

"Thank you," Ceepak says and we scuff our heels across this gigantic marble-and-glass foyer. You can see the sea and sand dunes through the three-story windows in front of us, and all the furniture is either white or tan so it looks like it's made out of sand, like the beach rolls in, right through the windows.

"We're in here!"

She sounds even friendlier and bubblier than she did at the station, and the sun pouring into the solarium makes her dazzling smile seem brighter too.

Now I remember. Years ago, when I was kid, she used to be a weather girl on TV. Betty Something. Betty Bell. She met Reginald Hart at a charity bazaar where she was the emcee and he was the highest bidder, so to speak. I know—I spend far too much time reading in the checkout lane.

I remember watching Betty Bell "Your Friendly Weather Gal" when she was on TV. She had this sweet and sexy way of pointing at her weather map or rolling her arms to let you know a cold front was tumbling into town. She was chipper and perky and her suns always had smiley faces drawn on them and she wore these really tight pink sweaters all winter long. Fuzzy, soft sweaters that hugged her up top, which is all you can really see on TV anyhow. I was only nine or ten at the time, but seeing her in those cuddly pink sweaters, rolling her arms, pointing at cold fronts, kind of made me wish winter could last all year.

"Please, officers, have a seat."

Betty Bell Hart hasn't been on TV in years, but she could be. She's blonde, poised, and gorgeous. I'm sure she's had "work" done, but her workers did a very good job.

"I apologize for making you gentlemen drive all the way down here," she says.

"No problem," Ceepak says. "We understand."

I nod, glad to be included among the understanding.

"When they called, I—"

"You were up in the city?"

"That's right. Usually Ashley and I come down here together on summer weekends."

We listen intently.

"But Ashley's father requested one summer weekend with his daughter, so I let him borrow my beach house. I stayed in the city."

"That's where you and Ashley live?"

"It's our primary residence. I was granted sole custody. Mr. Hart, however, retained certain visitation rights."

Much to my surprise, she opens a box on the coffee table and takes out a cigarette. She lights it with this big clunky thing that I thought was a decorative rock. It stinks. Real bad—worse than cigarettes usually do. Clove has never been one of my favorite odors, not since second grade when I punctured my thumb on one pressing it into an apple for my mom to hang in her closet.

"Do you mind?" She, of course, only asks after her stink bomb is burning like a wet pile of leaves and the solarium goes partly cloudy.

Ceepak shrugs. He could care less.

"So this was your ex-husband's weekend with Ashley?"

"That's right. From time to time he might arrange to take a weekend off and spend it with his daughter." Betty exhales slowly to give us time to realize what kind of father Reginald Hart must have been.

"Then he would typically hire some bright young computer person to play video games with her, as he himself would be busy with all the work he brought along in his briefcase. . . ." She made a quick grimace. "Of course, Reginald also remained very proud of Ashley's many accomplishments. Even if he was rarely able to attend any functions at school."

"I was Emily in *Our Town*." This from Ashley now.

"Grover's Corners," Ceepak offers. "Thorton Wilder."

This display of dramatic trivia is impressive and the two blondes beam. Here's a manly man who knows his Broadway and isn't afraid to admit it.

"I only wish her father could have seen the play. Unfortunately, he was otherwise engaged. Hong Kong, opening another new hotel."

"So, the two of you spent time together out here?" Ceepak says encouragingly. "You and your dad?"

Ashley nods.

"Did he do any work this weekend?"

"Yes. Some. He and Ms. Stone were pretty busy most of Friday. So I swam in the pool and read and stuff. He worked on his laptop."

"We'd like to look at that," Ceepak says to Ashley's mom. "His computer?"

"Certainly. I'll ask James to find it for you."

James. The butler's name is James. Figures. I wonder if it's his real name or one he just uses for work. You know—like The Rock. I'm sure The Rock's parents didn't put "The Rock" on his birth certificate.

"Can you tell us what happened?" Ceepak says to Ashley. "This morning? At the Tilt-A-Whirl?"

"He's still out there, isn't he?" Ashley's eyes swing around the glass-walled sunroom. "The man who shot my father. He could be right outside these windows right now. . . ."

"Don't worry," Ceepak tells her. "I won't let him hurt you. I won't let anybody hurt you."

"Promise?"

"Yes, Ashley. And you know what?"

"What?"

"I always keep my word."

Ceepak actually raises his right hand, like he's making some kind of sacred vow, which, I guess, he is.

TEN

shley takes a deep breath.

"I woke up around six 'cause I heard Miss Stone giggling in the kitchen. I went in and Daddy said, 'Today's our day.' Usually, once every summer, we like to sneak into Playland before it's open."

"Can I ask why?" Ceepak is curious. So am I.

"I dunno. It's just kind of fun."

"But the rides aren't running, the arcade's closed. . . ."

"I know. It's sort of stupid, but it's just something we like to do."

"If someone else writes the rules," Betty explains, "Reggie likes to break them."

I figure that means wedding vows, too.

"We liked to be there while it's still quiet," Ashley continues, "before the beach fills up and gets all crowded."

"What do you two talk about when you're together, like this morning?"

"I dunno. Stuff. Like how he thinks I'm too young to have a boyfriend . . . even though I do. . . ."

"But why the Tilt-A-Whirl?"

"He bought her a turtle once," mom offers.

"Excuse me?"

"When I was like four or five? Daddy bought me this little turtle. I called him Stinky because he pooped all the time."

"You should see her room in the city. Stuffed turtles everywhere. Turtle wallpaper . . . custom-made in Milan. . . ."

"I see," Ceepak says. "I think that's kind of neat. But, tell me—how exactly did you sneak in?"

You gotta admire how Ceepak can push a runaway train of thought back on track.

"There's this tunnel under the fence," Ashley says.

"Under the board?" I say, remembering the square of plywood that looked like it was used for a lid to cover the hole under the fence.

Ceepak turns to look at me.

I never did tell him what I saw. Never told him about the trapdoor. Oops.

Ashley nods. "Yeah. Other people can get in that way, too, I guess." Her mother grips Ashley's hand tight now.

Ceepak waits patiently.

"We were sitting there talking and stuff and this man . . . he came out of the bushes."

"Which bushes?" Ceepak asks.

"Behind this big picture of, you know, the sun-faced guy? Clyde, I think they call him. The cartoon surfer?"

"Unh-hunh."

"We weren't looking that way because, well, it kind of blocks the view so we were looking the other way . . . out to the ocean and all."

"Right."

"He looked crazy and then he started waving this gun at us. A pistol. He looked all dirty and I could smell him . . . even when he was, like, ten feet away. I think he was on drugs, like the homeless people on TV. He told my father to hand over his wallet and my father told the man to 'calm down and not do anything stupid. . . .'"

"Then what?"

"Dad gave the guy his wallet. The crazy man opened it and pulled out all the money. Then he looked at the credit cards and stuff like he was going to steal them but he didn't, he just, you know, read them. 'You're Reginald Hart?' the guy said '*The* Reginald Hart?' My father said, 'Yes, let's talk about this. . . .'"

"Typical Reggie," Betty interjects. "Trying to work a deal."

"What'd the man say, Ashley? When your father said they should talk?"

"Nothing. He just laughed and looked at me. Then, he raised his gun up and pointed it at Daddy's chest and started squeezing the trigger and shooting. He squeezed and fired and squeezed and fired . . . over and over . . . until all the bullets were gone. The gun started clicking and I started screaming 'cause I thought he was going to start shooting at me next, but he didn't. Like I said—I think he ran out of bullets because he fired so many at my father . . . there was so much blood. . . ."

I figure she's seeing it all again on the instant replay of her mind. Poor kid, billionaire's daughter or not.

Ceepak waits. Then he speaks, real soft—a gentle nudge.

"And then?"

"He just sort of smiled this freaky smile at me and told me to count to like a thousand or whatever, like we were playing hide and seek. I tried to count but I couldn't because I was crying and I knew he didn't really care how high I counted 'cause he just ran back to the hole and crawled under the fence and ran away."

"Which way did he go?"

"I'm not sure. I ran behind the turtle to hide. I'm sorry. . . ."

"That's okay. You were smart to hide."

"I was scared."

"Did you see him drop the gun?"

"No. Before he crawled back under the fence, he tucked it back into his pants. Those dirty blue jeans I told you about?"

"Right."

"He put it in, like, the waistband. He didn't have on a belt. He had a string. Twine? Like you wrap up boxes and stuff with? He had twine for a belt, I forgot that part until just now. . . ."

Ceepak makes a note.

"Did he say or do anything else?"

"No. I don't think so. No. Wait. . . ."

Ashley looks at her mother.

"He used the F-word," Ashley says.

"How so?" Ceepak asks.

"Go on, sweetie." Her mother gives her permission to swear. "Tell them what he said."

"He said to me, he said, 'You should know—your father was a fucking slumlord.'"

ELEVEN

I figure Ceepak is totally pissed at me.

We're sitting in the car in the driveway with the engine shut off, so that means the AC is off too and the temperature is 110 inside the Explorer thanks to the sun everybody comes down here to worship.

Ceepak's not saying anything. Not telling me where to drive next. He's just sitting there, staring out the windshield at those ugly pompon poodle bushes.

"Tell me what you saw," he says after what feels like four hours of slow roasting in the Ford E-Z Bake Oven.

"Inside? With them?"

"At the fence."

"You mean the hole?"

"This lid. This plywood lid you say you saw."

"Oh. Okay. Sure. It was, you know, a square. Probably two feet by two feet. It was covered with sand, from where the sweeper raked over it. . . ."

"What was the condition of said tunnel?"

"It was only like three feet long. Enough to scoot under the fence."

"How deep?"

"Foot or two."

"And the bottom?"

"What do you mean?"

"Was it loose? Packed down?"

"Packed down."

"Like people had been crawling in and out every day?"

"Yeah."

Ceepak nods.

"You see why this should be considered important?"

"Yes, sir. Sorry."

Ceepak nods again. I don't think he ever loses his temper. I wish he would. This quiet routine gives me too much time to realize just how royally I screwed up.

"Notice anything else that might be important?"

"At the beach?"

"Or anywhere. Take your time."

Okay. Now I'm actually kind of pissed at *him* for staying so calm, cool and collected. At least when my dad's mad he screams at me and I get a pretty colorful and complete description of what I did wrong. Not with Ceepak. Maybe he wants me to stew in my own juices, go to my room and think about it, all that kind of crap. Well, screw him.

Did I notice anything else that might be important?

I suddenly recall the rust marks I saw on the wall in the men's room at The Pancake Palace, maybe because Ashley said the crazy guy with the gun smelled like pee-pee and maybe my astute observation could also be considered urine-related.

Then I remember the perfume.

"The lawyer? Cynthia Stone?"

"Yes?"

"She smelled like that perfume. The Victoria's Secret stuff."

"Interesting."

"You think she was there? At the Tilt-A-Whirl?"

"It's a possibility."

I do the head-bob nod this time, like I've figured something out.

"But," Ceepak says, "the more likely scenario is that the odor emanated from Mr. Hart's own clothing, suggesting he had contact with Ms. Stone earlier in the morning or late last night. Perhaps they were romantically involved. Good work, Danny."

I can tell he means it, too.

"Thanks."

He flips through his notes.

"Possibly our 'crazy man' was a tenant at some point in one of Mr. Hart's buildings . . . or knows someone who was."

"On account of what he said to Ashley about her father being a slumlord."

"Presents us with a long list of names to check. . . ."

"Thousands."

"We can also conjecture that the perpetrator used a semi-automatic weapon."

"Because he had to keep squeezing the trigger?"

"Exactly."

That one was pretty easy, but I smile anyhow. I'm starting to feel better.

Ceepak looks at his watch. It's 2:45 P.M. My shift is supposed to end at three but I'm willing to work overtime if it will help dig me out of the hole I think I dug for myself when I forgot to tell Ceepak about the lid over that other hole.

"I want to see Officer Kiger. The officer on beach patrol this A.M. . . ."

"Sure. No problem. I'm cool with pulling some O.T., won't even put in for it. . . ."

"Danny?"

"Yeah?"

"You're not in trouble. You made an honest mistake. You should have told me about the trapdoor, but you did not. Now, however, you have, so we move forward. I harbor no resentments. We all make mistakes. That's why my pencil has an eraser. I make mistakes too."

"Yeah. Okay. Cool."

"Now then, do you know where Officer Kiger lives?"

"Adam? Sure."

Ceepak checks his watch again.

"I suppose this is when he typically sleeps."

"Too bad," I say, feeling juiced. "Let's go wake him up."

"Roger that."

I crank the ignition and blast on the air conditioner.

Ceepak is staring out the window, mumbling. I can barely hear him over the fan blowing cold air into my face.

"'The greasers they tramp the streets or get busted for trying to sleep on the beach all night. . . .'"

He's quoting Springsteen again. Now I know why he wants to see Kiger.

If Adam drives up and down the beach in his ATV every morning looking for vagrants, chances are he's met the greasers who frequent the Tilt-A-Whirl. He's busted a few tramps "trying to sleep on the beach all night."

Maybe even the ones in charge of under-the-fence-tunnel maintenance.

On the ride over to Kiger's place, the chief radios to let us know that the State CSI team is at Betty Bell's beach bungalow retrieving Reginald Hart's computer and briefcase.

"You'll be happy to hear Lieutenant Slominsky is no longer with them," the chief says. "He went home a little early. . . ."

"How's that?"

"We got lucky, I guess."

"Did you make a few calls?"

"Maybe one or two."

"Roger that. Do we know where Ms. Stone is staying? Hart's lawyer?"

"Chesterfields—a hoity-toity place in town. Don't worry. We'll keep her on a short leash."

"Check. We're heading over to talk to Kiger. See if he's ever bumped into our suspect."

"Give Adam my best when you wake him up."

"Roger that."

"Squeegee," Adam Kiger says when he looks at the sketch of our suspect.

We did, indeed, wake him up. But we stopped at Dunkin' Donuts on the way over and the black coffee was, as advertised, "just the thing." Especially since we also grabbed Adam a couple of those cakey chocolate doughnuts I know he loves.

"Yeah. That's Squeegee. I mean it sure looks like him."

Adam wolfs down a hunk of doughnut.

"You've rousted him before?" Ceepak asks, folding up his copy of the sketch.

"A few times. He likes to crawl under the fence there at the Tilt-A-Whirl. A lot of our local druggies do the same thing. That's why I never took away their trapdoor or filled in the tunnel. Makes it easy to find 'em."

"Check," Ceepak says.

"One-stop shopping." Adam chomps off some more doughnut. "Like a big roach motel."

Adam Kiger is a little older than me, younger than Ceepak. He's been full time with the Sea Haven police for three or four years. He has the short, shaved-head haircut. The muscles. He and Ceepak look like cops.

"They the only ones who sneak in there? The users?"

"In the morning. Late nights, you get your high school and college kids looking for a dark place to make out. They crawl under the fence, too. But that's more a night-shift problem. Some guys catch all the luck. They get lovers' lane, I get the pharmaceuticals convention."

"So why do you call him Squeegee?"

"He used to work at the car wash sometimes. You know the place—just off Ocean Avenue?"

"Cap'n Scrubby's?" I say.

Ceepak rolls his eyes. I don't think he'll ever get used to the cutesy-poo nautical names in Sea Haven.

"Yeah," Adam says. "Scrubby's. Squeegee used to be one of the towel guys at the end of the line working for tips. He'd rub down the inside of your vehicle, swipe his towel around your seat cushions, wipe the water off your windows. . . ."

"Like a squeegee." Ceepak gets it.

"Right. And he was so skinny, the name kind of stuck. He looks like a long, skinny pole. . . ."

"Have you seen him lately?"

"About a week ago I did a swing by the Tilt-A-Whirl, gave him a wake-up call. It was raining, so he and a few of his buddies were up in the turtles. They use the ride for a shooting gallery because all the cars have those roof deals up top. You know, where the turtle necks stick out? Makes an excellent crash pad. Roof keeps 'em dry."

"Do you know where he lives?"

"Up and down the beach. No known address. We don't even know his real name."

"Check. So what happened this morning?"

"Approximately 0630, I get called off the beach. Had to go deal with that stupid tricycle theft up on Rosewood."

"Right."

"Missed all the fireworks."

"Have you ever seen your friend Squeegee carrying a weapon?"

"What? A gun? Knife?"

"Perhaps a semi-automatic pistol? Maybe nine-millimeter?"

"Not that I ever saw. But I wouldn't put it past him. For a long-haired hippie, Squeegee's sort of short on 'peace, love, and under-standing.' He is one angry old dude. Extremely confrontational. Paranoid. Thinks everything is a Republican plot against him. Always gives me grief when I wake him up."

"How so?"

"He's just a nasty hunk of humanity. Called me a 'lackey tool of the capitalist pigs.' Got up in my face real close, made me smell the sour booze on his breath. Liked to hiss stuff at me, like he was some kind of snake."

"What kind of stuff?"

"'Stupid slumlord stooge.' Stuff like that."

Slumlord. We're hearing that word a lot today.

TWELVE

A round six, I drop Ceepak off back at the Bell beach house.

"You want me to stay here with you?" I ask. "In case you need a ride somewhere?"

"No thanks. I'm staying put tonight, walking the perimeter."

"Guard duty?"

"I gave that young lady my word." He says it with a grin and looks much happier because I think he feels like we're finally getting somewhere.

Squeegee's our man.

"Go home and get some sleep, Danny. Big day tomorrow."

"Roger that," I say, sounding just like Ceepak. "You too."

"Right."

But I can tell he has other plans. I don't think he ever sleeps much—especially not when he's on guard duty.

"See you tomorrow," he says. "0730. Here. Sharp."

"Sharp," I say.

Ceepak salutes "so long" and marches up to the top of the driveway to check in with the two state police. They point here and there, plot their positions.

CHRIS GRABENSTEIN

I figure Ashley Hart's going to sleep peacefully tonight.

She's got armed guards—and one of them is John Ceepak.

I'm feeling kind of pumped, like I clutched victory from the jaws of defeat and ended the day on a high note.

I turn in the cop car, punch out at headquarters, jump into my own wheels, and head home to lose my work clothes and grab a quick shower. Then, I think I'll head down to The Sand Bar, see what I can see, download my day.

I'm starting to think maybe I could be a cop. A real one, not just this part-time deal for the summer. Ceepak? He'll do that to you— he'll make you start thinking about being all you can be, like they used to sing in those old Army commercials.

The Sand Bar is buzzing.

It's 8:30 P.M. and I'm out on the deck with a few of my buds (most of whom are drinking Buds) watching the sun slip down behind the docks and sailboats on the bay side of the island. There's a screened-in porch with picnic tables, and sometimes we like hanging out here better than inside at the bar. You can hear most of the music but not as much of the bull people at the bar start spewing after their third or fourth beer.

Everybody wants me to tell them about the murder but I say "No comment," like I've seen lawyers do on cop shows.

"Who do they think did it?"

"No comment."

"You have some suspects though, right?"

"No comment."

Sounds like I know everything without having to say anything at all.

Some of my friends wonder if Sunnyside Playland will ever reopen. And if they do, will they tear down the Tilt-A-Whirl? This one girl, my friend Becca, who works at her family's motel on Beach Lane, she thinks they have to.

"Would you want to ride on a ride where somebody was murdered? How gross. . . ."

"No comment," I say.

"Jesus, Danny—is that all you're gonna say all night?" It's Jess. He's right. I sort of sound like a skipping CD somebody needs to whack so I'll move on to the next track.

"Can't you say anything else?"

"How about another brewski? I'm buying."

"Okay. That's better."

"Much better," Becca adds. "And grab some popcorn."

"Roger that," I say.

"Who's Roger?"

I forgot I'm with civilians.

"Nobody. You guys want to eat?"

"Sure."

"Grab some menus. I'll grab the beers."

"10-4, good buddy," Jess says. He's confused. By adding "good buddy," he's doing Truck Driver instead of Cop. This stuff is kind of subtle.

I work my way inside and move through the crowd to the bar. It's noisy. The speakers hanging off the ceiling are thumping something fierce.

Down at the far end of the bar, I see this Abercrombie-Fitch type kid with a tray of Jell-O shots. He looks to be seventeen. Maybe sixteen.

He shouldn't be in here buying booze.

So I do what I think Ceepak would do.

"Debbie?" I yell loud enough so my friend the bartender can hear me over the Saturday night racket. Debbie looks particularly fetching in her tattered-neck Sand Bar T-shirt and torn-off short-shorts. Add a parrot, she could be a pirate wench.

"Hey. What's up, Danny Boy?"

"That kid down there? I hope that's the Jell-O jiggler sampler you just served him. Something he could share with the whole class when he goes back to kindergarten in the fall. . . ."

"Hey, man—I checked his driver's license. Says he's twenty-one. Says he's cool."

"Is that so? Well, I got a piece of paper back home that says I'm Star Wars TIE-Fighter Commander on account of I drank enough Pepsi at Pizza Hut. . . ."

"You goin' all-cop on me, Danny Boy? Taking this summer job seriously all of a sudden?"

"I just don't want you guys to lose your liquor license. That's all."

"Then ease up."

"What if that kid gets in a car wreck?"

"He won't."

"How do you know?"

"His father probably took away his keys. In case you haven't heard, there's this killer on the loose and nobody wants their kids driving anywhere until the cops catch the creep. *If* they can catch him. If they're not too busy running around town hassling people, checking fake IDs. . . ."

Debbie can dish it out pretty good.

"I need three beers," I say.

"Buds?"

"Yeah. Long-necks."

Debbie moves back down the bar to the cooler.

I'm thinking about asking the kid with the fake ID a few questions like Ceepak would do. *"So — you're twenty-one? What year were you born? How many touchdowns did Mickey Mantle score that year? Hah! Gotcha. Mickey Mantle never played football. . . ."*

The kid's cell phone rings. He sticks his finger in his empty ear, looks at his watch, says something like "right now?" (from what I can read on his lips), and snaps his flip phone shut.

"Gotta bounce."

I hear him say good-bye to the high-school buddies clustered behind him.

"I'm late for a blow job."

I hear that one, too. His buddies slap him on the back and the kid slurps down a Dixie pixie cup of (I'm sure) vodka-soaked red Jell-O and walks out the door.

Debbie brings me the beers in a plastic bucket filled with ice.

"You got some ID, Danny?"

She's still busting my chops, but I play along and whip out my wallet.

"See? We card everybody in here."

"Good for you, Debbie."

And to think—we used to date. Back in high school, when I was the big man with the fake ID. Maybe Debbie's right. Maybe I'm taking this cop thing too seriously.

I uncurl five extra bucks and leave them on the bar as a tip so Debbie knows I'm sorry if I was acting like an asshole.

"You need popcorn?" she asks.

"Yeah. Popcorn would be great."

She scoops me up a bucket and smiles. All is forgiven.

I hug both buckets and hustle out to the porch where my thirsty friends wait.

Becca, per usual, regales us with lurid stories of sordid motel guests. She works at the front desk, so she sees and hears everything. This week, she says, it's "Latino Soprano" week at The Mussel Beach Motel.

"We've got all these tough customers hanging out around the pool. Mendez. Ramirez. Echaverra. And you should see the tattoos—which I, of course, did." Becca is known to admire the sculpted male physique. Probably why she and I don't date. "This one guy? Virgilio Mendez? His chest and arms look like an art museum. He's pumped to the max and has the Blessed Virgin Mary inked on his right shoulder . . . Jesus with the crown of thorns on his left pec. . . ."

Halfway through the beers—my second, their third—we decide it's time to order dinner. So we flag down a waitress and order some fried shrimp and fried clam tenders and a French-fried lobster.

The fried food always comes to the table fastest.

I'm just getting started on my clam strips and curly fries when my cell phone rings.

I figure it's Ceepak, calling to make sure I'm tan, rested, and ready for our big day tomorrow.

Caller ID confirms my hunch. It's my 9:30 tuck-in call.

"Yes sir?"

"Danny—how many beers have you had?"

"Two."

"That'll work. I need you down here at the beach house."

"Is everything okay?"

"Negative. Ashley Hart is missing."

THIRTEEN

've never seen so many cop cars.

Red and white lights are swirling everywhere. The road is clogged with armed troops lugging all kinds of heavy firepower. I even see some guys with black Kevlar helmets and full body armor. I swear—it looks like we're about to invade the next town down the shore.

I see Adam Kiger. He's got another Dunkin' Donuts coffee going. This one's iced, one of those slushy Coolatas they sell, because it's still hot and muggy and the wind isn't even blowing.

"Guess I'm never gonna get any sleep," Adam jokes when I catch his eye.

"Yeah. You seen Ceepak?"

"Out back. That's where the girl snuck out."

"Thanks, man."

Snuck out? The plot thickens.

I find Ceepak in the back yard, out near the pool.

"She snuck out," he says. "To meet her boyfriend."

He points up to a small balcony on the second floor. There's a sliding glass door up there and it's open. The balcony's right near this trellis deal made out of four-by-fours and latticework with grapevines or something growing all over it. It'd be an easy little hop from the balcony to the top of the trellis and then a quick shimmy down to the ground. It's like Ashley has a backyard "Romeo and Juliet Playset" instead of the more traditional jungle gym.

"Is the boyfriend here?"

"Negative," Ceepak says. "We heard his story, then his father hauled him home."

"Mayor Sinclair?"

"Roger that. The boy will be available for further questioning, should we need to talk to him later."

"So what's his story?"

Ceepak pulls out his little notebook.

"Ben Sinclair says Ashley Hart called him from her cell phone and stated she needed to see him right away. She was so 'totally freaked' by everything that happened today, she asked him—no, he said she 'begged him'—to meet her back here by the pool. He hopped on his motorcycle, left town around 2045. They waved him through at the guardhouse gate. . . ."

Figures. Guess being the mayor's son gives you an E-Z Pass through life.

"Sinclair arrived here at approximately 2100 hours. The state police officer guarding the northern perimeter let him pass when he explained who he was." He does a two-finger point to the south. "I was patrolling the far perimeter. Wasn't alerted to his arrival. The young man waited approximately fifteen minutes. Sat there."

Ceepak points to a chaise longue on the patio surrounding the kidney-shaped pool. I see one empty and one half-empty Heineken sitting on a small round table next to the chair.

"How old's this boyfriend?" I ask, looking at his beer bottles.

"Sixteen. Maybe seventeen. Apparently, he knows where they stow the alcoholic beverages."

Ceepak nods at a refrigerator tucked into the brickwork of a massive backyard barbeque. I'm not talking Weber grill and sack of charcoal here. This is one of those stainless-steel professional jobs built into a garden wall.

"So the kid sat sipping beer for five, ten minutes," I say, picking up the narrative.

"Right," Ceepak says, piecing it all together for me so it becomes clearer for him. "Then, when Ashley still doesn't show, he starts 'getting pissed.' He walks over here . . . to the pergola—"

"The what?"

"The arbor. The trellis."

"This thing? With the vines?"

"Right. He comes over here and tries calling up to Ashley's room . . . tosses a pea pebble or two at her bedroom window. . . ."

"And he realizes her balcony door is open."

"Exactly," Ceepak says. "That's when young Mr. Sinclair starts, as he puts it, 'to shit a brick.' He runs back up to the road, yells at the state police officer, says, 'Ashley's gone! Ashley's gone!' Her mother hears the boy, comes running out the front door. She proceeds to scream as well. At 2125 hours, I call for reinforcements, initiate a hard target search."

That would be 9:25 P.M.

It's almost ten now. Took me fifteen minutes to drive down from The Sand Bar. I drove slow because, well, I'd been drinking.

"Ceepak?"

It's the chief.

"What the hell happened?"

The chief is wearing a big mesh T-shirt, like a football jersey if they played football in July instead of the fall. He's got on gray sweat-pant shorts and flip-flops and looks like he was home in his comfy chair, ready to kick back, pop the top on a cold one, and watch some ball when this new thing started going down.

"Nothing definite yet, chief."

"Well, find something definite, okay? Find it fast."

"I'm all over it, sir."

The chief does one of those quick looks around, like he wants to make sure nobody is eavesdropping.

"This thing? It could . . . you know . . . it could get messy. State police. FBI. I need, you know . . . I need your best, John."

"It's all I'll ever give you, sir."

"Great. Okay. Great. Thanks."

Something about the way Ceepak says stuff, like he truly means it, always puts people at ease.

"Where's the mother?"

"Inside. Jane is sitting with her."

"Okay. Good. Smart. I'm going up to the road," the chief says. "Reconnoiter with the troops. Work out a search grid. You coming?"

"In a minute. I want to nose around down here first."

"Yeah?"

"Yeah."

"Holler if you find something . . . anything."

"Roger."

"I'm putting out an Amber Alert."

Ceepak nods. This means the TV and radio will urge anybody who thinks they see Ashley, or has any information about her at all, to call the police.

The chief lugs his bulk around the side of the house and starts screaming at our guys assembled up at the top of the driveway. When we can't hear him yelling any more, Ceepak motions for me to follow him—away from the pool, down to the beach.

The back yard of the beach house sort of flows right into the sand, making it look like whoever owns the house also owns this piece of the ocean too.

"Where we going?" I ask.

"Down to the beach. They've got the road covered. Sending out search teams. But—we had the front and sides of the house under surveillance when Ashley went missing. There's also the gatehouse at the entrance to the subdivision. The guard only granted admittance to the mayor's son because he knew him. So. . . ."

"So whoever did this came up the beach?" I catch on fast.

"He or she. But at this juncture, we don't even know if there was someone."

"What? You think Ashley went for a moonlit stroll on the beach? Without her boyfriend?"

"Like I said, at this point, anything is possible." Ceepak is walking with his head down, studying the ground in front of his feet. "And everything will remain possible until we find evidence that eliminates certain of those possibilities."

"Like what?"

"This."

Ceepak pulls out his Maglite and twists the lens.

He saw the bootprint without the light. I see it now.

"Timberland?" I ask.

"Looks like." He follows the prints down to the tide line, where the waves wash everything away.

"It's our same guy," I say.

"That is one possibility. Remember, Danny—don't jump to conclusions; there may not be anything solid for you to land on."

That line is so corny, it must be something Ceepak's father told him. My own dad always said, "Never assume: It makes an ass out of 'u' and 'me.'" I think they must go to night school to learn the corny stuff they're supposed to say to their sons in certain situations.

"So," I ask, "how did this boot-wearing person sneak in?"

"Good question."

Ceepak swings his flashlight around.

"You think he was, I don't know—some kind of Navy SEAL or something? Scuba-dived up to the beach? Dragged Ashley away. . . ."

"It's a possibility," Ceepak says, only half-listening. Maybe he knows I stole my idea from this Steven Seagal movie I rented once.

"How about a boat?" I say. "Maybe the guy or girl . . . the doer . . . maybe they had a boat."

"More probable than a car or ATV. However, I suspect we might have heard the approach of any motorized craft. So if it was a boat. . . ."

"It was a rowboat . . . or a kayak . . . or a rubber raft. . . ."

CHRIS GRABENSTEIN

"Or, our perp might have simply walked along the shoreline, using the waves to wash away any trace of his or her movements."

He swings his flashlight up and down the beach. Left, then right, then left again.

He stops on a patch of beach grass just beyond the high-tide line.

There's this one trampled section. Ceepak walks over to it. I'm right behind him.

"Careful where you step."

"Right," I say, remembering my morning lesson, walking only where Ceepak has already walked.

"Interesting," he says.

The coarse grass is spread open, matted flat, and reaches a V-shaped point like a wedge was dragged across the weeds. A wedge or an aluminum fishing boat.

Ceepak hunkers down and holds his flashlight near his head. He looks like a coal miner digging for sand crabs. I see him snap open a pants pocket and pull out his magnifying glass.

"Danny, do you have the digital camera?"

"Sorry. It's in the Ford and I drove my own vehicle, because. . . ."

"Roger."

Ceepak examines something caught in the grass.

"Surfer bracelet," he says.

"Purple and green?"

"Check."

I remember it. "It's Ashley's."

"You had no one back here?"

The chief is yelling at the state police, but Ceepak is the one hanging his head and staring at his shoes. He's taking this hard, like it's entirely his fault. Like he broke his promise and let Ashley down because he should have anticipated a sea-based attack.

I wouldn't have thought about it.

Who'd ever expect an angry junkie to be smart (and sober) enough to launch some kind of amphibious assault?

And why didn't Squeegee just kill the girl?

Or maybe he did and we just don't know it yet. Maybe he hid her body somewhere, buried it in the sand, dumped it in the ocean.

But if he was trying to get rid of the one witness who could place him at the scene of his earlier murder, why didn't he just shoot her the minute she dropped into the back yard? We know she was alone. The boyfriend didn't show until she was already gone.

So why aren't we doing another crime-scene analysis of Ashley Hart's bullet-riddled body?

Maybe somebody else grabbed the girl, not Squeegee. Somebody else wearing Timberland boots in July? Doubtful. But like Ceepak says, "it's a possibility."

"We need to contact the FBI," the chief says. "This guy's going to ask for money. It's a goddamn kidnapping."

"That's one possibility."

"You got a better theory?" the chief snaps.

"No, sir. Not yet."

The chief sounds and looks pissed because, basically, he is. The last two things a tourist town like Sea Haven needs is a murderer *and* a child-snatcher running up and down the beach, because that sort of thing can really scare folks away, make them want to stay at home in their crime-stricken cities where they feel safe.

"I suspect," the chief says, "that once our guy realized whom he shot this morning, he also realized he could ring the cash register a second time by grabbing the girl and scoring an even bigger payday."

"That would explain why he didn't shoot Ashley this morning," Ceepak says, helping the chief flesh out his theory.

"Right. Exactly. Good." The chief seems happy that Ceepak is back on board. "He figured the girl was more valuable to him as a hostage held for ransom."

"It's a possibility," Ceepak says again, and the chief flashes him a look that makes my shoulders hunch up, like somebody's going to smack me. "A very distinct possibility."

"Yeah." The chief stares out at the sea. "Okay. Makes sense. I tell you one thing—this guy, Squeegee? He must be doing some very serious drugs. The kind that make you smart. Real smart."

FOURTEEN

t's all over the eleven-o'clock news.

"Authorities in Sea Haven have issued an Amber Alert for Harriet Ashley Hart, the twelve-year-old daughter of murdered billionaire Reginald Hart. . . ."

They flash her picture. And her first name is Harriet? No wonder she calls herself Ashley.

"The young girl apparently witnessed her father's brutal murder earlier today. Now it appears she may have become the victim of foul play herself. . . ."

Yep, folks—been a busy day down in beautiful Sea Haven. Murder. Abduction. Foul play aplenty. And you thought people came here to relax.

Up pops the police sketch of Squeegee. He looks plenty scary, with big blank eyes that don't give you any clue what the hell his whacked mind might be thinking. He looks like a skinnier version of Charles Manson, only without the swastika scratched into his forehead with a safety pin. Squeegee's scowl will probably give the folks watching at home all sorts of raw material for their nightmares tonight.

Now they're showing video footage taped earlier in the day. We see the mob of people in T-shirts and shorts, some licking ice-cream cones, outside the fence at Sunnyside Playland. Guess this was the thing to do on vacation today: Grab the kids, head on down to the closed-off crime scene, prop your boy up on your shoulders, and see if he can sneak a peek at the Tilt-A-Whirl where, as the TV reporter on the scene so colorfully puts it, "Reginald Hart's whirlwind life came spinning to a stop."

"Danny?"

Ceepak motions for me to join him at what I guess is the wet bar.

We've set up a mobile command center inside the rec room, a big space right off the pool through sliding glass doors about twenty feet tall.

"Yes, sir?"

"Does this look like the bootprint we found behind the bushes this A.M.?" Ceepak shows me what looks like a smooshed dinner plate somebody stomped on while the clay was still wet, like the plaster handprint I made for my mom one Christmas that still hangs above the cabinets in her kitchen.

"Did this come from the beach?"

"Check. The State boys took a plaster cast of the bootprints we found in the sand."

"It's a Timberland," I try out. "Just like we found this morning."

"Check. But remember—it's a very popular, very fashionable brand of boot. Lots of people wear them."

Ceepak refuses to eliminate too many possibilities.

"Still," he admits, "it's a link. A strong connector. . . ."

Ashley's mother comes into the room. She looks like hell on toast. She sees all the police putting pins in maps and talking into hand-held radios. Then she sees Ceepak.

"Why aren't you out searching for her?"

Ceepak puts down the bootprint plaster. I hope Betty doesn't use it for an ashtray. She's smoking again and there are gray ash flecks dusting the front of her black sweater. Her face looks ashen too, like it's been gray and drizzling all day and there's more precipitation in the forecast for tomorrow.

"You said you'd protect her. When you raised your hand and made that vow? Ashley believed you. So did I."

The chief comes up behind her and places his big beefy hand on her shoulder. She turns to look up at him. He towers about two feet above her blond head, but he's a gentle giant and his touch seems to comfort her.

"Ma'am, believe me—Officer Ceepak and all the other officers, in here and out in the field, will do everything they can to find your daughter. We're sorting through clues and organizing a massive search-and-rescue operation. We've called in the Coast Guard, the Rescue Dogs. We're setting up roadblocks, sending out a call for volunteers to assist in the search. . . ."

The woman nods her head. She understands.

"Thank you. It's just that. . . ." She takes a deep breath. "I'm afraid."

"Just let us do our jobs? Please?"

She hesitates, then pulls herself together. "Of course, Chief. Of course."

They both nod their heads. The chief steps away.

She turns to Ceepak.

"Ashley really liked you."

"Don't worry. We'll find her."

She turns to go back to her bedroom and cry some more, when one of the State Crime Scene Investigators comes over carrying a small Dell computer.

"Excuse me, ma'am?"

She slowly turns around.

"Yes?"

"Sorry to bother you with this. . . ."

"Will it find my daughter?"

"It could."

"All right."

"We've been working on your ex-husband's laptop. Trying to

access his calendar, address book. See who he might have had recent contact with. . . ."

Betty closes her eyes for a second, like she needs to collect her thoughts to keep from screaming at this cop for worrying about a computer when he should be outside, finding her little girl.

"You really think *this* will help you locate Ashley?"

"Like I said, it could."

The chief now marches back to her side, looking every bit the big-hearted commander.

"We think the murder and the disappearance are linked," he says, using his confident coach voice—the one that tells you he knows exactly what play to call to win the game in the final five seconds. "So we really need your help."

"Of course." She gives him a tense smile.

"Any idea what his security code might be?" the crime scene guy asks. "It might help us crack into his database faster. . . ."

"BUSTER," she says.

"Ma'am?"

"Buster was his dog when he was a boy. B-U-S-T-E-R is his security code for everything. ATM card, E-mail . . . everything."

"Thanks." The guy with the laptop plops down on a sofa and starts tapping keys.

"Thank you," the chief echoes softly.

"You're welcome. I think I'm going to lie down now. The doctor gave me some pills . . . I'm starting to feel a little groggy. . . ."

"Good. Sleep is good."

"Officer Ceepak?"

"Yes, ma'am?"

She steadies herself, wanting to say whatever it is she needs to say before her brain closes up shop for the day.

"You made a very special connection with my daughter today. Somehow, I think she needs you more than all these others. She put her trust in you . . . told me you were her protector, her special champion."

Poor Ceepak. He's being pegged as Ashley's only hope, her knight in shining armor.

He nods. I guess he sees himself the same way. The Code? It'll do that to you.

"I'll find her," Ceepak whispers. No "we" any more. This is personal. "I give you my word."

"Thank you."

Betty leaves the room, her five-day forecast looking extremely gloomy, indeed.

"Ceepak?" It's the chief.

"Yes, sir?"

"I want you and Danny on the morning shift."

"Fine. We'll work straight through. . . ."

"No. You need to go home and grab some sleep. Now. Both of you. I want you fresh and at your best tomorrow morning when we'll probably have more substantial leads."

"Roger." Ceepak, as always, recognizes an order when he's given one.

"Anybody know a Virgilio Mendez?" the guy working with the laptop asks the room.

"Mendez?" The chief moves to the couch to look over the guy's shoulder.

I think I've heard of him. Isn't that the guy Becca mentioned back at The Sand Bar? The Latino Soprano with the tattoos. But I'm sort of out of my league in this room so I stay quiet, let the big dogs bark first.

"Hart met with Mendez on Friday. Noon. Place called The Lobster Trap. He had another meeting scheduled with him tomorrow. 10 A.M. Chesterfield's."

"Swankiest dining room in town," the chief says.

I nod. I've never actually been inside Chesterfield's. It's this three-story gingerbread Victorian painted purple and pink that hired a fancy chef from the city for its kitchen. That's why the scrambled eggs cost like twenty bucks.

"So who is this Mendez?" Ceepak asks.

The chief's on top of it. "Dominican. Works for the top boys in Ocean Town. Connected to the casinos. . . ."

"What's his relationship to Mr. Hart?" Ceepak asks.

"I don't know," the chief says.

"I do."

When nobody was looking, our New York lady lawyer had slipped into the room.

Cynthia Stone is standing there, doing that thing with her hands on her hips and her chest all pushed forward. She reminds me of this bird I saw once on a National Geographic special, always puffing up its breast, trying to scare everyone else away from the worm it wants.

"Mr. Mendez has, in the past, done some work for Hart Enterprises as a real estate expediter," she says.

"Expediter?" the chief groans. He doesn't like words like expediter.

"He handled certain matters for us. However, that calendar is incorrect. All scheduled meetings with Mr. Mendez were subsequently cancelled."

"Ms. Stone?" the chief says. "That's your name, right?"

"Correct."

The chief moves real slow so she can see what a big, scary man he is. But she isn't buying into it. She stands there just like her name: rock solid—a concrete saint in a cement birdbath.

"Thank you for the information," the chief says, leaning in so he's about six inches from her face. If she wanted to, she could count the pores on his nose. "Now, I must ask you to leave. As you may know, Ashley Hart is missing. . . ."

The woman doesn't flinch.

"Yes."

"We are very goddamn busy here and I don't see how any of this is any of your business—"

"That's where you are wrong. It is my business. In fact, as a corporate officer, I have a fiduciary responsibility to—"

"You have a what?"

"Fiduciary responsibility."

"Oh? Really? Paint me a picture."

"Certainly," she says. "Reginald Hart's will specifies a single beneficiary. His daughter."

"So?"

"So as of 7:15 A.M., the time of death pronounced by the Ocean County Medical Examiner, Harriet Ashley Hart inherited everything her father owned. Your missing person? She is also my new chairman and CEO. Ashley owns Hart Enterprises."

FIFTEEN

Suddenly, Squeegee—or whoever grabbed Harriet Ashley Hart—looks like a genius. He's nabbed himself a kid who just inherited several billion bucks.

I know what Ceepak is thinking: Squeegee isn't the only one who'd be interested in that kind of dough. Anybody who knew about the will is suddenly one of his "distinct possibilities."

We're out the front door and heading up the road to where I parked. All the good spots were already taken when I got here.

When we're about two hundred yards away from the house I let Ceepak know what I think I know.

"Ceepak?"

"Yes, Danny?"

"I think this Mendez guy is still in town."

"How so? Gut feeling?"

"No. This friend of mine? Becca Adkinson? She works the front desk at her family's motel . . . The Mussel Beach Motel."

"Mussel Beach?"

"Like, you know—the seafood?"

"Okay. Go on."

"Becca said she saw these tough guys hanging around the pool all day."

"Tough guys?"

"Yeah. You know—tats everywhere. Muscles. Scars." I add the scars part because I think it makes the story a little better and besides I bet at least one of them had a scar—somewhere. "She thought they were a gang or something."

"I see. And what makes you think one of these gentlemen is our Virgilio Mendez?"

"He was her favorite."

"Excuse me?"

"Becca liked Mendez's tattoos best. I think they, you know, talked about them. Anyhow, she mentioned his name. . . ."

Ceepak stops walking.

"Good work," he says, sounding proud.

"Thanks. So why would Ms. Stone insist Hart's calendar was wrong? That all meetings with Mendez had been cancelled? We know he's in town. . . ."

"Perhaps Mr. Mendez knows some things Ms. Stone would rather we did not."

"You think?"

"It's a possibility." He winks, letting me know he's saying it for the ten millionth time on purpose. "Excellent work, Danny. Awesome intelligence."

"So—what do we do? Go back in and bust Ms. Stone?"

"This motel? The Mussel Beach? Do you know where it is?"

"Sure."

"I'd like to head over there right now. However, the chief ordered us to stand down for the evening."

"So?"

"We'll contact your friend."

"Becca."

"Ask her to ascertain whether Mr. Mendez is still a registered guest."

"Then what? She can't bust him or anything. Not unless he pulls a tag off a mattress or something. . . ."

"We'll ask Officer Kiger to keep an eye on the motel during his overnight shift. Tomorrow morning, first thing, we'll swing by the motel ourselves, have an early-morning chat with Mr. Mendez."

We reach my car. It's a hand-me-down I bought "pre-owned" from my mom. A minivan. That's the bad news. The good news? Ceepak has plenty of legroom.

We both climb in. I make the call. Becca tells me Mendez is still there. Went to bed early. I don't ask her how she knows this, she just does. I tell her Adam Kiger will be cruising through her parking lot a bunch tonight. She giggles. Becca digs Adam Kiger. I think they used to date. Maybe they still do.

"So," Ceepak says when I finish with the phone, "where does one grab a beer at this hour?"

I check my watch. It's almost midnight.

"You want a beer?" I'm in shock.

"Might help me sleep."

"Yeah. Okay. We could hit The Frosty Mug. It's on the way into town. They're open 'til two or three. . . ."

"That'll work. Let's roll."

The Frosty Mug isn't very popular with tourists.

It's a dimly lit tavern that smells like spilled beer and fried fish. There's dark maple paneling on the walls made even darker by fifty years of tar and nicotine. Most of the booths have patches of duct tape where the imitation red leather is ripped or torn. No "beachy" decorations to be seen except this one Budweiser neon in the window, which has a glowing green palm tree bent into its glass. If you're hungry, The Mug serves fried fish fillets and French fries and these greasy wads they call Shark Knuckles. If you want vegetables, order the fried cauliflower and dip it in the imitation cheese sauce. It's what I do.

Most tourists think The Frosty Mug is a dump.

That, of course, is why we locals love it.

My buddy Mike Sullivan is behind the bar where two old dudes, wearing flannel shirts in the middle of July, are nursing shots with beers back. They look and smell like fishermen.

We order two bottles of Bud and grab a booth near the window, right under the rotating Clydesdale clock.

I order fries because I see Mike pulling a fresh basket out of the oil vat and shaking on salt.

Ceepak doesn't order food but he unwraps a Power Bar he had stowed inside his cargo pants. I swear, one of these days he's going to pull a meatball sub or an accordion out of one of those pockets.

"MRE," he says, chomping on the waxy bar. "Meal, Ready to Eat."

"Like in the army?"

"Roger that. Chief Cosgrove and I choked down some awfully bad food in the service of our country. . . ."

"You guys were together in Germany?"

"Right. MPs. In joint training exercises with our European counterparts . . . NATO troops. . . ."

And chasing child-molesting chaplains, I could add, but I don't.

"Why'd you quit?"

"Quit?"

From the frown on his face, I can tell Ceepak doesn't like the word "quit." Quitters never win, winners never quit—that whole deal.

"I mean, why didn't you re-enlist?"

"My time was up." He shrugs and sloughs it off. "I rotated home."

"But you were in the Army for . . . what? Ten, twelve years?"

"Something like that."

Ceepak pretends like he doesn't know the precise number of days, hours and minutes he served in the military, that he's forgotten about the ton of medals he earned and never talks about. If I was Ceepak? I'd have those medals pinned to my chest even when I wasn't wearing a shirt.

"I would've figured you for a career guy," I say after we've both had a few swigs of Beechwood-Aged goodness.

"Yeah."

It gets quiet at the table.

"Danny?"

"Yeah?"

"We need to find Ashley." He takes a long pull on his bottle and empties it. Then, he starts peeling off the label, scratching at it with his thumbnail.

"Sure."

"We must not lose another child. . . ."

I wasn't aware we'd lost any children, that Ashley would somehow be "another."

"Sure."

I don't say much because I'm getting this feeling that Ceepak wants to do all the talking tonight.

"We do this to protect children, right?"

"Sure. I mean partly. Yeah."

"We defend those who cannot defend themselves. . . ."

I hold up two fingers to let Mike know we're going to need two more beers.

"We went over there to help . . . to make a difference. . . ."

Ceepak's back in Iraq. I can see it. He looks like he did after the grenade attack this morning at the dumpster.

"Sure. . . ."

"This morning . . . that explosion . . . the M-80 in the dumpster . . . I feel I owe you an explanation for my behavior."

"Nah, that's okay."

"We're partners, Danny. You need to be able to trust me. I apologize for reacting as I did. . . ."

"The 'grenade!' deal? That did spook me a little. 'Grenade!' Maybe if you just don't yell it in my ear like that any more. . . ."

I'm trying to make it a joke. He isn't smiling.

"The children of Iraq. I still see their faces. The first day we rolled in? Children were lining the road, cheering us, asking for food, money, water—anything. This one boy had cut his foot. I hopped off our Humvee and rendered first aid. He kissed me on the cheek and said something. I don't know what, but I'm pretty sure it was all good. . . ."

Ceepak smiles remembering, but then his face gets somber again.

"Some of the locals didn't want us there. We knew that. We knew it was a bad place where bad things happen. . . ."

"Of course."

"These three MPs? Friends of mine? They were on routine patrol and the hajis, that's what we called the bad guys, the hajis were up on the rooftops with rocket-propelled grenades and AK-47s. It's why I still check out the tops of buildings when we drive by. . . ."

"Yeah. . . ." I say, like I even have a clue.

"My three friends came home in body bags."

He sips from the fresh beer Mike just brought over. I can tell Mike's eavesdropping. So are the two old guys at the bar. It's impossible not to, but you have to listen hard because Ceepak's kind of whispering.

"Two weeks later, we're heading up ambush alley. I'm driving. We're in this convoy. Everybody's on edge. Over there, the hajis can take some C-4 and turn a doorbell into your death sentence."

"Remote-controlled bombs?"

Ceepak nods.

"They daisy-chain explosives and hitch them up to a trigger . . . maybe an old doorbell . . . they push the button and you're done for. Anyhow, we're in this convoy. I'm driving. Looking left, looking right, looking not to get blown up. A guy named Wallace is riding shotgun on the M249."

"Machine gun?"

"Roger that. He's locked and loaded. . . ."

Ceepak squints again. He's seeing whatever he saw back then.

"We're the lead vehicle. Left-hand lane. Convoy of Deuce-n-Half diesels coming up behind us. We see any locals on the road in front of us, Wallace starts thumping the side of the vehicle and yelling: 'Move it or we'll run you down and shoot what's left!' He means it, too. He'd shoot them all. We're five minutes outside the wire, almost home free. There's this explosion. . . ."

"Jesus. . . ."

"IED. Roadside bomb. The truck behind us takes the initial impact, blows sideways. I glance back and see red spraying all over the inside of the truck's windshield, blacking it out like someone let loose with a can of paint. A taxi tries to pass us on our right. It's racing away from the blast site. Wallace sees the cab, sees it speeding up like it's trying to escape, and he starts to unload. He starts screaming: 'You sons of bitches! You fucking Fedayeen motherfuckers!'"

The two old guys on the barstools are frozen. Mike's in mid-mug-wipe. You could hear a peanut shell snap in here right now.

"He's discharging his weapon, smoking them, running through his ammo belt. The taxi swerves right and rolls off the road. Wallace keeps firing. I bring us to a stop and Wallace is still on the gun. I yell at him to cease fire but he sees movement in the back of the taxi and lets loose with another burst. Cease fire! I give him a shove! God-dammit, cease fire! He empties what he has left into a sand bank."

Ceepak stares at his torn beer label.

There are beads of sweat on his forehead, even though Mike keeps the thermostat set at 65 and The Mug feels like a frosty icebox.

"Were the bombers in the taxi?"

"No, Danny. It was a family. The father was a taxicab driver. His wife was up front in the passenger seat. The two in the back moving around were their children. A ten-year-old boy and his six-year-old sister. They were coming home from the hospital where the boy went for his asthma treatments. The others went with him . . . so the boy wouldn't be afraid. The two children were dead on the scene. The parents died about an hour later. We wiped out the whole family."

The old guys at the bar pick up their beer bottles and take long, slow drinks and wish they had another shot of whiskey to chase. Mike folds his towel and shakes his head. Ceepak stares at his hands.

He's quiet but I'm still listening.

"If I hadn't been driving . . . if I had been the one manning the weapon . . . maybe I could've seen it sooner . . . seen it was kids . . . maybe. . . . "

I nod.

I understand.

It won't happen again.

He won't be the one driving and we will not let another kid get hurt.

SIXTEEN

I crawl out of bed at 7 A.M. on Sunday. I've had about five hours of sleep.

I wonder if Ceepak's had any.

I go to the station house and sign out the Explorer. There's this newspaper vending machine on the sidewalk near our parking lot.

"HART BROKEN!"

The Sunday papers have found a clever way to link the two tragedies—run a big four-color photo of Betty Bell Hart's anguished face under a bold banner headline. On one side of the photo is a story about her ex-husband's murder. On the other side, a two-column spread about the disappearance of her daughter. In the big photo, you can see the former weather girl's mascara running in black globs down her cheeks. They're going to sell some papers this Sunday.

I read as much of the Ashley story as I can without actually depositing four quarters in the tin box and buying the thing.

They suspect the young "heiress" was kidnapped and is being held for ransom. Sounds like the reporter got his scoop from Chief Cosgrove.

"It's one possibility," I mumble out loud.

Ceepak and I will probably look into a few others.

The Mussel Beach Motel is a family-owned and operated establishment on the sandy side of Beach Lane. It's a clean, two-story, horseshoe-shaped stucco box with a sign out front advertising a "newly furnished pool." Becca's dad, Mr. Adkinson, decorated the place, so that's why there's this three-foot-long stuffed fish in the lobby. It's hanging right next to the window air conditioner Mr. Adkinson decided to mount through the wall because the window was too far from an electrical outlet.

If your motel room is on the first floor, you can park two feet from your front door. If you're upstairs, you have to lug your suitcases and beer coolers up a flight of metal steps but the room rates are cheaper. Every room comes with its own air conditioner and coffee-maker, and another one of Mr. Adkinson's trophy fish. They hang between factory-made oil paintings of seascapes and lighthouses bolted to the walls.

Like the Web site says, there's plenty of parking on the premises, so we pull into an empty spot out front.

It's 8:15 and Becca's in the lobby behind the bright blue counter sipping coffee out of a styrofoam cup. Her dad must've gotten a good deal on that countertop because I have never actually seen that particular shade of royal blue marble. It kind of looks like bowling ball blue.

"Hey, Becca."

"Hey. He's still here. Mendez."

"Cool. This is John Ceepak."

Becca likes what she sees.

"It's awesome to finally meet you. Danny talks about you all the time. . . ."

"It's good to meet you too."

Ceepak does a cheek-dimpling smile, shakes Becca's hand, and she falls in love. Big John doesn't notice.

"Is Mr. Mendez awake?" he asks.

"Yep."

"How do you know?" I ask, wiggling my eyebrows suggestively. This is a motel, after all.

"Because, you skeeve, I just took some towels out to the pool and Mendez is up on the sundeck doing these freaky exercises." She demonstrates in slow motion.

"Tai-Chi," Ceepak says.

"Could be. Or maybe Tae-Bo? Like that guy on TV?"

"Sure. That'll work."

"We'd like to talk to him," I say.

"Fine by me. You guys want some coffee? Pastry? I'm putting out the breakfast buffet."

She's also putting out the Sunday papers. Ceepak sees the screaming headlines and knows he has no time to waste on danish.

"No, thanks," he says. "Danny?"

We head for the sundeck.

"Nice to meet you, Officer Ceepak."

He smiles back, and Becca almost drops her Raspberry Crumble Cake.

The deck is out back, overlooking the beach. You have to go around the pool and climb up some stairs to reach it. On one side of the deck, there's a row of Wal-Mart white vinyl chairs. The other side faces the ocean.

Mendez is wearing boxer shorts and a white nylon doo-rag that makes the top of his head look like a nurse's kneecap. His eyes are closed as he stretches and toasts his brown body in the early morning sunshine.

I can see the Blessed Virgin's face stretching up on his shoulder every time he flexes those particular muscles. The guy is a regular tattoo gallery, but there's no dragon up on his neck. I looked. He has a flaming heart with a knife jabbed through it.

Ceepak clears his throat to let the guy know we're here.

"Mr. Mendez?"

Mendez stops in mid-leg-lift and opens his eyes just enough to see we're cops. He doesn't care.

"Yo. Wazzup?"

"Sorry to disturb you, sir. We need to ask a few questions."

"Now? Damn, son—I'm in the middle of my moves. Tryin' to start the day right, you know what I'm sayin'?"

"Yes, sir. Again, I apologize for any inconvenience. If this is a bad time. . . ."

"What if I said it was?"

"We could arrange to meet at a more convenient hour."

"Nah-uh, nah-uh. What you need to know?"

"We'd like to talk to you about Mr. Reginald Hart."

"Now deceased?"

"That's correct. Have you ever done business with Mr. Hart?"

"Shit, son. You got that ass-backwards, you know what I'm sayin'? Mr. Hart? He do business with me. See what I'm sayin'?"

"Yes. Thank you for the clarification. You're an independent contractor?"

"That's right."

Ceepak rubs his eraser around in his notebook, like he's correcting some faulty information someone gave him.

"What type of business activities did Mr. Hart hire you to perform?"

"He, you know, he hired my firm to perform what you might call real-estate consultation-type activities."

"Your firm?"

"That's what I said, isn't it?"

"Very well," Ceepak says. "So . . . your firm? What sort of real-estate services do you provide?"

"You know—little this, little that."

"Groundskeeping? Sprinkler maintenance?"

Mendez looks hurt.

"Nah-uh, man. Tenant relations."

"I see. In his new buildings?"

Mendez smiles, and I can see the glint of bling-bling: he has a small gold cross implanted in his upper left incisor. This guy is seriously Catholic.

"Nah-uh—we worked mainly in the old buildings. The ones Hart was fixing up but, you know, he couldn't get started without a little spring cleaning. That was back in the day. Now we be, you know, branching out."

"Diversifying?"

"Yeah. Diversifying. I'll show you something you might be interested in. . . ."

He goes to a pile of clothes in front of one of the vinyl chairs and pulls a slick brochure out his jeans.

"Project we be working on."

He hands Ceepak the brochure.

"The Sea Palace?"

"Yeah. Old hotel up on the North Shore we be renovating. Gonna turn the rooms into condos, vacation-type time-share units and all."

Ceepak flips the brochure over and studies its back.

"Awesome location. Nice beach."

"Yeah, yeah. Check it out."

I can't believe this guy. He's talking about a disaster zone. There's nothing up at the north end of the island except an abandoned lighthouse and a rundown resort hotel no one (except rodents and sea gulls) has stayed in for sixty years.

Now, once upon a time, when dinosaurs roamed the earth and railroads hauled bathing beauties in wool swim trunks over from the mainland, The Palace was a hot spot because the North Shore was where the train tracks terminated. The Palace was one of those huge hotels built around 1912, when people spent a month or two at the shore because the cities were sweltering and air conditioning hadn't been invented. William Howard Taft was president. I only remember this stuff because Taft was the fattest president ever elected, weighing in at 350 pounds, and he stayed at The Palace when it first opened. In fact, you can still buy black-and-white post cards of Taft squeezed into his bathing suit, one of those numbers with a top and a bottom and lots of horizontal stripes. The guy might've been president, but he sure looked like a fully inflated beach ball.

There's nothing left of The Palace Hotel now but three hundred ratty rooms nobody's known what to do with since 1942. The last I heard. . . .

"Hart bought The Palace."

"Come again?" Ceepak says.

"It was in *The Sandpaper*," I say. "Couple years back. Front-page story. Reggie Hart was going to turn the old hotel into a luxury condo complex. . . ."

Ceepak casually flips the brochure over and studies a small logo near the bottom of the back panel.

"Hart Enterprises. . . ."

"Yo—them's the *former* brochures. Old man Hart couldn't cut it, you know what I'm saying? He sold that sucker to me. Ten cents on the dollar. I'm the one be putting in jacuzzis, whirlpools, fitness center, sushi bar. . . ."

"All that's what Hart was going to do," I say.

Mendez glowers at me.

Ceepak tucks the brochure into his back pocket.

"You know," he says, "I once toured a time-share unit in North Carolina."

"Yeah. So?"

"Your project intrigues me."

"Smart man."

"So when will your condos be offered for sale?"

"We be working out the final details and all right now. Soon."

"Good. Ms. Stone certainly knows her way around a real estate deal."

"Yeah. She's worth the big bucks I'm paying her."

Ceepak is good. He just linked Mendez to Ms. Stone in two seconds flat.

"Well, we don't mean to delay you any further, but"—Ceepak unfolds his sketch of Squeegee—"can I ask you one more question?"

Mendez waits.

"We're asking all the leading businessmen in town the same thing. . . ."

"Yeah," Mendez nods, happy to be included.

"Do you recognize this man?"

"Nah-uh."

"You're certain?"

"Don't know him."

"Perhaps he's applied for a position with your firm?"

"Nah-uh."

"Maybe he's done some day labor for you or your associates?"

"Nah-uh."

"Have you ever seen him around town?"

This could take hours.

"Car wash."

"The car wash?"

"Yeah."

"Which one?"

"Off Ocean Avenue there. Cap'n Crunch's?"

"Cap'n Scrubby's?" I say.

"Yeah."

"Thank you," Ceepak says and folds up the sketch.

Mendez checks his watch. It looks like a huge chrome-rimmed hubcap.

"Damn. Got me a breakfast meeting with my lawyer. . . ."

"Chesterfield's?" I say, employing the ol' Ceepak "slip it in" move.

"Yeah—you ever eat breakfast there, son?"

"No."

"Didn't figure you did." He goes to his clothes pile and reaches for his shirt and his jeans.

That's when we see them.

Buried under everything else.

His Timberland boots.

SEVENTEEN

"**Y**ou saw those boots, right?"

"Affirmative," Ceepak says. "Remember, Timberland is a very popular brand."

We're sitting in the Ford out front of The Mussel Beach Motel, sipping coffee Becca was kind enough to pour in go-cups for us when we said our good-byes.

"Do you think?"

"That Virgilio Mendez killed Reginald Hart to get his hands on the Palace Hotel and who knows what other real-estate assets?"

I nod.

"It's a possibility."

"But Ashley described Squeegee. Maybe Mendez and Squeegee worked together. . . ."

"Another possibility."

"So how do we dump some of these goddamn possibilities?" I usually don't swear in front of Ceepak, but my brain was hurting trying to make sense of all this stuff.

"We keep working the puzzle. Picking up pieces, fitting them into place."

"Okay—Ms. Stone. What's she up to? Double-crossing her boss? It sure looked like she and Hart might have been, you know, romantic. So how come she's suddenly got Mendez as a client?"

Ceepak doesn't answer.

"What time does the car wash open?"

"Ten. Maybe eleven."

"Drat." Now even Ceepak's swearing—or as close as he ever gets. It's not even nine A.M. yet. The puzzle pieces aren't cooperating. "We need to talk to people at Captain Bubbles. ASAP."

"Cap'n *Scrubby's.*"

He nods.

The car wash is where two people place Squeegee. First, Officer Adam Kiger. Now, respected real-estate tycoon Virgilio Mendez.

"Some of the other employees, particularly the other transients, these towel men, they might know where Squeegee lives or where he goes when he means to disappear. . . ."

"We could grab some breakfast or something . . . kill a half an hour."

Ceepak looks at me like I'm crazy. Breakfast? What's that? I don't think we'll be eating again until Ashley Hart is safe.

Our radio squelches.

"Ceepak? Goddammit, Ceepak?"

It's the chief.

Ceepak picks up the mike.

"Yes, sir?"

"We just heard from the State Ballistics Team."

"And?"

"They made a match."

"Nine-millimeter?"

"Yeah."

Ceepak nods. It's what he figured.

"So now we know what we're looking for?"

"Yeah," the chief grumbles. "Goddamn Smith & Wesson. Semi-automatic. One of ours."

"Come again?"

"It's one of ours! Goddammit—it's Gus's goddamn gun. Get your asses over here! Now. Move it!"

Cap'n Scrubby will have to wait.

"He lost it," the chief says.

"He *lost* it?" Ceepak's jaw is halfway down his neck.

We're in the chief's office. Gus is outside in the hall, waiting. When we passed him, he looked whiter than a fish belly, like he'd just seen his own ghost—probably because he knows the chief is about to kill him.

I always thought they took Gus's gun away from him when he went on desk duty. Now it looks like he went on desk duty because he was careless with his sidearm. They demoted him for being a fuckup.

"How does an officer *lose* his lethal weapon?" Ceepak refuses to believe such things are possible.

"Last winter? Gus was sitting in his squad car and his belt was hanging so loose on his bony butt, the gun kept sliding up, pinching him in the side. . . ."

Ceepak closes his eyes. I don't think he wants to live in a world where cops take off their pistols because they rub them the wrong way.

"Gus?" The chief screams at the door. "Get your ass in here!"

Gus sort of shuffles into the room, afraid to look the chief, Ceepak, or even lowly me in the eye.

"Yes, sir?" I've never heard Gus sound so meek, like a kid in the principal's office. Usually he's ready to bust your chops the minute you waltz through the front doors.

"Tell Ceepak."

"You mean—about my gun?"

"No—about how good the goddamn stripers are running this morning. Jesus! Give us the fucking fishing report, why don't you?"

Gus turns to Ceepak.

"It was back in March. One of those days when it sort of feels like spring even though it's winter, you know?"

Ceepak nods.

"It was freaking hot, too. Muggy. Unseasonably warm, like they say on the radio. And I'm half-Greek, so I always feel kind of hot and sweaty, you know?"

Gus smiles.

Ceepak?

God bless him, he smiles back.

He's ready to move on. I guess he figures he's wasted enough time being disappointed. Now he wants to see if there is something he can do, some positive action he can take.

Gus feels better. I can tell by the way all the air trapped in his chest seeps out when his neck muscles finally relax.

"Anyhow, the freaking gun kept riding up on me. Every time I'd sit, it'd slide up some and pinch me. It cut into me . . . right here. And was I having a day? This call, that call. Go here, get out, get back in, go somewheres else. So I put the gun in the glove compartment."

"The glove compartment?"

"Yeah. I'm not so stupid I'm gonna leave it lying out on the freaking seat there. . . ."

It seems even Gus has his limits.

"You were alone?" Ceepak asks.

"Yeah. It was late winter—we always cut back some on personnel, pull solo patrols. It's mostly basic stuff that time of the year—swinging by the bank when the Brinks truck comes to town, writing up fender-benders, helping out with the school zones. Don't really need two-man patrols in March. . . ."

"So where'd you go? After you put the gun away?"

"I'm not really sure. . . ."

"Focus. Do the best you can."

"Yeah. Okay. I went by The Pancake Palace. Had an early lunch. Went by the Surf City Shopping Center on account of they were having some trouble with their freaking alarm system. Remember, chief? It was your day off and you were looking in the window of that jewelry place?"

"Yes."

"Gonna buy your wife a present, remember? I said go with the earrings? The ones shaped like sandals with diamonds in the toes? I said she'd get a kick out of those—"

"Gus?" The chief is impatient, big time.

"Right. After that, I'm back in the car. Make a few more stops. Here and there. Piddling little stuff, but duty calls, you know? I walked up and down Ocean Avenue, wrote up some parking tickets at expired meters . . . this one had gum jammed in the slot . . . damn freaking kids, you know?"

"When did you realize your gun was missing?" Ceepak asked.

"Second time I ran into the chief."

"When was that?"

"I was parked outside Driftwood Floral. Our anniversary was coming so I was thinking about maybe picking up some flowers or something. My wife doesn't need any more earrings. She's got a million of those. Anyhow, the chief is picking up some cold cuts or whatever from the deli next door and he sees me coming out the flower shop. . . ."

"It was a Tuesday," the chief remembers.

"Yeah." Gus agrees. "Your regular day off, right?"

"Right." The way the chief says it I get the feeling he'll never take one again.

"Anyhow, the chief here says, 'Where the hell's your goddamn weapon?' He's looking at my holster and it's freaking empty, you know? So I say, 'Oh, shit' because, at first, when I put it in the glove compartment, I'd put it back in my holster every time I got out of the car. Only this time I guess I forgot. Might've forgot some other times, too. So I say to the chief, 'It's in the car.' The chief says, 'Where?' I go to show him, pop open the glove compartment, no gun. It's gone."

Ceepak turns to the chief.

"Did you report the missing weapon to the proper authorities?"

The chief sort of looks from side to side—like it's his turn to tell us what he did wrong.

"No. I did not."

He rubs his nose with the back of his big hand. Then he pushes both hands back through what little hair he has left on the top of his head.

"Why not?"

"Because I'm a goddamn big-hearted idiot, okay?"

Ceepak's eyebrows do that quizzical puppy dog thing: Hunh?

The chief sniffs in enough air to explain.

"Here's Gus—what? Six, seven months from retirement. I don't have it in me to blow his whole goddamn pension. To write him up. Losing your gun? You don't just get a slap on the wrist for that one. So I yank him off the street, stick him behind the desk where he can't lose anything else. Then I have a quiet word with the guys. Ever since, we've all been nosing around town, keeping an eye and ear out for Gus's goddamn gun. . . ."

"But you never found it?"

"No. We never did."

Until today, I want to say, because I'm the resident wise-ass. But I don't.

"Why didn't you tell me, chief?" Ceepak says. "I could've helped look for it."

The chief doesn't answer right away.

I know what he'd say if he were being totally honest: He didn't tell him because Ceepak would have turned them all in. Ceepak won't lie, cheat, or steal, and he won't tolerate those who do. Even the ones who do it to save an old cop's pension. The chief knows all about Ceepak's Code.

"Hey, you were new," the chief says. "Just back from that other shitbox. The war. I didn't want to drag you into this, load you down with our old crap. You needed a fresh start. I figured me and the other guys . . . I figured we'd find it sooner or later. . . ."

The chief lets that one hang there. I think even he's thinking: *"We sure as Hell found it now, didn't we?"*

"Are the ballistics conclusive?"

"Yeah. Smith & Wesson semi-automatic nine-millimeter. We know that's what Gus lost four months back. You do the math."

"Okay. Gus? We need a complete calendaring of everywhere you went that day. Look at your log, check with dispatch, rack your brain. Don't leave anything out."

"Okay. Sure. I can do that. I remember most of what I did that day. . . ."

"Good."

"Pretty hard to forget." Gus lets out another nervous chuckle bubble. "I mean, it's not every day you pull a bone-headed stunt like that, you know?"

"Write it up for us, okay?"

"Sure, Ceepak, sure. No problem. I can write it up. Because, like I say, I remember pretty much everything. March 9th. What a freaking shitty day. Right before my anniversary. And it rained the day before. Poured."

"Good," Ceepak says, looking at his watch. I don't think he meant for Gus to give him an oral report *right this minute.*

"Write it up. Chief?"

"Yeah?"

"New development. Virgilio Mendez?"

"The guy in Hart's calendar?"

"Yes, sir. Ms. Stone was being disingenuous with us last night. *She* is meeting with Mendez. 0-10 hundred. That same restaurant."

"Chesterfield's," I say.

"What for?"

"Apparently," Ceepak says, taking the folded brochure out of his pocket, "they're planning for a future without Mr. Hart. Real-estate development."

He hands The Palace condo flyer to the chief.

"Goddammit," he growls. "How'd you find out?"

"Danny," Ceepak says. "He was listening carefully and made some right connections."

"I think Mendez hired Squeegee," I blurt out, bucked up by Ceepak's praise. "To kill Hart!"

"What?"

"It's one possibility," Ceepak backs me up. "Greed is always a good motive."

"Shit," the chief says, like he's the one riding the Tilt-A-Whirl, not knowing what to expect next. "I want you two there. At the meet."

"Roger that."

"Gus?"

"Yes, chief?"

"Go write up your goddamn diary."

"Sure. I can write it up. No problem. I remember everything. I remember the car was filthy, 'cause of the rain and the mud and all. Remember, chief? At Surf City? You said it looked like a 'rolling mud pie.' So I swung by the car wash. . . ."

He's got our attention again.

"Which one?" Ceepak asks.

"What?"

"Which car wash did you use?"

"Cap'n Scrubby's," Gus says. "They give us a discount."

EIGHTEEN

t's right before ten on Sunday morning.

The chief will meet Mendez and Ms. Stone for brunch at Chesterfield's. We're on our way to the car wash. Sounds like Gus could have lost his gun at the one place everybody who recognizes Squeegee says they've seen him.

The car wash is fast becoming one of Ceepak's more definite possibilities.

Maybe our prime suspect did an extra-good job cleaning out Gus's car. Maybe, while wiping down the dashboard, he even tidied up the glove compartment.

On the way to Cap'n Scrubby's, we drive past a few church parking lots. They're fuller than usual. Most people take a little vacation from the Lord while they're down here taking a vacation from everything else. But this Sunday, people seem to be out in force, undoubtedly praying for the safe return of Ashley Hart.

When we stop at traffic lights, I can see flyers stapled to the telephone poles.

MISSING.

Under that big, scary headline is the face of the pretty blond girl we met yesterday. I look up Ocean Avenue. The flyers are nailed to every single pole, taped to every light post.

Traffic seems kind of heavy for Sunday morning. I notice a lot of cars are taking the turn for the Causeway and heading home. I guess people checked out of their rentals early because they'd rather lose their deposits than their children.

We pass the entrance to Sunnyside Playland.

The ground is blanketed with bouquets. Bunches of tissue-wrapped roses—the kind you can buy in the refrigerator case at the A&P. A couple of teddy bears and some stuffed green turtles are stuck into the chain-link gate. The newspapers had told everybody how much young Ashley and her father liked turtles, why they were on the Turtle-Twirl Tilt-A-Whirl before it even opened. They'd worked all the human-interest angles pretty good.

There's a sheet draped over a section of the Playland fence, covering up some of the "Fun In The Sun" slogan. It's the kind of banner we used to paint for high-school homecoming games. Only this one says, "Please Come Home Safe Ashley!" and has a smiley face in the dot under the exclamation point.

We're on our way to Cap'n Scrubby's to see if we can help make that wish come true.

"Gosh, I was just thinking about calling you guys."

The manager of Cap'n Scrubby's Car Wash looks like he took the job right after a quick stint managing the local Blockbuster because he's wearing the same basic uniform: pleated khaki pants and an oxford blue button-down shirt. He also has on, I kid you not, a tie with foaming soap bubbles printed all over it. His name is Steve. Says so right on his nametag. I figure the guy's a little older than me. Maybe even thirty. He was just opening his doors when we marched in.

"You recognized the sketch?" Ceepak says.

"No, I'm not a hundred percent certain, or I would have called. The towel boys are a very transient labor force."

"And this man?" Ceepak pushes the Squeegee sketch across the desk.

"Like I said, he kind of sort of looks familiar. But frankly, a lot of the vagrants out back look like this. Unkempt. He might've worked here. Maybe."

"Do you keep employment records?"

"Sure."

He pulls out the metal file drawer on the right side of his little desk. It squeaks.

We're sitting in the lobby. The manager's desk is in the far corner, near big plate-glass windows, tucked behind a low cubicle wall to give him a little privacy, to make him think he actually has an office. There are a pair of tiny American flags stuck into a wooden holder on his desk, part of the Proud American Deskset they sell at Office Max.

A cashier is stationed up front, near the lobby door. She's dressed in khakis and a blue polo shirt with Cap'n Scrubby's face embroidered where the alligator or polo player usually sits. The Cap'n's head is a big soap bubble under a Jolly Roger pirate hat. His moustache? It's a scrub brush.

The lobby is also where you buy air fresheners to hang on your rearview mirror. They've got the classic pine trees in all ten colors, Yosemite Sams, Garfields, Playboy Bunnies—they hang alongside other car crap like fuzzy dice and leatherette steering-wheel wraps, stuff you might just purchase while you're waiting for your car to finish its automated bath.

"Hmmm," Steve says after flipping through a few file folders.

"Problem?"

Ceepak is not interested in "hmmms" this morning.

"Well, as I say—some of our labor force is transitory in nature. Migrant workers, if you will. . . ."

"You don't have records?"

"Not anything, you know, official. Not for the drifters and homeless folks."

"Pay stubs?"

"Well, we don't really, you know, 'pay' the towel boys per se. They're not actually employees."

"They work for the tips? That's it?"

"That's right. But we provide them with the treasure chest."

"The tip box?"

"Yes. We had it made up to look like a pirate chest. Adds to our whole nautical ambience . . . maintains Cap'n Scrubby's imaging system. . . ."

The guy must've taken a marketing class back at community college.

I've had my car cleaned at Scrubby's a couple times. (They charge extra for minivans.) Once the mechanized track drags your vehicle through the scrubbers and sprayers and drying curtains, you meet it out back where a gang of seven or eight guys goes at it with tattered towels.

These guys have a padlocked box with a slit on top for tips. I usually stuff a buck or two into it when they finish rubbing wet towels around my windows and smearing them up worse than they were before they started. It's like you're paying them to stop. Please.

My guess is Steve has the keys to the tip box and he's the one who divvies up the dough. I wouldn't even be surprised if ol' Cap'n Scrubby takes a cut of the tips meant for his hardworking mateys out back.

"Have you ever heard of the minimum wage law?" Ceepak says to Steve.

"Oh, sure. You bet. But technically, the boys out back? As I said, they aren't employees. So technically, they are not wage earners, nor are we in violation of any labor laws."

"What about the spirit of those same laws?"

My man Ceepak doesn't like folks who skirt around a law by scoping out its loopholes.

"As I said, Cap'n Scrubby's is in full compliance with all state and federal labor laws."

Sounds like another seminar Steve took.

Either that, or Mr. Sinclair, our mayor, who also happens to own this fine car-washing establishment, told him what to say if anybody ever asked. It's why Steve gets to wear the tie and call men twice his age "boys."

"Mr. Sinclair feels he is providing a charitable public service by allowing the towel boys to work here for tips. Better than having them beg on the beach, he says."

"Steve?" Ceepak stands up. He has that subtle cop way of leaning on his holster so the leather creaks and you remember that he has a gun, *you* don't, and that maybe you ought to listen very carefully to what he's about to say.

"Yes, sir?"

Ceepak slides the sketch back across the tiny desktop.

"One more time. Do you recognize this man?"

"As I stated earlier. . . ."

"I know. He wasn't an employee. But was he part of your social outreach program?"

Steve picks up the sketch. Studies it.

"Yes. He was a troublemaker."

"How so?"

"Patrons accused him of theft. Coffee mugs. Cell phones. Loose change. Anything that wasn't nailed down inside their cars. The police were called here on several different occasions." Steve pushes the sketch back at Ceepak. "Eventually, we asked him not to come back."

"His name?"

"Don't know. As I said, many of these boys —"

Ceepak's suddenly not listening any more. He sees something outside.

A guy who looks like an old hippie carrying a dirty bath towel.

NINETEEN

I t isn't Squeegee.

The guy outside doesn't have a beard and his hair is red and curly, like a Bozo wig, not white and scraggly.

But he sure looks like he could be one of Squeegee's best buddies, like they might hang out together on beanbag chairs and pass the bong around. The way the guy is weaving? I'd say today was a bong-for-breakfast kind of day.

He looks to be about fifty-something and has on these green corduroy shorts with stringy threads where he cut off the pants. His legs are so filthy, they're caked with dirt, as if he took a mud bath a month ago and forgot to rinse. He's also wearing a rainbow-colored tie-dye shirt like we know Squeegee likes to wear. Who knows—it might be their fraternity uniform.

"Excuse me," Ceepak says and starts for the door.

He's thinking what I'm thinking—the hippie burnout in the parking lot probably knows Squeegee.

"Danny?"

I'm right behind him.

"Is there going to be some trouble?" Steve sinks a little lower in his swivel chair, nervous. The flags cover his face.

"No," Ceepak says. "We intend to remain in total compliance with all state and federal laws."

He unsnaps his holster.

I can hear Steve whimpering, "Wait!" in the background as we head out his front door.

The old hippie looks like he's lost. Like he can't remember how he usually walks around to the back of the building. Does he go left, or right, or maybe left-then-right?

"Sir?"

Our quarry turns to face us. His eyes are like blurry slits underneath his giant red Afro.

"Yeah?" he says with an effort.

"I wonder if we might have a word with you?"

"Me?" Again, he answers as if it's extremely hard work.

"Yes, sir. You." Ceepak steps toward him. I stand ready to radio for backup.

"We need to talk to you—"

"Fuck!"

He starts running. He's old and fat and wearing worn-out Birkenstocks, but he can waddle pretty fast.

However, he makes a real stupid move.

He heads *into* the car wash.

Looks like he's finally going to get those legs washed, maybe even waxed: he tries to lose us by running alongside somebody's sudsy Pontiac.

Ceepak shakes his head and tries not to laugh. No way are we running into the car wash after this freak.

"Go left," he says calmly. "I'll swing around the right."

I race back into the lobby, past the cashier, and up to the windowed walkway where you can watch your car moving down the line.

I see our friend inside. He's not running any more.

He's soaked and sort of squeezing through these big fluffy spinning roller-buffers.

When he gets past those, he's sprayed by high-pressure water jets that pin-needle him so hard he has to close his eyes and that means he can't see what's coming next: big flapping straps of cloth that swish back and forth and scrub him down good. While he's slapping against the flaps, he also gets some undercarriage rust protectant shot up his shorts.

Now he's in the rinse cycle where the water's mistier, less like bee stingers.

By the time he reaches the end of the line, his curly red hair is shooting straight back, plastered in place by the turbine-powered blow dryers.

He tries to run past the towel guys and negotiate a sharp turn into the street, but his sandals are so slick he slides sideways, loses his feet, and plows into the rolling table with the pirate chest on top. The tip box goes flying while our fugitive sleds across the tarmac on his butt.

"Freeze!" Ceepak booms.

I can tell he's trying very hard not to laugh, but it's not working.

The redheaded guy sits in a soapy, oily puddle and raises both arms to surrender.

Ceepak walks forward shaking his head. His pistol is still in its holster.

"Why'd you run away, sir?"

"I dunno, man." He rubs his knee where it got roughed up in the tumble. "Seemed like a good idea at the time. . . ."

Ceepak turns to the towel guys standing in a circle, having the best laugh they've probably had in weeks.

"Can I borrow some of your towels? We need a couple."

A few of the guys oblige.

"Thanks," Ceepak says. "Gracias." He hands the towels to the man on the ground.

Then Ceepak stuffs a ten-dollar bill into the pirate chest. Doing better than me—just like he always does.

❖ ❖ ❖

Ten minutes later, we're sitting with our captive at Do Me A Flavor, the ice-cream shop next door to Cap'n Scrubby's. I think Mayor Sinclair owns this place too.

Ceepak buys our new pal a jumbo mug of black coffee and a gigantic hot-fudge sundae with two scoops of mint chocolate chip, two scoops of moose tracks, marshmallow sauce, nuts, sprinkles, Oreo crumbs, whipped cream, and maraschino cherries.

We're the only ones in the ice-cream parlor this early in the morning. The girl in pink scooping up the sundae? Jenny. A friend of mine for years.

The guy is shoveling the ice-cream concoction into his face, smearing sauce down his chin.

"You might want to slow down, sir," Ceepak suggests. Bozo digs faster. The man loves his sugar. Probably because he also loves booze or heroin or both.

He has to slow down when he belches.

"Sorry I ran, man," he says during the quick break between bites.

"No hard feelings," Ceepak says. "What's your name?"

"Red." He digs into the ice cream again.

"That your real name?"

The guy stares blankly at Ceepak.

"It's the name I choose to use, man."

"Okay, Red."

Ceepak lets him eat some more.

"So, why'd you run?"

"You're the fuzz, man." Red is licking as much of his face as his tongue can reach, trying to lap up all the sticky stuff available.

I haven't heard police called the fuzz since my father made me watch a re-run of *The Mod Squad.*

"I always run from the fuzz. Ever since 1968. Chicago. They'll stone you if you're a stoner who likes to get stoned, man."

Ceepak nods. "Bob Dylan once expressed a very similar sentiment."

"You dig Dylan?"

"Certainly. Bob Dylan was quite an influence on the young Bruce Springsteen, my favorite recording artist."

"Springsteen? Springsteen ripped Dylan off! Just rhymed words to hear them rhyme." Red chomps a cherry and licks whipped cream off his spoon. "'Some go-kart Mozart checking out the weather chart?' What the fuck's that supposed to mean? Where's the poetry, man? Springsteen sucks."

"Thank you for sharing your opinion," Ceepak says. "Now — talk to me about Squeegee."

"No can do."

"Why not?"

"Hey. If Squeegee hears through the grapevine that I squealed, turned ratfink on him? He'd hurt me, man. Hurt me bad. Dude is the devil. I'd be buying the stairway to heaven."

"Is that so?"

"You seen that sketch? In the newspapers?"

"Yes."

"That dragon crawling up his neck? Squeegee told me it could fly off his flesh to devour his enemies with hellfire and brimstone, if he so exhorted the beast! Like a funeral pyre, he'd set the night on fire!"

Oh-kay. I'm wondering exactly how many spliffs Red had for breakfast this morning.

He takes a loud slurp on the coffee.

"Pass the sugar, man."

I slide the sugar jar across the table. It's one of those glass jobs with the little metal gate that swings open when you pour. Red doesn't bother using a spoon or measuring. He just pours the white stuff in until his coffee thickens up like Karo Corn Syrup.

"So where is your friend now?"

"Squeegee?"

"Squeegee."

"Are you even listening to me, man?" Red holds up his hands and shakes them near his head like his brain is about to explode. "He's no friend of mine. I have zero sympathy for that devil. The dude tried to kill me."

"When?"

"After he stole my old lady."

"You had a domestic dispute?"

"He came after me with a rusty blade, man! A machete! Said if I didn't back off, he'd go get his gun!"

"Squeegee has a gun?"

"Hell, yeah! How do you think he shot the billionaire on the beach? Don't you guys read the papers?"

"Where does Squeegee live?"

"Same place as me, man. Here, there, everywhere."

"You're homeless?"

"Ever since the night those brown bastards drove us down."

"Who?"

"The Dominican death squad, man! They said they'd smoke us out."

"Really?"

"Yeah. And we had such a groovy thing going. Had the whole hotel to ourselves! You could take ten bedrooms if you didn't mind sharing space with Mother Nature's children . . . seagulls and shit. . . ."

"Where was this hotel?"

"Up north, man. The Palace! It was like Camelot, and Gladys was my Guinevere!"

"Gladys?"

"My ex. My old lady. It was paradise, man."

"What happened?"

"Reginald Fucking Hart. He pushed us out, man! The white man pushes out the Red man once again. . . ."

Red is, of course, a Caucasian. The only minority he belongs to is old guys who eat too much ice cream and do too many drugs. While he shakes his head and fumes, he also clinks his spoon against the sides of his sundae glass, trying to scrape up any melted ice cream or cherry juice or chocolate fudge he might have missed on the first pass.

"Squeegee was working for The Man."

"For Hart?"

"No—the jack-booted thugs. I figured he had some plastic-fantastic deal worked out with Mendez. . . ."

"And who is Mendez?"

"Come on, man—keep up with me, okay?" He does the head-exploding shaking hands thing again. "Mendez was the leader of the pack. El jefe grande. Squeegee cut a deal with Mendez, I know he did. I swear that's why my old lady left me. Thought she could really be princess of The Palace by shacking up with King Squeegee. But whatever he told her? It was totally bogus. Squeegee got squeezed out, too. We all did."

"What happened?"

"Couple weeks ago? We had to split. Mendez said he'd torch the building and use us for kindling if we didn't vamoose. So we packed our shit and split, hit the beach. I slept under the boardwalk. On the beach. Spent a couple nights on a cot in a church. . . ."

"Have you seen Squeegee since you vacated The Palace Hotel?"

"Here and there. Here and there. I try to avoid him because of the bad vibrations that emanate from his aura. But I'll be honest—we both have substance abuse issues."

Ceepak does this "really?" expression, pretending like this is some sort of news flash.

"So, sometimes, by sheer necessity, I have to deal with the devil, dig? Squeegee's always got good shit. The best."

"Where does he procure his merchandise?"

"Where do you think? The Dominicans, dude! They have their fingers in every pot and, like I said, Squeegee worked out some kind of deal because even though he had to leave the hotel, he still has this primo powder, dig? And my old lady? She says they have plans. Big plans. You ever notice, man—chicks dig the dark, dangerous dudes like the Squeege? Even the bikini babes? From the beach?"

"Yeah?" He's got my attention.

"They dig him 'cause he's like this wild sex beast they want to ride and tame. Oh, yeah. I see the young chicks crawling under the boardwalk with ol' Squeege all the time, promising to unsnap their jeans. . . ."

"Springsteen," Ceepak says.

"What?"

"'Chasing the factory girls underneath the boardwalk where they all promise to unsnap their jeans.' That's from a Springsteen song."

"No, man. Not factory girls. These are like college co-eds. High-school chicks."

Ceepak lets it drop.

Apparently Red's head is so fried, it's like an iPod somebody toasted in the microwave and the MP3s have melted together into one huge playlist shuffling randomly through his brain. He has no idea where the songs are coming from or which one's about to cycle into his consciousness.

"You ever see him at the Tilt-A-Whirl?"

"What? Having sex with factory girls?"

"Or doing anything."

"Sure. He sets up shop there some nights. His own little drug store. I only go see him when I'm desperate, because lately the dude's been extremely cranky—ever since they canned his ass at the car wash on account of his thieving ways. He stole loose change from ashtrays. Groceries out of back seats. Shit, he even stole this little girl's stuffed dog from her car seat and then told everybody it was me who copped it."

"Why'd he steal so much," Ceepak asks, "if he had the drug income like you say?"

"Why does the devil keep on keepin' on? Evil is writ large upon his soul. Squeegee is Beelzebub in disguise, telling dirty lies. . . ."

I have no idea whose lyrics Red's ripping off this time.

"When was the last time you saw him?"

"A week ago. I needed some shit, and he was already lit up and talking about righteous retribution. How the last were going to be first and the first would be last. You know—that Jesus shit. Said judgment day was nigh and all slumlords would soon be summoned forth to pay."

"Is that what he called Hart? A slumlord?"

"No. Squeegee never called Hart a slumlord. Him he called a *fucking* slumlord.' Can I get another one of these?"

Red slides his empty ice cream dish across the table.

Ceepak pulls out a ten-dollar bill.

"Get yourself two."

TWENTY

"What's your 10-38?" Ceepak asks the chief.

"I'm at HQ. Ready to roll to Chesterfield's."

Ceepak tilts the radio microphone to check his Casio G-Shock. It's 10:32.

"I thought the breakfast meet was set for 0-10 hundred?" Ceepak says, releasing the mike button to hear the chief's reply.

"Roger that," the chief growls back. "But I had to go home and put on a goddamn tie. They want me on TV in an hour. I have to give a statement. Stand up in front of all those goddamn cameras and give a progress report. We got any?"

"Yes, sir. I think so."

"What?"

"A witness."

"To the murder?"

"No, sir. An acquaintance of Squeegee's who links him to Mendez. We need to go to Chesterfield's and Mendez needs to be there."

"He is," the chief says, sounding excited. "I have Malloy and Santucci stationed out front. They saw him go in. Ms. Stone is registered upstairs. Neither one has come out."

"Excellent," Ceepak says. "We'll meet there."

"Ceepak? The mayor is crawling up my butt. People are packing suitcases and leaving town. You see the beaches this morning? They're goddamn empty. We need to wrap this up quick. Now!"

"Roger that. Just don't let Mendez leave the restaurant."

"10-4."

"Our ETA is five."

"Good. Move it!"

Ceepak clicks off the radio and does one of those Hollywood "Cavalry, Ho!" hand gestures.

I stomp on the gas.

We proceed to haul some ass.

We arrive three minutes later.

Malloy is sitting out front in a cruiser with Tony Santucci. Santucci's behind the wheel, chomping more gum and looking like a total hardass. He wears those mirrored sunglasses like redneck sheriffs do in movies and rolls his short sleeves up so you can see more of his muscles.

Chesterfield's is a big Victorian bed & breakfast with gables and peaks and gewgaws. It's the kind of place my mom would love and my dad would only enter with a gun pointed at his head.

Or on Mother's Day.

I double-park the Explorer near the cruiser.

"You puke your breakfast again this morning?" Santucci asks, cracking his Dentyne.

I'd say something witty in reply but Ceepak is bounding up the front steps and I'm right behind him.

Two seconds later, I hear the Chief's big Expedition screech to a stop in the street.

"Inside, Malloy. Santucci? Off your ass! Move it! Move it! Go, go, go!"

The coach is sending in the whole team. Behind me, I hear the sound of heavy men thundering up the porch steps, jangling all the tinkley wind chimes hanging off the ceiling.

Chesterfield's front foyer is stuffed with antique furniture. Doilies and little glass candy dishes sit on top of everything.

Room number two features wingback chairs on oriental rugs in front of green-striped wallpaper and oil paintings of hounds and horses. Cozy.

Ceepak looks completely out of place, making his way to the main dining room, his pistol hanging by his hip in his hand.

He reaches the hostess at the double doors. Do we have a reservation? She studies her big burgundy binder while Ceepak looks over her head, trying to locate Mendez.

"May I help you, sir?"

She's wearing some kind of costume with a frilly shower cap, like she just came inside from churning butter.

"Yes, ma'am," Ceepak says firmly, yet politely. "Please vacate these premises immediately."

"I'm sorry?"

"Danny?"

"Out here, ma'am," I say.

"Ceepak?" The chief is lumbering up the hall behind us. Malloy and Santucci are with him. They all have their weapons in their hands.

"Mendez and Stone are the only diners," Ceepak says. "I'm going in. Cover me."

"Roger that," the chief whispers.

Ceepak makes a swing move into the dining room.

We swarm in after him like we're on military maneuvers. A waiter sees us and drops his tray. Muffins go tumbling everywhere.

"Upstairs," Ceepak yells to the waiter. "Now. Go!"

The guy thinks about picking up his muffins for a second and then hightails it out of the room.

Cynthia Stone and her companion are sitting at a corner table under a brass wall sconce with a flickering glass globe that's lit kind of low to set a more romantic mood. They were both sipping mimosas before we so rudely interrupted.

"Mr. Virgilio Mendez?" says Ceepak.

"Yeah?"

"Keep your hands on the table, where I can see them."

"Yo. Why you actin' like G.I. Joe all of a sudden? Take it easy, son."

"Officer?" Ms. Stone swivels around to face Ceepak. She sees the small army assembled behind him. "I hope you gentlemen have an explanation for this unwarranted intrusion."

Ceepak ignores her. His beef is with Mendez.

"Mr. Mendez, in my book, a man's word is good as gold—until he breaks it."

"You got that right."

"You were dishonest in your dealings with me this morning."

Mendez looks insulted.

"I will not tolerate a liar."

"Say what?"

"You stated you had never met nor had any contact with the man we are searching for, the street person known as Squeegee."

"I say I might, you know, see him around, here and there, maybe over to the car wash. But, yo—I do not *know* the dude. . . ."

"You two never had discussions concerning his need to vacate The Palace Hotel?"

"You tellin' me he's one of those skanks squatting up there?"

"You tell me."

"Damn, they all be lookin' the same to me. Every shaggy-assed crackhead junkie one of them."

The chief bulls forward.

"What's the story here, Ceepak?"

"At the car wash, Danny and I interviewed a witness who stated Mr. Mendez here had several conversations with our suspect."

Ms. Stone started to say something, then thought better of it.

"Mr. Mendez was working for Mr. Hart," Ceepak continues. "Removing unwanted tenants from an abandoned property. . . ."

"Nah-uh, I was, you know—measuring the windows for curtains and shit. . . ."

"This witness went on to state that Squeegee was attempting to work a deal with Mr. Mendez. Some way he and his girlfriend could remain in The Palace Hotel. They were negotiating."

"Say what?"

"Did you work out a deal, Mr. Mendez? A way for this junkie, as you call him, to pay his rent? Was Squeegee your hired assassin? Your hitman? Did he murder Mr. Hart for you?"

"What? What's a deal like that gonna do for me?"

"Maybe allow you to sell me a time-share." Ceepak pulls the Sea Palace brochure out of his back pocket. "When did Mendez Enterprises take possession of this property? Yesterday? Sometime shortly after 7:15 A.M.?"

Mendez almost leaps out of his chair to go nose to nose with Ceepak.

"Don't answer that," Ms. Stone now says. "In fact, don't say another word."

"Mr. Mendez?" Ceepak and Mendez are both about the same size. Same height. Same build. They stare into each other's eyes. Mendez blinks first.

"She don't want me talkin' to you 'cause she the one who call me. That's right. Yesterday morning. Say she got the damn power of attorney. Until they pro-rate the dead dude's will and all, she in charge of every damn thing Hart owns. His whole damn empire. You want you a casino or some shit like that? Maybe a shopping mall? She'll cut you a deal, bro . . . cheap too."

I hear the chief start breathing real loud, his nose hairs whistling like he's a lobster in a pot about to boil.

"All right," he says. "That's enough. Ceepak?"

"Yes, sir?"

"Good work. Malloy?"

"Yes sir?"

"You and Santucci—run these two clowns down to the station."

"Don't be preposterous." Ms. Stone smoothes out her skirt like she's ready to order her eggs benedict and skim the Sunday funnies. "On what possible charge?"

"I don't know," the chief grumbles. He looks like one of those guys in the antacid commercials, like his stomach is ballooning up with gas and his face is going to turn green, then explode. "I'll think of something later. Haul them out of here. Hustle! Move it!"

"Yes, sir." Malloy and Santucci go to the table. "Sir? Ma'am?"

Ms. Stone stands.

"Chief Cosgrove, I am going to sue your ass and nail it to a cross—"

"Get them out of here!" the chief hollers.

Malloy and Santucci escort Ms. Stone and Mendez to the front door.

"Ceepak?"

"Yes, sir?"

"Check out this hotel. This Sea Palace place."

"Yes, sir."

"Chances are, Squeegee is holed up nearby. See if there's a dock up there, too. Find the goddamn boat he used."

"Will do."

"Move it. Go."

The three of us stomp out, rattling curio cabinets and shaking Hummel figurines as we go. When we hit the porch, Malloy waves for the chief to come over. Quick.

"What?" The chief stomps down the steps. "What is it now?"

"Dispatch," says Malloy. "You just received a fax at the house."

"What? Another damn newspaper reporter?"

"No, sir. It's from Squeegee. It's a ransom note."

TWENTY-ONE

"**I** was simply carrying out Mr. Hart's wishes," Ms. Stone is saying. "It's what Reginald would have wanted."

The ex-Mrs. Hart just smiles.

"Were you sleeping with him?"

"I don't see how that is relevant."

Lucky me.

I'm stuck in the chief's office with the two of them.

Ms. Stone is waiting to be processed on whatever charges the chief cooks up.

Betty came to hear what the ransom note says.

"Ladies?" I say. "Would either of you like some more coffee?"

Trust me—caffeine is the last thing these two women need right now. They're pacing around, twisting the chief's paper clips, rubbing their arms, doing all kinds of itchy, twitchy stuff. But this is my assignment. Stay with the ladies. Get them what they need, keep them comfortable, and keep them away from everybody else while the chief and Ceepak and this guy from the state police study the ransom fax.

"When will we see the ransom note?" Betty asks. "Hear this man's demands?"

"Soon. I promise. They just want to have a few experts, you know, comb over it for clues. . . ."

"I see." She smiles. Her eyes twinkle.

"Experts?" Ms. Stone chuffs. Her eyes never twinkle. They burn like flares at a car wreck. "Hah! Who? That idiot from the state police? The slob on TV yesterday?"

"No, ma'am. Mr. Slominsky went back to—"

"Who then? That goody-two-shoes Ceepak?"

Stone sits. Betty paces to the window.

"Tell me, Ms. Stone," she says while she stares out at the ocean, "did Reggie actually say he was going to marry you?"

"Again, I refuse to answer any questions—"

"He would've left you, you know. Eventually. It would only be a matter of time." She's staring out the window like she sees herself a few years back. "Reggie was always looking for someone younger. He liked his girls young. Did you know that? The younger the better. . . ."

"Well then, if I were interested, that would certainly give me an advantage over you, wouldn't it?"

Meow. Hiss.

"Ladies? Let's try to remember why we're here, okay?"

"Why we're here?" Ms. Stone snorts at me. "I am only here because you and your friends stormed into a restaurant where I was simply attempting to—"

The door opens.

The chief and Ceepak march in. The chief has a xerox of the fax.

"It's Squeegee," the chief says. "Please sit down."

Betty slips demurely into the chief's big rolling chair. She has one of those Sally Field attempting-to-be-brave looks on her face.

"Does *she* need to hear this?" Ashley's mother pulls rank. You can tell she considers this matter a private, family-members-only type deal. I think Betty also regards Ms. Stone as a nympho-floozy, law degree or no.

"We might need her assistance as chief counsel of Hart Enterprises

. . . to help us meet the kidnapper's financial demands," Ceepak says. "However, if you'd be more comfortable. . . ."

"No. Fine. Let her stay. Read it."

The chief has on these reading glasses he's never let anybody see him wear before.

"Okay. It's words he cut out of old magazines . . . pieced together. . . ."

"Like in the movies?" Ms. Stone sighs, unable to not butt in.

The chief ignores her and reads.

"I HAVE YOUR DAUGHTER. YOU WILL PAY ME TEN MILLION DOLLARS AT NOON TOMORROW OR I WILL KILL ASHLEY WITH THE SAME GUN I USED TO KILL HER FATHER."

Ashley's mother gasps.

"He's confessing to the murder?" Ms. Stone sounds amazed. "I don't believe it. What an imbecile. Who's giving him his legal advice?"

"I . . . I don't have ten million dollars," Betty says. Her voice is faint. "Reginald only paid me an allowance . . . ten million dollars . . . I don't have ten million dollars. . . ." She closes her eyes.

The chief turns to Stone. "Harriet Ashley Hart, however, does. You told us her father left her everything? In his will?"

"Yes, but. . . ."

"We need to probate that will. Immediately."

"Impossible."

"Judge Erickson is standing by."

I know that probate is something a court does to prove a will is valid. But when the will involves billions and billions of dollars, dozens of companies, tons of real estate and airlines and shopping malls—I guess they usually like to take their time.

"We don't have much time," Ceepak says. "Noon tomorrow. A little over twenty-four hours."

"I'm sorry," Ms. Stone says, "but—"

"The bank is going to help," Ceepak says to Betty. "We contacted Don Nelson from First Federal. He's helping us pull together the actual cash."

Ashley's mom nods.

"Thank you," she says.

I'm wondering if we're going to use a suitcase stuffed with twenty-dollar bills like you always see when someone gets kidnapped on TV. If we do, I hope the suitcase has wheels. Ten million dollars probably weighs a ton. We might need a truck, like Saddam Hussein's kids did when they robbed the Iraqi Central Bank.

"Mr. Hart's executor is Arnold Bloomfield," Ms. Stone says, still stuck on the will. "I don't know if. . . ."

"We've already contacted Mr. Bloomfield," the chief says. "He's on his way. Corporate jet."

"I see. But surely you don't intend to give this criminal, this murderer ten million dollars—"

"We intend to do whatever it takes to ensure Ashley's safety," Ceepak says.

"You just make sure Ashley has complete access to her entire inheritance," the chief instructs her. "Understood? Or do you want another Hart to die this weekend?"

"No. Of course not." Sounds like our reluctant attorney is finally on board. "We'll make the necessary transfers."

"We've called the FBI," the chief says.

Betty nods.

"Of course."

"Kidnapping is a federal crime."

"I know."

"They'll help us figure out how to handle the ransom drop."

"Do we know if this man has . . . hurt Ashley?"

"No, ma'am," Ceepak says. "We do not. But, ma'am?"

"Yes?"

"I won't let him."

Ceepak doesn't say how he's going to stop Squeegee from hurting Ashley. But no one doubts him.

"Chief Cosgrove?"

One of the State CSI guys sticks his head in the door. I recognize him from the crime scene, even though he's not wearing his hairnet today.

"What've you got?"

"This fax? We tracked down the number."

"Yeah?"

"Came from the Sea Spray Hotel."

"The front desk?"

"No, sir. One of their in-room fax machines."

TWENTY-TWO

'm starting to think our friend Squeegee has fried one too many brain cells. He's not being too savvy about this whole ransom demand deal.

The Sea Spray Hotel is like only six blocks up the street from police headquarters—right on Beach Lane.

And doesn't he know every fax machine in the world prints the sender's phone number up on the top of the page in what they call a header, unless you program it not to?

Guess they didn't have in-room fax machines at The Palace Hotel when he and Red were squatting there. Hope Mr. Mendez remedies that when he takes over.

We're racing up Beach Lane. I'm doing about 60 m.p.h. on a road that's mostly used for bike riding, jogging, and pulling kids around in little red wagons.

Ceepak slips a fresh clip of ammo into his Smith & Wesson, the same pistol Squeegee's probably packing. Chances are slim Squeegee will bump into Ceepak in the lobby of the Sea Spray. After all, the fax came in about a half-hour ago, while we were all down at Chesterfield's. But Ceepak wants to Be Prepared, just in case he sees

Squeegee running down the beach and has a chance to pop him in the leg and slow him down.

We're one of four cop cars that simultaneously scream up to the canopied entranceway of the Sea Spray.

"Room 162!" the chief says. "Now! Move! Go! Move!"

Ceepak takes the lead, and seven cops follow. Pistols come out of holsters. Radios burble with static.

The Sea Spray is one of our biggest hotels—probably five hundred rooms. This is where businesspeople come for conventions and seminars so they can sit in conference rooms and stare out at the ocean when the PowerPoint presentations get boring.

The lobby is wide and extremely green, like a carpeted football field.

"Room 162?" Ceepak says to the lady behind the concierge desk.

She gapes and gawks. I think she's sort of in shock. Usually, she helps people book restaurant reservations and deep-sea fishing expeditions. Her typical day doesn't involve many heavily armed SWAT teams asking for directions.

"Room 1-6-2?" Ceepak says again.

Other people in the lobby have started to notice our weapons. I suspect panic is soon to follow.

The concierge points to her left.

"First floor," she says. "Go to the elevators, turn right."

"Danny?" Ceepak says over his shoulder, as we run past a stand of potted palms.

"Yes sir?"

"Bring up the rear. You're the last one in, understand?"

My partner's looking out for me, the guy without a gun.

"Yes, sir."

We make the turn and head down a long hall. There are trays sitting on the floor outside doors, the remnants of room service, half-eaten breakfasts hidden under warming lids and pink napkins.

"Stand back!" We're in front of 162.

I take Ceepak's advice. I'll let him and Malloy kick down the door.

They both have good steel-toed shoes and, even better, they both have guns.

The door doesn't budge with their first whack. It's steel. Deadbolted.

Santucci's lugging this one-man battering ram that must weigh about fifty pounds.

"Do it!" the chief says.

Santucci grabs both handles and swings the cement-filled pipe with everything he's got plus a grunt.

The door pops open.

Ceepak's first in, gun held forward in front of him.

"Clear," he yells.

That's when it's okay for me to enter. I see curtains blowing near the sliding glass door that leads out to a small beachfront patio.

Ceepak checks it out. The patio's empty.

"Nothing," he says.

The State CSI guy moves to the fax machine sitting on a desk.

"Inn-Fax," he says, recognizing the make and model of the beige box.

He pulls on his latex gloves and punches a button.

"Log," he says. The guy is such a pro, he doesn't waste time speaking in complete sentences. "Printing now."

The machine whirs and groans and spits out a sheet of curling thermal paper.

"What's the story?" the chief asks.

"Auto-Send."

"Come again?"

"The machine's time delay function."

"So we got the fax a half an hour ago," Ceepak says, "but when did he load it in?"

"10 A.M."

Maybe Squeegee has more unbaked brain cells that I gave him credit for.

"Damn," the chief says. "Dust the keypad for prints. Search the room."

"Watch where you step, gentlemen," Ceepak says. "Could be evidence underfoot—"

"May I be of any assistance, officers?"

"Stay where you are!" Santucci shouts, training his weapon on this old guy in the door.

It's the hotel's security chief. I can tell because he's wearing gray polyester pants and a blue blazer with an embroidered patch on the pocket. He holds up his hands so nobody in the room will shoot him. The radio clipped to his belt squawks and he thinks twice before lowering one hand to twist any knobs. When the squelch is silenced, his hand goes back up.

"Who was in this room?" the chief asks.

"Nobody," the security guy answers.

"Nobody?"

"It's been empty for weeks. Fly infestation."

Now that he mentions it, I notice dozens of little black specks scattered across the bedspread and the pillowcases and the carpet. Guess they aren't raisins.

"We've been fumigating, letting the room air out."

"Did you purposely leave the patio door unlocked?" Ceepak asks.

"No," the security guy says. "But unless you throw the safety latch up top there, you can pop it open from the outside with a screwdriver. I told maintenance we should change that."

"Yeah," Ceepak says, examining the u-bolt latch. "So our guy can come in off the beach . . . if he has a screwdriver. . . ."

"Or a Popsicle stick," the chief says, shaking his head.

"Hey, like I said. . . ."

"We're not mad at you, sir," Ceepak says. "We're mad at the situation."

The security guy nods. "This have to do with that missing kid?" he asks.

"Yeah," Ceepak says, adding, "You don't have to hold your hands over your head like that."

The guy lowers his arms.

"Are there security cameras? Outside?"

"No. I told management we should put in a system. They gave me their standard answer—costs too much."

"Yeah."

"You want I should block off the hallway here? Reroute foot traffic?"

"It'd be much appreciated." Once again, Ceepak stays calm while the angry storm swirls around him.

"Watch it near that door," the State guy now says, indicating that Ceepak should step away from the patio. "High potential for footprints in that quadrant."

Ceepak moves back and looks down at the tight weave in the industrial-strength carpet. "Boot print impression near threshold."

"Timberland?" the state guy asks.

"Affirmative."

"Malloy?" This from the chief. "You and Santucci go out the exit at the end of the corridor and circle back to the beach outside this patio. See if you can pick up any trace of our guy. See if he dropped anything, left any more boot prints. . . ."

"We're on it."

They bolt.

"Jesus." It's the state guy. He just slid open the drawer in the desk under the fax machine. I have a hunch he isn't reacting to the free Sea Spray Hotel post cards he has just found in there.

"What is it?" Ceepak asks. We all move a little closer, watching where we step.

He dips into the drawer with his tweezers and pulls out a sheet of Sea Spray stationery. I can see there's a Polaroid taped to it.

It's a photo of Ashley Hart.

Squeegee must have forced her to put on makeup: lipstick, rouge, mascara—the works. Then he had her tease up her hair so it looks all slutty. In the bleached-out Polaroid, Harriet Ashley Hart looks like something off an Internet porno site. She's wearing a beaded tank top with skinny spaghetti straps that hugs her chest and shows us she's definitely reached puberty.

You can read the fear in her eyes.

Below her small breasts and bare midriff, she holds this morning's newspaper. The one with the big photograph of her mom crying on the front page.

The Polaroid proves Ashley was alive this morning when the paper came out.

What's scribbled beneath the picture proves Squeegee is totally twisted:

BRING ME MY MONEY OR
I'LL MAKE HER PAY
IN SOME OTHER WAY.
XXXOOO
"SQUEEGEE"
P.S.
SEND THE MONEY WITH CEEPAK
ASHLEY SAYS I CAN TRUST CEEPAK

TWENTY-THREE

"**Y**ou need to be the one on TV," the chief says to Ceepak. Ceepak nods.

We're standing around the police cars parked higgledy-piggledy in front of the Sea Spray Hotel. Several state police and some local guys are scouring the beach, looking for clues.

Our man was here. Not so long ago. Popped in through the patio door and helped himself to the inn-fax. Who knows—maybe Squeegee even ordered room service. Anything's possible with this screwball.

There's a long line of tourists standing next to suitcases and luggage carts outside the lobby doors. The line snakes back inside, past the concierge desk. Everybody's waiting for the valet parking guys to bring their cars up from the garage so they can get the hell out. Squeegee seems to have that effect on people. So does seeing a SWAT team running through your hotel lobby. It's only July 11th, but summer might be over in Sea Haven.

The chief checks his watch.

"We were supposed to do the press conference at 1100."

"Let's do it at 1130," Ceepak says.

He's talking to the chief but looking up and down the road, searching for any sign of the enemy. The picture of Ashley was the last straw—this thing is extremely personal now.

"The FBI should be at headquarters. . . ."

"Yeah."

Ceepak scans the horizon.

"Let's wait to see what they say," the chief suggests.

"Yeah."

"They deal with these kidnapper loony-tunes all the time. And we need some goddamn specifics. Where the hell do we make the drop and pick up the girl? The scum is pretty damn vague about the goddamn particulars."

Ceepak is only half-listening.

He turns to the chief.

"There's only one way to be certain," he says quietly.

"Yeah. I know. You need to take him out, John. Eliminate his potential to do more damage."

Ceepak stares across the road at a plastic bag blowing in the branches of a tree.

"I have an M23 SWS in my office," the chief says.

"How's the scope?"

"Dead on."

"That'll work."

I figure SWS must be military mumbo-jumbo for some kind of rifle, because I remember one of Ceepak's many medals.

Marksmanship.

"I'm Christopher Morgan."

This big man in a dark suit is waiting for us when we return to headquarters.

"FBI Critical Incident Response Group. You Ceepak?"

"Yes, sir. This is my partner, Danny Boyle."

"Boyle." Morgan nods in my general direction but fixes his atten-tion on Ceepak. It's easy for these two guys to see eye to eye because they're both six-two and look like they play on the same football team. If Morgan wasn't black, he could be Ceepak's brother.

"We're here to help," Morgan says.

"Appreciate that."

"The FBI's primary objective in these instances is always the safe return of the victim. Once Ashley Hart is home, we'll move on to phase two: nailing the bastard who did it."

"That'll work."

"Any idea why the bad guy wants you involved?"

"I'm not sure."

Morgan flips through some pages in his yellow legal pad.

"You talk to her mom?" Ceepak asks.

"Yeah."

"How's she holding up?"

"Good. All things considered. I told her to grab some air, take a quick walk around the block."

"What about the reporters?"

"She can handle them," Morgan assures us. "Used to be in TV, herself. Told me she carries a wig and an ugly-ass floppy hat in her handbag at all times. Helps her avoid her adoring public when she's not in the mood to be adored."

"Smart lady."

"Well," Morgan says, "the media awaits. You ready for your close-up, Mr. Ceepak?"

"Sure. Right after you tell me what I say."

Morgan hands him a sheet of paper. "Make it your own, but those are your talking points. This guy Squeegee? He'll be watching. Or listening. They usually do. It's how they get their rocks off. They like to watch you squirm a little before their big payday."

"So I'm talking directly to him?" Ceepak says, his eyes skimming the page of notes.

"Right. Just look him in the eyes and let the son of a bitch know you're his best friend in the whole damn world."

✳ ✳ ✳

There are about a hundred microphones set up in front of our porch steps.

Mayor Sinclair, Chief Cosgrove, Christopher Morgan (very FBI with his Ray-Ban sunglasses and suit), and Ceepak stand on the second step, looking like some kind of four-man boys' choir.

The TV people are all over our lawn. Thank God it's gravel. If it were grass, it'd be dead. Behind the circle of reporters is an army of big guys lugging video cameras and fuzzy microphones on poles. Behind them are the other TV people—the young ones with clipboards, the ones who stare at monitors and keep a cell phone stuck to one ear at all times.

Mayor Sinclair speaks first.

"Thanks for coming out, everybody. Well, we have good news and bad news."

Did I tell you—our mayor can be a real jerk?

He's wearing khaki shorts, a polo shirt, and snazzy sunglasses dangling around his neck on a Croakie because he's the young, hip mayor of Fun-In-The-Sun City.

"First, the bad news. We recently received a ransom demand from Ashley Hart's kidnapper. The police will have more to say about that in a second. The good news? Well, the ransom note means Ashley is alive. It also means Sea Haven's pristine sandy beaches are once again safe for everybody else to enjoy! Folks, this whole tragedy is a *personal* matter between the killer-kidnapper and the Hart family. So come on down, enjoy your stay, and have a sunny, funderful day!"

The doofus is beaming, proud of how he worked in the Chamber of Commerce's slogan like that.

"And now—Chief Cosgrove?"

The chief gives the mayor a look. Thank God he's never used it on me.

"Thank you, Mayor Sinclair. I'm going to turn this thing over to Officer John Ceepak, who is heading up the task force on our end."

Ceepak takes the microphone.

"Thank you, Chief. First, as the mayor stated, we are in possession of the kidnapper's monetary demands. I assure you we are taking all steps necessary to facilitate Ashley Hart's safe return. We intend to do whatever needs to be done. You have my word on that."

I'm watching the video feed on a monitor set up on the lawn. The Code is oozing out of his eyes.

"As I said, the monetary demands are clear and appear quite doable. However, what remains unclear are the details. The where. The how. You mention a very specific time frame. . . ."

Now everybody knows he's talking directly to the kidnapper.

". . . and we hope to meet it. However, to do so, we require more information. Any clarification would prove most helpful. Thank you."

Ceepak steps back.

"Are you using us to talk directly to the kidnapper?" a reporter shouts from the crowd.

Morgan steps forward and eases Ceepak to the side.

"We have nothing further to say."

Now all the reporters are screaming.

"Are you paying the ransom?"

"How do you know the girl is alive?'

Morgan simply turns his back on the crowd, gestures to everybody else on stage to do the same, and the choir walks up the porch steps and goes back inside.

We're sitting inside the interrogation room—Morgan, Ceepak, and me.

The mayor is out walking the beach, personally encouraging everybody he can to stick around town.

On the table in front of us are copies of the ransom fax, the photograph, and the scribbled note that came with it.

"I've sent all this material to Quantico. We'll run a handwriting analysis, try to work up a psychological profile. . . ." Morgan has circled the phone number in the header with a felt-tip pen.

"Your man drops a lot of clues, doesn't he?" he says to Ceepak.

Ceepak nods. "You think he wants us to catch him?"

"You mean is this one of those 'stop me before I do this again' calls-for-help you see in the serial-killer movies?"

"Right."

"Nah." Morgan takes a sip of coffee. "I think he's trying to be clever. Show how smart he is. He knew you'd trace the fax number in about five minutes flat. That's why he did the auto-dial deal. Why he left the picture for you to find. He's Hansel, dropping bread crumbs like crazy."

Ceepak rotates his copy of the Polaroid to show Morgan where he's been doodling on it with his pen, outlining something blurry in the background.

"More like a bread loaf, I'd say."

"What you got? Lighthouse?"

"Could be."

"The north shore," I say.

"Danny's a local," Ceepak explains. "Knows this island like nobody's business."

Morgan hands the photo to me.

"Yeah. Okay. That looks like the old Ship John lighthouse. See how it's got this big band painted around the middle of the tower, here? Makes it look like a barber pole or a rugby shirt: white stripe, red stripe, white stripe. Makes it a daymark too."

"Where's Ship John?" Ceepak asks.

"Bottom of the ocean. They named the lighthouse after a ship that sank in the shoals. That's why boats needed to see the lighthouse day and night . . . the shoals. . . ."

"Hence the red band."

"Right."

"You know how to find this lighthouse, Danny?"

"Sure. It's been closed for years, but I know where it is."

"Excellent." Ceepak actually claps me on the back. Then he turns to Morgan. "Looks like he's sticking pretty close to familiar stomping grounds. We know he used to squat in an abandoned hotel up that way. Might be prudent to do some RST up that way. Reconnaissance, Surveillance, and Targeting."

"I don't know." Morgan leans back in his chair and rubs his eyes.

"You don't want him going all jumpy. Don't forget—the guy's a junkie. No matter how smart he thinks he is, when he's wired he could do something pretty damn stupid."

"That's why we'll go up tonight. Cover of darkness."

Morgan looks at Ceepak for a second.

"You want me or my guys to go with you?"

"No, sir. Like you say—a big crowd will only draw unwanted attention. Danny and I can handle it. We're just going up for a look-see. Get our bearings for tomorrow. We have to figure the money drop will be somewhere in the general vicinity—"

Gus sticks his head in the door.

"Uh, excuse me, fellas. Ceepak?"

"Yeah?"

"Chief said to grab you guys. Another freaking fax is coming in."

TWENTY-FOUR

"**Y**ou got the number?" Morgan asks.

"Yeah," the chief says. "We're on with the phone company . . . pinpointing the location."

We're all standing behind Gus's desk, staring at the fax machine as it prints out page number three.

"It's a self-serve machine on Ocean Avenue," Jane Bright yells from a desk phone. "Boardwalk Books. 1733 Ocean Avenue."

"Helen?" the chief barks into the dispatcher's cubicle. "Who's close to 1733 Ocean?"

"Cochran?" Morgan's yelling at one of his men.

"Pescatore and Murphy," the dispatcher yells back to the chief.

"Send them!"

"Boardwalk Books!" Morgan's bellowing at a guy who must be Cochran. "1733 Ocean. Take the forensics team. Go!"

"Sir?" Ceepak says to the chief.

"No, you can not go. We need you here."

Ashley's mother walks through the front door. She's wearing her black wig and floppy hat, and she freezes when she sees all of us standing behind the front desk staring at a beige box grunting out paper.

"What's going on? Is it him?" Is it the kidnapper?"

"We think so."

"What does he want now?"

"It looks like he's honoring our request for more specifics," says Ceepak.

"Is that good news?"

"Yes, ma'am. I believe it means we're one step closer to bringing Ashley home."

"Can I read it?"

"No need," the chief says. "We'll handle it from here."

"Are you sure?"

"It's for the best," Morgan chimes in, giving the official FBI seal of approval to the chief's suggestion.

"In fact," the chief suggests, "you might be more comfortable at your own home. I can have Officer Bright drive you."

"All right, Robert. You know best."

Ceepak and me look over at the chief, who's sort of blushing.

We've never heard anybody call him "Robert" before.

Of course Pescatore and Murphy found no one at Boardwalk Books. The coin-operated fax machine is tucked in a corner, hidden behind bookcases filled with beach reads. The sole employee was up at the cash register. Business was extremely slow, so he was sipping cappuccino and reading. He hadn't seen the fax sender walk in or out. Preoccupied with his froth. End of story.

Also, the bookstore doesn't believe in security cameras. The owner, this guy I've met a couple times, is a big fan of George Orwell's *1984* and doesn't want us "to go down a slippery slope" to governmental mind control or world domination, I forget which. Besides, what kid is going to shoplift *books* on his summer vacation?

Cochran, the FBI guy, dutifully dusted the fax machine for prints. He even impounded all the quarters in the money box. I'll bet you there's three or four in there without any fingerprints on them at all.

That would be our guy's loose change.

So all we have is the fax.

Once again, we have copies, and the interrogation room looks like a Barnes & Noble, everybody hanging out reading. The chief, Morgan, Ceepak, and me—we're all studying what the kidnapper wants us to do next:

Mrs. Hart.

Listen carefully! We have your daughter and have not yet harmed her in any way even though I have been tempted.

If you want your daughter to stay safe and unharmed you will put ten million dollars in cash in several rolling suitcases. $100 bills are fine so are $1000s but please give me some $20 bills too.

You are to place the suitcases inside the Ship John Lighthouse at noon tomorrow. The first floor. Just inside the door. The padlock and chain have been removed and you will be able to enter. When you do so, you will find instructions as to where to find your daughter at precisely 2 P.M.

Yes. Sorry. You will have to wait two hours.

I have friends who are with Ashley.

Any deviation from these instructions will result in the immediate execution of your daughter.

The friends watching over your daughter did not like your late husband so do not provoke them.

Ceepak is to bring the money and then leave and not look back.

If he stays, if he brings the FBI agent with the sunglasses, if he even brings a dog, your daughter dies.

If the money is marked or in any way tampered with she dies. If the Coast Guard tries to stop me from leaving the island, she dies.

You stand a 99 per cent chance of killing your daughter if you try to out smart us. Follow our instructions and wait until 2 P.M. and you stand a 100% chance of getting her back. Don't try to grow a brain. Don't underestimate us. It is up to you now.

Victory!
Squeegee

Everybody finishes reading about the same time. We know we will have to show this to Betty, just not right away.

"*We*," Ceepak says. "*Us*."

"Yeah," Morgan chimes in. "Saw that too."

"Stands to reason he'd have associates," the chief says. "Ten million dollars is a lot of money."

"I thought you guys told me Squeegee was a junkie." Morgan is leaning back in his chair.

Something doesn't smell right.

"We found drug paraphernalia near the Tilt-A-Whirl," Ceepak says. "In the spot where we know the man in the Timberland boots was hiding."

"Right. Behind the bushes."

"What's your problem, Morgan?" the chief sounds grouchy, upset at Morgan for slowing things down.

"It just doesn't make sense."

"I know what you mean," Ceepak says.

"What doesn't make goddam sense?"

"Chief Cosgrove," Morgan speaks in this slow, easy rhythm. "Since when is a junkie capable of pulling off something this big? Most junkies can't even mastermind their next score or their next bath, let alone an elaborate scheme like this. Yet, every step of the way, this thing's been carried out with military precision. The hit at the Tilt-A-Whirl. The grab on the beach. The smooth nautical getaway. The photo. The timing of the faxes."

"What's your take, Chris?" Ceepak is interested.

"Let's run this thing down," Morgan says. "If Squeegee is in the bushes because, let's say, he tailed Mr. Hart and his daughter to the Tilt-A-Whirl, why doesn't he just nab the girl then? If the ten-million-dollar ransom money is his ultimate motive. . . ."

"Don't forget," the chief says, "he called Hart a 'fucking slumlord.'"

"I remember. So first he takes a little revenge and pops seven bullets into Hart. Fine. Then, he wants to sweeten his revenge by grabbing the daughter and ripping off the slumlord's estate for ten million bucks. Okay. But if that's the plan, why doesn't he just grab the girl at the amusement park? He's got a gun. The girl's in no state to resist. Why didn't he grab her then?" Morgan asks it again. "Why does he wait?"

"Only about fourteen hours," the chief answers.

"Still, he waits."

"He knew," Ceepak says. "About the will. The probate. The potential for delay. The need to find the executor, contact the insurance companies. . . ."

"Exactly," Morgan says. "Sound like typical junkie thinking to you guys?"

"No, sir."

"Sounds more like the mob," the chief is getting with the program now.

"Or a gang," Morgan adds.

"Danny?" Ceepak swivels in his chair. "Your friend Becca? What was it she told you?"

"You mean about Mendez and his crew?"

The chief stands up. "His crew?"

"Yeah. He and his buddies were hanging out around the pool, flexing their muscles. . . ."

"Danny? Focus, okay?"

"I remember some of the names. Mendez. Ramirez. Echaverra. All these tough dudes, she said."

"Gentlemen," Morgan says, "we may have found us our *'us.'*"

TWENTY-FIVE

Good thing we have Mendez locked up in the back. Unfortunately, the chief never did cook up a good charge against Cynthia Stone, so the lawyer went back to her room at the B&B to plot her revenge.

"I will make myself available at 3 P.M."

Her steel-tipped voice now emanates from the chief's speakerphone.

"We'd prefer to talk with Mr. Mendez sooner," Morgan says. "We'd prefer to talk to with him sometime closer to now!"

"I'm sure you would, Mr. Morgan. However, he will not speak to you without his lawyer present. Me."

Ceepak nods. He knows it's the right way to proceed.

"It is currently 1:15," Ms. Stone says. "I have a few final matters to attend to, regarding the transfer of Mr. Hart's assets into Ashley's name."

"Three is fine," the chief barks. "Not a minute later."

"I'll be there. You have my word."

The chief jabs the speaker button to make sure Ms. Stone is gone. I don't think he likes her.

"Gentlemen?" Morgan moves toward the door. "If you'll excuse me, I think I'll go grab a quick bite with my guys. There's something I want them to look into. . . ."

"What?" the chief asks. "Anything we should know?"

"No. Don't think so. But if it turns out to be something, I'll let you know. Probably won't. Just . . . I don't know. I'll keep you posted. Where's a good place for a sandwich?"

"Just head over to Ocean," I suggest. "There's sub shops and delis up and down the street."

"Thanks, Boyle. We circle back up at, say, 1445?"

"Make it 1420," the chief says.

Morgan leaves.

"Close the door, Boyle."

"Yes, chief."

He waits until I do it before he speaks again.

"Ceepak?"

"Sir?"

"I want you up on the north shore tonight."

"That's my plan."

"Good. Mendez and his gang might be involved, but I don't think those gangbangers are the kind that get their rocks off with teenaged girls."

"Check."

"Squeegee, on the other hand . . ."

The chief walks over to a locked closet. He slips in the key and opens the door.

There's a long case sitting on the floor. It looks like the kind of hard-sided storage box you'd pack your power tools in if you had some tool that was about three feet long.

The chief props the case up on his desk and snaps open all four latches.

I was right about SWS. It's a rifle.

Inside the case, tucked into specially cut foam slots, are all the pieces of an Army issue M-24. The stock, the barrel, the scope, even a silencer. I see Dymo-pressed label tape: "M-24 Sniper Weapon System."

SWS.

"Just in case," the chief says.

Ceepak snaps the latches shut and picks up the case.

"Danny?"

"Yeah?"

"Let's go grab some lunch."

We almost go out the front door. Then we remember the reporters. Ceepak is sort of a poster boy for this case, talking directly to the kidnapper on TV and all. If the newshounds see him, they'll start screaming questions again and chase after us like twelve-year-old girls on the heels of Justin Timberlake or whoever they're squealing after these days.

We slip out the back.

I take Ceepak to this totally out-of-the-way restaurant.

Actually, to call The Rusty Scupper a restaurant is a stretch. It's really just this four-table grease pit with a grill and a waitress over on the bay side of the island that practically nobody ever goes to except starving people with boats because it's located right off the public dock. In fact, you can smell the salty air and listen to the water slap against the barnacle-crusted pilings while you wait for your burger to be burnt.

I come here to ogle the waitress. Gail.

She's at the "staff table" painting her toenails. She has her bronzed leg up on a chair, her back arched, her long hair hanging forward. She is incredibly tan and likes to wear a skimpy bathing suit on the job so she can stay that way.

Two tables have customers, chewing their burgers over and over and over, nibbling droopy fries out of red plastic baskets with tissue paper dotted with grease blots. The décor is simple: red-and-white vinyl tablecloths with tomato-red rings wherever a dirty-bottomed ketchup bottle sat in the past week. Gail is not a big table wiper.

"Hey, Danny."

"Hey, Gail."

Gail shakes her frosted hair out of her eyes and sees Ceepak.

"Ohmygod. You're that guy from TV!"

"Yes, ma'am."

"How totally cool! You were just on TV."

Gail is a few fries short of a Happy Meal, as they say. She's sort of forgetting *why* Ceepak made his television debut earlier in the day.

"Ohmygod," she repeats, unable to believe she's about to serve a greasy hamburger to a television star.

I sort of wish I had taken Ceepak someplace else.

"I'll have a burger," Ceepak says.

"Hunh?"

"Two burgers, Gail." I say, trying to snap her out of her adoring daze. "Okay?"

"Oh, right."

Gail scribbles on her green pad.

"How'd you like that cooked?"

Ceepak does a quick survey of his surroundings. Sees the flies buzzing in and out through the holes in the screen door. The lipstick stains on the tops of our clean water glasses. The grill cook wiping his nose and chewing a toothpick on the other side of the kitchen pass-through.

"Very well done," he says.

"You want him to like cook the shit out of it?"

"Yes, ma'am. I surely do."

"Cool." Gail twirls on her heel and bounces over to tell the cook what kind of meat to massacre next.

"Like I said, nobody much comes here."

"She a friend?"

"Yeah."

Ceepak nods. He can see why.

"That Morgan's pretty sharp, hunh?" I say, trying to start some idle conversation that might help us forget about our increased risk of contracting mad cow disease.

Ceepak nods again. He's thinking.

"Wonder what the other thing is he's checking out. . . ."

"Something in the note," Ceepak says.

"Really?"

"FBI guys read a lot of ransom notes. Something about this one struck him as peculiar."

"How do you know that?"

"Saw it in his face. Like he smelled bad fish."

Gail comes bopping back to our table carrying a crumpled newspaper.

"Hey guys—that girl? You know, the one whose father was like shot in Playland? Was she like kidnapped or something?"

"Yes, ma'am."

"Oh. . . ."

The fifteen-watt bulb in her brain is now illuminated.

"So *that's* why you were on TV!"

"Yes, ma'am."

"Cool. Funny, we get a lot of TV people in here lately. . . ."

"The reporters?"

"No. Just that weather girl who married Hart. The kid's mom." She taps her curved fingernail extension on the front-page photo of Betty Bell Hart. "She was all like secretive and like leave me alone-ish and all. I guess on account of what happened to her ex-husband and her daughter. She looked kind of sad, you know?"

"When'd she come in? Earlier today?"

"No. Friday."

"Friday?" Ceepak says before I do.

"Yunh-hunh."

"You sure?"

"Uh-yeah. She ordered fish sticks."

"And?"

"Duh! We only serve fish sticks on Fridays. For the Catholics or whatever. Makes sense she'd want to be left alone after all this. I know I would if my ex got killed or my kid got kidnapped. Not that I'm married or anything. . . ."

Neither Ceepak nor I mention that all "this" took place on Saturday. Not Friday. Not when Ashley's mother was, according to what she'd told us, at her apartment in the city.

"Danny?" Ceepak stands up.

"Yeah." I push back my chair and smile up at Gail. "We gotta run."

"Really? Your burgers are almost done."

I can hear the cook squeezing the sputtering life out of our chopped meat patties on his griddle. I give Gail ten bucks for our uneaten lunch.

"We'll take a rain check."

It's not that we're afraid of The Rusty Scupper's burgers.

We just need to talk to Ashley's mother about the fish sticks.

TWENTY-SIX

"**S**he *what*?"

"She was in town on Friday night."

"Fuck. . . ."

I can tell the chief is upset by our news flash. He doesn't usually swear like that over the radio.

"I'll meet you there," he barks. You can almost hear the acid indigestion churning up in his stomach. The guy is a Tums time bomb.

"No need, sir. Danny and I can cover it."

"I'll meet you there, goddammit!"

We reach the Beach Crest Heights subdivision's gatehouse and tin the rent-a-cop standing inside his hut. That means we show him our badges and he doesn't ask a whole lot of questions—he just opens the gate. I always wonder about these unarmed, white-shirt security guards. If they look at your driver's license and decide you're a bad guy, what do they do?

Whack you in the head with their clipboard?

We pull into the circular driveway. Ceepak rings the doorbell.

"Yes?"

It's that butler dude again. I wonder if he did it. He does everything else butlers do in the movies, so maybe he's the one who murdered Reggie Hart. Maybe he and Mendez were working together, too.

"We need to see Mrs. Hart," Ceepak says.

"She is temporarily indisposed."

"Tell her it's Officer Ceepak." With this, Ceepak simply sidesteps the loyal manservant and glides into the glass-walled front room. I glide in after him.

"But sirs . . ."

Ceepak folds his hands behind his back, up near the belt loops, standing at what they call parade rest, ready and willing to wait.

"We're kind of in a hurry," I say.

"Please wait here." Nose held high, the butler strides slowly to his right.

"Is she in the sunroom?" Ceepak asks.

"Sir, if you'll kindly wait. . . ."

Ceepak remembers the way. I bring up the rear. Behind us, I hear the chief make his entrance.

"Ceepak?"

"This way."

"But . . . sir . . . really. . . ."

Sounds like the chief is pushing past the butler, too. Maybe the poor guy ought to go back to working for Joe Millionaire.

"Yes. I was in Sea Haven on Friday night."

Betty is sitting on the couch sipping tea. She has on white pants that cuff above her ankles, white strappy sandals, and this white-and-gold top that sparkles in the sun.

So much for widows wearing black.

"I took a motel room—"

"Where?" the chief asks.

"The Smuggler's Cove."

"Jesus," the chief groans.

"What?" Ceepak is curious.

"The Cove? They rent out the same goddamn room ten times a night. It's a hot sheets hotel! Hourly rates. Adult movies. . . ."

"I see."

"They are also very discreet," Betty says defensively. "Gentlemen, I am not proud of my deception, but I fail to see how my being here on Friday has anything to do with Ashley's kidnapping. Why aren't you out searching for her? Why are you wasting your time here, questioning me?"

"So what were you doing here, ma'am?" The chief cuts to the chase.

"Looking out for my daughter."

"How's that?"

"He had her in the house here with him. In front of my daughter."

"Had who?" The chief puts his fist to his stomach like he just burped up a bubble of something nasty.

"The lawyer? He had her . . . here."

"Were Mr. Hart and Ms. Stone romantically involved?" Ceepak asks.

"Yes," Betty says and sets down her teacup. "She was Reginald's most recent conquest."

The chief rolls his eyes and mutters something that sounds a lot like "Jesus Fucking Christ."

If I was Betty Bell Hart? I'd talk to Ceepak and forget the chief who really looks like he's going to explode some time soon. He's hardly even sitting in his chair any more, his fists are digging into his thighs, and he's grinding his teeth louder than he knows.

Yeah, I'd talk to Ceepak.

"So," Ceepak says, "you were the one who had Ms. Stone's suitcases tossed out into the driveway?"

"Yes." Betty smiles slightly. "I'm afraid I was miffed."

We look at one another, Ceepak, the chief, and I. Miffed.

"Ashley said she heard them," Betty says. "Up in the master bedroom."

Ceepak closes his eyes. Some people severely disappoint him. I think Reggie Hart is now one of them.

"Prior to that," Betty says, "Ms. Stone was flouncing around the house in nothing but a frilly push-up bra, panties, and a garter belt."

"Ashley told you all this?"

"Yes. She called me and said it was like a Victoria's Secret fashion show out here."

"That would explain that perfume you told me about," the chief says to Ceepak. "That stuff you smelled on Hart?"

"Yes, sir," Ceepak says. "It sure might. They came up Thursday? Mr. Hart, Ms. Stone, and Ashley?"

"Yes. Thursday afternoon. Ashley amused herself. Swam in the pool. Her father did some paperwork with Ms. Stone. Went to a 'meeting' with her, somewhere downtown. Then they all went out to dinner. O'Riley's, I think. The fashion shows, the sexcapades? That all started Thursday night. After dinner."

"So you drove up on Friday?"

"I did."

"Do you use E-Z Pass?"

"Excuse me?"

"To pay the tolls. Do you have an E-Z Pass transponder unit installed on your windshield?"

"Yes. Why?"

"We'll want to run a check," Ceepak says. "Verify your whereabouts. The timeframe."

"What?" She tucks her legs up under her on the couch. "Don't you trust me, Officer Ceepak?"

Ceepak lets that one go unanswered.

"So, Ashley called you?"

"Of course she did. Snuck outside and used her cell phone so her father wouldn't hear. I told her I would come, but it had to be our secret. I knew what Ms. Stone was up to."

"Banging her boss?" The chief kind of blurts it out. "Sorry."

"Ms. Stone wanted Reginald to restructure his will."

"Why?" Ceepak asks.

"She probably told him it was in the best interest of the corporation.

That it wasn't prudent to leave everything to Ashley. However, I suspect Ms. Stone fancied herself the next Mrs. Hart."

"Were they that serious?"

"*She* might have been. Reginald, I'm certain, was not. She's not really his type. Oh, sure—he'd have his fun with her . . . for a while. But eventually he'd move on to something younger. He always does. . . ."

She'd mentioned this before. I guess all billionaires prefer that their trophies be youngish.

"He wouldn't change his will. Never. He simply loved Ashley too, too much to even consider it. And he certainly didn't need a new wife, no matter how fetching Ms. Stone may have appeared in her lingerie. I gave Reginald the only child he ever wanted. He could date any woman in the world. Why would he ever want to get married again?"

"Where were you Saturday morning?"

Ceepak has to ask it.

"You mean when Reginald was murdered? Is that what you mean, Mr. Ceepak?"

"Yes, ma'am. Saturday. Around 7:15."

"Let's see. I woke up. Brushed my teeth. Took a shower. Got dressed. Combed my hair. Put on my makeup. Made a cup of coffee right there in my motel room." The standard run-down, delivered deadpan. "They have a miniature Mr. Coffee machine in every room at The Smuggler's Cove. Did you know that, Officer Ceepak?"

"No, ma'am. After coffee? Go anywhere?"

"Yes. I went to the bank. The cash machine. I didn't dare use my credit cards for anything."

"Or we might find out you were in town when you weren't supposed to be?"

"Something like that." She tries to bat her eyes at Ceepak. It doesn't work.

"You know an ATM takes a photograph during every transaction?"

"Really?"

"Yes, ma'am."

"So if I'm lying, you'll soon know—won't you?"

"Yes, ma'am. I will."

"Isn't technology marvelous? First the E-Z pass, now the ATM? It's a wonder we don't all wear collars around our necks and send out radio signals, like some sort of endangered geese."

"Yes, ma'am."

"I was at the bank." Betty enunciates every word, like she's doing closed captioning for the hearing-impaired. "I withdrew two hundred dollars. But I suppose you'll verify that as well, won't you?"

"Yes, ma'am."

Ceepak makes a note.

She sighs.

"Look, I'm sorry I lied."

"Well, you should be!" the chief snaps.

"Won't you forgive me?" Betty looks at Ceepak the way she used to look at the baby bunnies when she did her Easter Sunday forecast. "Please?"

Ceepak is sorry she lied, too. I can tell by the way he bites his lip while he nods his head. He might forgive her, but he sure as hell won't forget what she did.

Guess that's how The Code works. If folks follow it, you can trust whatever they say, you can even follow them into battle. If they don't? If they lie? You have to watch your back any time they ask you to believe a word they say.

The chief stands up.

"Okay. The damage is done. We move forward. I'll get Santucci or somebody to do the bank and EZ Pass calls."

Ceepak stands, too.

I guess we're done with Betty.

"You'll bring my little girl home safe?" she asks, eyes moist.

"We'll do our best," Ceepak tells her stiffly.

"Let's head back to headquarters," the chief now says, checking his watch. "Time to talk to Mendez—"

The chief's radio squawks.

"Jesus. What now?"

I don't think the chief likes the way this Tilt-A-Whirl case keeps spinning him around and making his stomach lurch.

He stabs the radio talkback button with his thumb.

"Yeah?"

"It's Adam Kiger, sir."

"What you got, son?"

"Gus's gun. We found it."

"Where?"

"In the trunk of Mendez's car."

TWENTY-SEVEN

Ceepak is staring out the car window, watching the beach roll by, thinking.

He asked me to take the scenic route home—up 247, the coast road, which turns into Beach Lane when it hits the town limits of Sea Haven proper.

I'm doing a little thinking too.

I'm starting to wonder if crime one and crime two are even connected.

Maybe somebody killed Hart because, as they say down South, he needed him some killing. Then maybe somebody else pulled the kidnap, figuring the kid had to come into some pretty fat money when her old man's ticket got punched.

"'With her killer graces, and her secret places. . . .'" Ceepak's mumble-singing again. Another Springsteen song. I know this one. It's called "She's the One."

"Danny?"

"Yes, sir?"

"Two things. One. We need a warrant. I want to search that woman's car."

"What sort of secrets are we looking for?"

"Car-wash coupons. Air fresheners. Cash-register receipts. . . ."

"From Cap'n Scrubby's?"

"Roger that."

"You think *she* hired Squeegee?"

"It's certainly a new possibility. Two—let's swing by the bank."

"Now? We're with Mendez at three—"

"Mr. Mendez can wait. I need to use the cash machine."

The First Atlantic Bank is located on Ocean Avenue between Snapper's Grill and Mango's Swimwear, about three blocks down the street from The Pancake Palace.

I park out front and follow Ceepak into the lobby. He dips his card into the ATM.

"You need cash?" I ask.

Ceepak doesn't answer. He tilts his wrist and punches a button on his G-Shock.

"Okay," he says, "I'm taking out $200."

I'm a little jealous. Ceepak's actually got $200 to withdraw.

While he waits for the machine to spit out ten twenties, he smiles up at the black plexiglass over the ATM.

"Cheese," he says.

Ceepak tucks the bills into his pocket.

"Okay. Follow me."

He heads out the door and up the block to the corner of Ocean and Maple. The light is red. We wait for it to change.

When it does, Ceepak checks his wrist and says, "Thirty seconds."

We head across the street. On the other side of Ocean Avenue, Maple Street creates one corner of the Sunnyside Playland property. So the fence leading down to the beach is on our left; on our right, rental houses. Two blocks' worth. The closer we get to the ocean, the higher the rents.

The sidewalk ends, and now we have to walk up planks laid across the sand dune to reach the beach.

"Three minutes," Ceepak says. I can tell he's trying not to walk too fast or too slow — he's just walking with what they call a sense of purpose.

We're up and over the dune and on the beach.

The first thing I notice is how empty it is for a hot Sunday afternoon. Guess folks weren't listening when the mayor told them Sea Haven was open for fun in the sun again. As far as I can see, there are only maybe five umbrellas, and the little kids are building their sand castles pretty darn close to where mom and dad sit in their beach chairs, terrified to take their eyes off their children.

We head left again. The ocean's on our right. Playland's chain-link fence is on our left.

Behind the fence, I can see parts of Playland. First, the Kiddie Rides: "Hot Doggers Hot Rods," tiny race cars shaped like hot-dog buns that putter around in a circle; "The Beachball Express," a little train that chugs around in a circle; "The Sandpiper Cub High Flyer," little airplanes that sort of fly around in a circle.

When you're a little kid, having fun at an amusement park involves a lot of riding around in circles.

Now I see the Italian sausage stand, the funnel cake and zeppole wagon, the French-fry and Coke stands.

Next come the bumper cars, and the Flying Fish Boat, which rocks you back and forth and swings you higher and higher until you wish you had skipped the sandwich with peppers and onions back at the Italian sausage stand.

Finally, I see the Turtle-Twirl Tilt-A-Whirl.

We're standing outside the fence, near the little plywood trapdoor, still covered with sand. I see the yellow police tape I hung fluttering in the breeze. I also see that Sunnyside Clyde has sent out his cleaning crews. Gone is any trace of Mr. Hart's last bloody thrill ride. The turtle's all green again, no red anywhere.

"Seven minutes, forty-five seconds." Ceepak says, stopping his digital watch with a beep. "Two or three more minutes to crawl under the fence, get in position."

"So we're what? A ten-, fifteen-minute walk from the bank?"

Ceepak nods.

"We need to talk to the medical examiner. Calibrate a more precise TOD."

Time of death.

Looks like Betty is this close to becoming another possibility.

"Yo! Someone planted that, man!"

Mr. Virgilio Mendez is none too happy about what young Officer Kiger found in the trunk of his El Dorado.

Gus's gun is sitting on the table in front of him and his lawyer, Cynthia Stone. It's a Smith & Wesson 9-mm semi-automatic with an evidence tag tied to it so it looks like it's on sale at some cop's yard sale.

"We're running the ballistics," the chief says. "I'm sure it'll match the slugs we found at the Tilt-A-Whirl—"

"Like I'm really gonna be leaving my piece in the trunk like it's a beer cooler or some shit—"

"I agree with Mr. Mendez," Ms. Stone says. "In fact, I find this crude attempt to frame him laughable."

"Then why the hell aren't I laughing?" The chief and Kiger are the only cops in the interrogation room with Mendez and Ms. Stone. Ceepak and I are watching from the little room on the other side of the one-way mirror. Morgan from the FBI is with us.

"Why don't you advise your client to come clean?" the chief says to the attorney. "Tell us how he hired Squeegee to kill Reginald Hart. Then, him and his friends? Ramirez? Echaverra? They rented a boat—"

"What the fuck you been smokin'?"

Ms. Stone stands up.

"Chief Cosgrove."

"Sit down."

"Sir, I am an officer of the court."

"Not right now. Right now you're just a suspect."

"Excuse me?"

"Co-conspirator."

"What?"

"Do you have a lawyer, Ms. Stone?"

"Why?"

"Why? Well, let's see. We know you were sleeping with the deceased."

"Okay," Ms. Stone says. "That's it. We're done here—"

"No we're not. I'm just getting started. Sit down."

"You can't question me without my attorney being present."

"Fine," the chief says. "No more questions. You won't tell me, so I'll tell you. We'll work it that way."

The chief hikes up his pants. I can see sweat stains under his arms. The guy hasn't had much sleep since Saturday, and all the strain is starting to show. He might rip somebody's head off today.

"I think you were the brains, Ms. Stone," he says, raising his thumb, like he's going to start counting stuff down. "You set the whole thing up because you realized Mr. Hart would never marry you. So you worked out this other way to get at his money. His real estate. Ten million dollars in ransom money—"

"Mr. Hart was my employer. That is as far as our relationship went. As such—"

"I'm not asking you questions, so you don't have to say anything. Deal?" Now the chief's first finger pops up; the countdown continues. "You partnered with Mendez here, who was tired of doing nickel-and-dime work for Hart. Wanted a bigger slice of the pie."

Mendez drops his jaw. The chief stares him down.

"Mr. Mendez proceeded to hire Squeegee. What'd you pay him? A free condo in your time-share hotel? A dime bag of dope? The same shit you sell to kids up and down the beach?"

"You're out of your fucking mind . . . out to fucking lunch. . . ."

"Me? No, Mr. Mendez—I checked your record. Your rap sheet. You sell drugs to little children."

He slides a folder across the table. Mendez refuses to open it or even look at it.

"I done my time for that."

"You sell drugs to children!"

"Only them that wants it."

Wrong thing to say in front of John Ceepak.

I look over and Ceepak's squinting again, like he's lining up Mendez in his sniper sights.

"Did you know Squeegee was a sexual predator?" The chief sends another manila folder across the table. "Pulled *his* record, too. Did you two talk about how he likes to expose himself to twelve-year-old girls under the boardwalk?"

"I don't know shit about this Squeegee."

"Did you promise Squeegee he could have his fun with Ashley? Is that how you got him interested in the trigger job?"

"I told you I don't know this Squeegee. Maybe I run into him once or twice up at The Palace Hotel, but. . . ."

"Where is Ashley Hart? Where did your gang take her, Mr. Mendez?"

"Hey! I don't do no kidnappin'—"

"Where the hell did you take her?"

"I don't do that kind of shit!"

And they keep going around and around—just like those kiddie-car rides over at Playland.

In the back room, Morgan turns from the window when Mendez says he "ain't no kidnapper" for the umpteenth time.

"Neither is our ransom note writer," the FBI guy says.

"How do you mean?"

"Well, there's some indication he may want us to think he's more experienced at this than he actually is."

Ceepak twists down the volume knob in the wall so the ranting in the other room becomes soft Muzak in ours.

"What do you mean?"

"The ransom note?"

"Yeah?"

"Something about it. It sounded familiar. So I had my guys do a quick check."

"And?"

"Jon Benet Ramsey."

"Colorado? The six-year-old beauty queen?"

"Right. After she disappeared, the Ramsey family received a ransom note. Lot of people think it was a fake. Just a way for the killer to cover some tracks, misdirect the investigation."

Ceepak nods. He's obviously familiar with the case.

"Anyhow, I always remembered the phrasing. Sort of stuck in my head because I thought some of it sounded odd, you know? Ridiculous, even."

"And?"

"I think our kidnapper cribbed it."

"Our ransom note is a copy?"

Morgan nods.

"I think so. Some key phrases are lifted verbatim. 'Listen carefully!' 'You stand a 99 per cent chance of killing your daughter.' And that corny thing at the end? 'Victory!' Give me a break."

"So whoever wrote the ransom note. . . ."

"They cheated," Morgan says. "Had their eyes on their neighbor's paper, like teacher always told us not to. They wanted to make sure they sounded like they knew what they were doing, even though they did not."

"I never did no damn kidnapping, man!"

I can hear Mendez up in the ceiling speaker, faintly repeating himself.

"Check my sheet," he says. "My record's clean on that one. I never did no damn kidnappin' before!"

Apparently, neither did the guy who grabbed Ashley.

TWENTY-EIGHT

"I want this over! Tonight!"

Ten minutes after the interrogation of Mendez and Ms. Stone, the chief's mood hasn't improved much. Ceepak and I are in his office.

"You guys hear me? Fucking FBI . . . looking over my fucking shoulder. . . ."

The chief hasn't enjoyed working with Mr. Morgan as much as Ceepak and I, even though the ransom note being a rip-off sort of supports the chief's whole "Mendez Did It" theory.

"I want this thing over . . . the mayor wants it over. . . ."

"Yes, sir," Ceepak says. "Couple things."

"What now?"

The chief is downright testy.

"I'd like to search the mother's car."

"What? Why?"

"To see if we can find anything that might indicate that she frequents Cap'n Scrubby's Car Wash."

"What? Now you think *she* hired Squeegee?"

"It's a—"

Before he can say "possibility," the chief is punching numbers on his telephone.

"Goddammit. You should've asked her your goddamn questions while we were down there."

"Didn't think of it until—"

"Hello? This is Chief Cosgrove. I want you to answer a question and I want you to tell me the goddamn truth because we can search your car and you know it!"

Ceepak raises his palm to make a "wait-whoa-slow-down" gesture. The chief does none of the above.

"Where the hell do you get your car washed? Where? Sharky's Suds?"

Ceepak reaches across the desk and pushes down the speaker-phone button so we can listen in.

"They're on the other side of the causeway," Betty says in her smooth, honey-dipped voice. "In that mall with the Home Depot? I usually stop on my way back to the city, before I get on the parkway. I like to be away from the beach and all the sand before I pay to have my car cleaned. So I usually stop at Sharky's."

Ceepak sits down.

"You ever go to Cap'n Scrubby's?" the chief asks.

"No. Like I said . . ."

". . . you like to do it off the island."

"That's right. Why? Is where I wash my car important? Will it help us find Ashley?"

Ceepak shakes his head "no."

"We'll be in touch," the chief says and hangs up.

Ceepak sighs and rubs his eyes.

The chief, in his sleep-deprived, agitated, I-hate-the-FBI state, has blown any element of surprise.

If there was any evidence linking Bell to Cap'n Scrubby, clever Betty probably just flushed it down the toilet. We might need to get a search warrant for her septic tank.

"What the hell makes you think Betty Bell Hart is involved in this thing? Jesus, Ceepak. . . ."

"We need to consider all possibilities in the investigation of suspicious deaths. Especially the less obvious lines of inquiry."

"What? Why?" The chief is none too interested in Advanced Theories of Criminology right now. "Mendez had the goddamn gun. In his car. He had the murder weapon!"

"Correction," Ceepak says. "Officer Kiger *found* the gun in Mendez's trunk."

"Same difference."

No, it's not. Even I know that. The shooter could have planted it there, just like Mendez claimed.

Ceepak doesn't press the issue.

I have a hunch he won't be telling the chief about our bank-to-beach time trials this morning, either. His old Army buddy seems to have a serious case of Mental Overload bordering on Brain Burnout.

The chief slumps down in his big rolling chair.

"So," Ceepak says, "how can you have a file on Squeegee? We don't even know his real name."

The chief cracks a smile, the first I've seen on his face in about forty-eight hours.

"I lied a little," he says.

Oh, boy.

People keep saying the wrong things in front of Ceepak today.

"I stretched the truth." The chief opens the folder. "This is an unsolved case from two years back. We kept it quiet at the time. Didn't want to panic the tourists. Fourth of July weekend. Young girl by the name of Jennifer D'Angelo is lured off the beach and under the boardwalk by a quote skinny homeless man with big, buggy eyes end quote."

"May I see that?"

The chief hands the folder to Ceepak.

"I put two and two together. Sounds like our same guy. Sounds like Squeegee. So I just used it for leverage."

Ceepak is studying the file.

"He raped her," the chief says quietly.

Ceepak nods. I guess he just got to that part.

"Case is still open. Of course, two years ago, we didn't know from Squeegee. The doer didn't leave many clues."

"Except this," Ceepak says, holding up a copy of a crime-scene boot print.

Another Timberland.

"The girl was twelve, almost thirteen," the chief says, standing up and looking out his window.

"Same age as Ashley." Ceepak neatly tucks all the paper back inside the manila folder. He's seen enough. A cold look frosts his face.

The chief's door opens.

"Chief?"

It's Jane Bright.

"What you got?"

"E-Z Pass. It checks out. Her transponder left the city via the tunnel at 10:43 A.M. Friday. She got off at exit 15 of the parkway at 2:12 P.M."

Two and a half hours from the city to the shore? She made pretty good time. Must not be too much traffic that early on a summer Friday. The people playing half-day hooky usually don't hop in their cars until one or two in the afternoon, after, they figure, they've put in enough work so the Friday doesn't have to count as a vacation day.

"What about the ATM?" the chief asks Jane.

She places a sheet of paper on his desk. It's a grainy, black-and-white image of Betty tapping the First Atlantic Bank ATM keypad. She's wearing a dark scarf and sunglasses, but I can tell it's her. So can Ceepak.

"What's the time stamp read?" Ceepak asks.

"7:03 A.M. Saturday."

"Her story holds up," the chief sighs.

"So it seems," Ceepak says.

"Thanks, Jane," the chief says.

"Where do you need me next?"

"Run with the FBI down to this Mussel Beach Motel. The girl who works there. . . ."

"Becca Adkinson," I say.

"Right. She's working with an artist on some sketches. Ramirez. Echaverra. See if you can help her remember stuff."

"Yes, sir." Jane hustles toward the door.

"And Jane? Tell Santucci to swing by Chesterfield's and keep an eye on the lawyer."

"You didn't arrest her?"

"No. The gun was enough to make Mr. Mendez our guest for another night but we've got nothing solid on Ms. Stone."

"Will do."

Jane is gone. The door is once again closed.

"Can I be honest with you, Ceepak?"

Ceepak nods.

"Ms. Stone's probably clean. I was just using her in there to get at Mendez."

"You lied a little more?"

"Yeah."

"What's your theory?"

"Mendez is playing both sides against the middle. He orchestrated the Hart hit, the kidnapping. And he doesn't mind cashing in on Ms. Stone's penny-ante real-estate rip off either. I think that's all she's got the balls to do. Steal a lousy piece of beachfront property when nobody's looking. But Mendez? He sees himself taking Hart's place. Becoming the new-crowned king. . . ."

"But first he had to kill the old king. . . ."

"And steal the princess."

"Yeah."

Ceepak has that look again.

Like he's the judge, jury, and executioner in the matter of the People vs. Squeegee.

"John," the chief says, "you know these guys . . . these pedophiles . . . even when they're caught . . . they don't stop. They just go somewhere new and do the same old stuff. Hurt more kids . . . ruin lives . . . like that Baptist minister who turned up on the base in Germany. . . ."

"Yes, sir."

"Hell, you know this stuff better than anybody."

"Yes, sir."

"So you know what I'm saying, right? What we need to do?"

"Yes, sir."

Somehow, I don't think this fairy tale, this story of kings and princesses, is going to have the usual happy ending.

I don't think everybody involved is going to live happily ever after.

I don't think some of them will be allowed to live at all.

TWENTY-NINE

I thought we'd swing by Cap'n Scrubby's first. Maybe have another chat with Red and draw up a map of The Palace Hotel, get the lay of the land before we launch our reconnaissance mission.

Instead, we drive straight north.

I guess Ceepak doesn't want word getting back to Squeegee that The Man's coming after him.

About the only thing we did back at headquarters before hopping in the car was check the cargo bay of the Ford.

Ceepak wanted to make sure his Sniper Weapon System was locked and loaded, ready to go. He raised the tailgate and used it to hide what he was doing while he twisted all the pieces together, snapped the telescopic sight into place, screwed on the silencer.

We take the back streets. Ceepak wants to avoid the reporters, the vigil crowds outside Playland, the traffic streaming off the island in fear.

It takes about twenty minutes to reach the tip of the island.

We pass the Ship John Lighthouse with its white-red-white striping that makes it look like a stubby candy cane. Ceepak wants the

Explorer on stealth mode. I try to avoid potholes, skirt around gravel patches.

I see the profile of what's left of the old Palace silhouetted on the horizon. As the sun sets, the faded red turrets, all six of them, look like Santa Claus caps on top of sugar-cube towers.

"Coast."

I jam the transmission into neutral, shut down the engine, and drift downhill across the rutted asphalt field that used to be the hotel's parking lot.

"There." Ceepak is pointing.

There's still some remnant of a covered entryway, a crumbling canopy hanging off the second story. If we park under what's left of that, fewer folks upstairs will be able to see us.

Stopping the car takes my whole leg—the power brakes went out when I cut the engine. I practically pull a thigh muscle.

It's about 7:30. The setting sun makes the craggy stucco walls look kind of pinkish, like an Easter egg somebody already tapped and cracked.

I remember years ago when some local ladies in a club, The Very Rich Daughters of the American Revolution or something, formed a Preservation Society to save The Palace, what they called "The Dowager Queen" of seaside hotels. They made the governor declare this dump a Cherished State Landmark, and that means nobody can tear it down without jumping through all sorts of hoops and red tape.

There are hundreds of rooms, but only about a dozen look like they still have windows with any glass. I can see water stains and mold on the peeling wallpaper in the lobby. I suspect anything worth money— all the fixtures and oriental rugs and stained glass and carved furniture—was hauled out years ago.

"Let's take a little walk," Ceepak says and points to a dilapidated dock out back behind the sagging hotel.

We march through the lobby. I can hear water dripping somewhere. Must be why the whole place reeks of mildew.

We reach the doorjambs on the far end of the lobby. No doors. Just some rusty hinges where, I guess, doors used to hang.

We head toward The Palace's private pier.

"You see it?" Ceepak whispers.

Finally I do.

There's a small aluminum fishing boat tied up to an ancient piling. The dock creaks as we walk.

"Watch where you step."

"Right."

This time, I don't think Ceepak's worried about me stepping on evidence. I think there's a good chance one or both of us will step right through this rotting wood. I can see jagged holes where others already have.

We reach the post where the boat is tied up.

Ceepak lies down on his stomach on the deck.

"Danny? Grab my ankles."

"Sure."

I hold his socks, like I'm spotting him for a quick set of upside-down situps.

Ceepak leans down into the bobbing fishing boat. While he's hanging, he unsnaps a pocket, pulls out the Canon Sure Shot, and somehow snaps a digital photograph.

"Danny?"

He reaches back with the camera and I take it, using my knee to hold an ankle and temporarily free up a hand.

Meanwhile, his hand feels around his cargo flaps, snaps open a different pocket, digs inside, and fishes out the tweezers.

He lowers himself farther off the edge. If I let go now, he'll be head-banging the boat bottom and flipping into the drink for a dip.

"Got it!" he says. "Rotating."

I have no idea what "rotating" means until I feel his very strong legs move around inside my grip so he's upside down and backwards and able to do this incredible abdominal crunch thing that brings him up to a sitting position on the dock.

In his tweezers, he's snared another surfer bracelet.

Another breadcrumb.

We move along the back of the hotel, under what must have been the grand verandah back when William Howard Taft was here putting on the feedbag.

We reach the remains of an in-ground pool. The water's all green and slimy and filled with crap. Stinks too, like it's been a bird toilet too long. Poolside, there's nothing but flaky chunks of concrete, bleached dry by the sun that used to shine so bright back here.

It's like that Springsteen song about Atlantic City:

"Everything dies

Baby that's a fact

But maybe everything that dies

Some day comes back."

Then again, maybe not. Springsteen probably never saw The Palace Hotel's scummy pool.

Man—I can't wait until I see what even-more-depressing stuff we find inside. I think knowing Ceepak's sniper rifle is in the cargo bay of our cop car has put me in some kind of glum, gloomy mood.

I'm too young to think about death and dying. But I guess pretty much everybody thinks that way, no matter how old they happen to be.

"Looks like a restaurant," Ceepak says. "Or a nightclub."

We're standing in a big half-circle room surrounded by three tiered terraces for tables. I imagine this was the dance floor.

"Hungry?" Ceepak asks.

"Kind of."

Good. He wants to eat, not dance.

Ceepak pulls two Power Bars out of his left pants leg.

There are a couple of cocktail tables and rusting café chairs. We sit down to our foil-wrapped suppers.

Having skipped both breakfast and lunch, I wolf down half my bar in one bite.

Ceepak laughs.

"Hungry?"

"Starving." When I say it, it sounds more like "snar-vink" because I've crammed so much food in my face.

"You remind me of my little brother," Ceepak says.

My mouth is full of mashed protein powder and nuts, so I just make a "really?" kind of face.

"Yeah. He was always hungry. Ate fast, too. Afraid somebody would steal his supper."

"How old is he?"

"He would have been about your age now. Twenty-three. Twenty-four."

Would have been. Past tense.

Jesus.

More death.

Ceepak puts down his Power Bar and stares out at the ocean framed by tall arched windows behind the dance floor. He balls the wrapper up in his right hand and fidgets with it.

I think the waves are mesmerizing Ceepak, putting him into some kind of trance. I also think he's waiting for the sun to go completely down so he can do what he thinks needs doing under the cover of darkness.

"William Philip Ceepak. Billy."

"That your brother?"

"He killed himself. Put a pistol in his mouth . . ."

"I'm sorry. . . ."

"I was already in the Army, so I guess Billy was about eighteen. High school."

I can tell Ceepak wants to make certain he gets his facts straight, that it's important he remember the details of his brother's death correctly.

"My father is a drunk," Ceepak says matter-of-factly. "I remember how he used to roughhouse with us and all the cousins when we were kids. Down in the basement. You know—after

Christmas, Thanksgiving dinner. Everybody thought he was such a great guy—going downstairs to play with the kids while the rest of the dads stayed upstairs and watched the game and smoked. But the basement? That's where he hid his booze. He swore to Mom he had quit. 'Cross my heart and hope to spit,' he'd say. He'd wink at her and she'd laugh. But while we were downstairs, the kids all wrestling on these old mattresses on the floor, he'd sneak under the staircase to where he hid his stash. Whiskey. Vodka. He had quite a collection going, little airplane bottles tucked behind all the baby-food jars filled with nails and screws.

"I was the only kid old enough to know what he was doing. Sometimes he'd catch my eye while he sucked one of those little bottles dry. 'Don't tell your mother.' He'd wink at me the way he winked at her. 'Promise?' I'd say I promised, because, you know—he was my dad.

"A drunk can be fun. Funny, too. But then, a couple hours later, he usually gets sad and angry and things turn ugly. The wrestling is a little rougher and maybe somebody's head gets banged against the steel pole in the middle of the cellar and there's crying and somebody comes running down to see what all the commotion is about. Maybe your dad roughs up your mom later that same night for embarrassing him in front of all the aunts and uncles, the whole family, and you hear her in their bedroom sobbing and when you run down the hall to help her your father swats you across your face. . . ."

Jesus.

I wonder how long it's been since Ceepak let any of this stuff out.

"Anyhow," he says, giving me, I'm sure, the abridged version of his time spent in Hell, "what does Springsteen say?"

"About him and his dad?"

"Yeah. Lots of songs on that one. Sons and fathers. Same-old same-old, I guess. 'Nothing we can say is gonna change anything now. . . .'"

"So you left?"

"Joined the Army. Went overseas. I wasn't around to protect Billy or Mom any more. I deserted my post. . . ."

"No, you were. . . ."

"I wasn't there. Eventually, Billy got out. Sort of. Started hanging out at the church. This new priest came to town and organized a youth group. And the priest? Oh, he was a swell guy, Danny. Young. Cool. Athletic. He had keys to the church school gym, so Billy and his buddies could play basketball any time they wanted. He took the boys on camping trips. Baseball games. Made them into movie stars. . . ."

"Movie stars?"

"He had them pose naked. Do things to each other. Do things to him. The priest put it all on tape and sold it on the Internet. One of the boys? He told his folks what was going on. That takes guts, you know? To tell your parents what this holy man, this great guy, what he's really up to? The cops bust the priest, there's a trial, and pretty soon everybody in town sees the tapes.

"Billy? He toughed it out for three years. Everybody snickering about what that priest did to him. My father? Oh, he was a real champ. Said Billy got what he deserved. Said God, the almighty Father on high, God himself was punishing Billy for trying to run away from his *real* father."

Ceepak tightens his grip on the Power Bar foil in his fist.

"My father? He's not a real father, Danny. A real father does everything he can to protect his children. He doesn't terrorize his family because he's thirsty for a drink. A real father risks his life to make the world safer for his sons. My father? He called Billy sissy boy. Porno queen. It's like he put the bullets in the gun and all Billy had to do was squeeze the damn trigger."

Jesus.

I think Ceepak just told me why he has to kill Squeegee tonight.

I don't know what to say.

So I keep quiet and let him look at the ocean.

The sun is gone. The stars are starting to come out. The waves keep rolling up on the beach.

Finally, I feel I should say something.

"So, where's your dad now?"

Ceepak looks at me.

"Don't know, Danny. We sort of lost track of each other."

"Yeah. Sure. And your mom?"

"She's safe."

He bites into his Power Bar.

That's all I'm going to get tonight, probably more than anybody has heard in years. Maybe even more than he told the chief, back when they were hunting down that chaplain in Germany. I see now, of course, why Ceepak was so motivated on that particular military mission.

"Well," Ceepak says, standing up, dusting the crumbs off his lap. "Guess we've wasted enough time. . . ."

"Yeah."

"Let's start working the hallways. See if—"

We hear a dog bark.

Then this woman's voice.

"Oh, fuck!" she shouts.

In the shadows I see a figure with frizzy hair. It's so dark, I can't see much of her, except her feet. She uses brown paper sacks for socks.

She also has a mangy German shepherd on a leash made out of twine.

The dog barks again.

"I know, Henry. It's the motherfucking fuzz!"

THIRTY

"**M**a'am?"

For an old lady, she's fast.

She and the dog run out a door and up what I guess is a hall.

Right now, they have the advantage. They've been here before; we haven't. We're first-time guests and they appear to be long-term residents. So they know where the hell they're running. We don't.

"Danny?"

"Right behind you, boss."

We both pull out our flashlights and tear up the tiered terraces to the exit she used.

On the other side of the door, I bang into this rickety old grocery cart loaded down with trash bags, nickel-deposit bottles, an old moving pad, books, and an eyeless stuffed panda bear with dirt on its nose.

We hear the dog barking somewhere up the corridor.

"Leave it, Henry! Leave the fucking rat alone!"

Now that she mentions it, I can hear the scratchy-toed devils scurrying around inside what's left of the plaster walls.

"Put him down!"

Wonderful. Henry's a "ratter." But his assorted barks and snarls act like a homing beacon, helping us figure out which way they're running.

Ceepak leads us up a long, dark corridor lined with rooms. Like most hotel hallways, there are no windows. That means there's also no light. No moonlight, no nothing. Our tiny flashlights shoot jittery spotlights across the walls as we run. I half expect a rat in a top hat to jump out and tap-dance like that frog on the WB.

The carpet squishes under our feet as we run. Guess the roof leaks. Or the toilets.

After about fifty yards, we come to a landing where the grand staircase swoops up from the lobby. Tall casement windows in the stairwell let in just enough light for us to see a few shadows and dim outlines.

I smell gasoline.

So does Ceepak. He goes to the staircase. Most of the planks have been ripped out and all that's left are the stringers on the sides and the support joists in between. Guess the floorboards, the treads, were mahogany or oak or something worth stealing.

"C-4," Ceepak says, looking at what appears to be a brick wrapped in black plastic and duct-taped to a crossbeam. His finger traces the red and white and green wires snaking from the plastic explosive up and down the steps to, I guess, more wads of C-4. There's a gas can sitting in the windowsill.

"Arson?" I say.

"Looks like."

"Why? There's not much left to burn."

"More like a demolition."

The dog barks.

"Come on," Ceepak says.

There's another bark. And another. A whole series.

"Henry? Shush!"

Now Henry tosses in a couple of howls, like he's singing opera. All the noise comes from below.

"Come on! Down the steps!"

We head down the grand staircase, stepping on the crossbeams and stringers because, like I said, there aren't any actual stairs any more. Once again, I have a really good chance of slipping through a gaping hole and landing on my butt.

We make it to the second floor and hear a long, slow dog yawn.

Downstairs.

I grab hold of the banister and try not to look down where the floorboards used to be. It's like running down a steep railroad track, stepping only on the ties. The boards bang my arches and sting like hell. Before this is over, I know I'm going to make some bone doctor a very rich man.

"Henry? Come on! Henry!"

Now she sounds like she's right below us.

"Henry?"

Sounds like he isn't cooperating.

We reach the lobby. She's tugging on that twine leash, but Henry is lying like a lump in the middle of the floor, all flopped out, breathing hard.

"You need a nap? Now?"

"Ma'am?" Ceepak moves toward what I'm guessing is a crazy homeless person. His hand never goes anywhere near his gun. "Ma'am?"

"Shhhh! Henry's napping. Can the noise, would ya?"

"Yes, ma'am."

"Jesus," she huffs. "Some people. Yak, yak, yak. Ma'am, ma'am, ma'am."

In the lobby, I get a better look at our quarry. She's tiny. Not even five feet tall. She has on Converse basketball shoes with the canvas toes ripped out and, like I saw earlier, brown paper bags for socks. She's wearing about three different skirts, plaid and denim, with a petticoat underneath. There's a tie-dyed shirt up top over what I figure, from all the bumps circling her like spare tires, is a goose-down vest. Her silver hair is wiry and dirty and wild and curls around her head like a worn-out scrubbing pad.

"You're not going to shoot me, are you, fuzz?"

"No, ma'am."

"Good."

"Is that your dog?"

"No. That's Henry."

"Yes, ma'am. That's a pretty shirt," Ceepak says. It's tie-dyed all kinds of colors—just like the one Ashley said Squeegee was wearing when he shot her father.

"My boyfriend loaned it to me. I was cold."

"Does your boyfriend have a name?" he asks. He's made the tie-dye connection, too.

"Jerry. His name is Jerry."

Ceepak nods, the way you nod when you're visiting the mental ward and a patient tells you the ashtrays have been saying mean things about them lately.

"Jerry Garcia?" Ceepak says, playing along.

"From the Grateful Dead?" the bag lady says.

"That's right. He wears a lot of tie-dye shirts."

"Jerry Garcia?" she says again.

"That's right. Did Jerry Garcia loan you his T-shirt?"

The bag lady stares at Ceepak like he's an idiot.

"Jesus. Jerry Garcia died like, what? Ten years ago. Don't you read the papers? Watch TV?"

"I thought, perhaps. . . ."

"You need to stay better informed. Especially in your line of work. . . ."

"Yes, ma'am."

"Jesus. My friend's name is Jerry Shapiro. You know. . . ."

She reaches into what I can only imagine is a dirty brassiere rigged up under that T-shirt and down vest and who knows what else she has piled on top of her sagging cleavage.

"Jerry Shapiro!" She pulls out a folded piece of newspaper. "He's famous."

She unfolds the newspaper and of course it's the sketch of Squeegee.

"You know Squeegee?" I blurt out.

Now it's my time to get the look.

"Squeegee? How fucking insulting. Jerry is a man, not a tool one uses for washing windows. What do they teach you kids in school? To demean those who labor with their hands? Nobody calls him Squeegee except the fuzz and the goons and bulls who run the capitalist car wash."

"Red calls him Squeegee," Ceepak says.

"Red Davidson?"

"I never actually caught his last name."

"Red hair? Like Bozo the clown?"

"Yes, ma'am."

"Figures. Red is an a-hole. He's pissed because I won't hop in the sack with him any more. That's over, you know? Red and me? That's history."

I'm getting a little queasy imagining this lady hopping in the sack with anybody.

"He kicked Henry," she says.

"Your dog?"

"Red kicked Henry in the butt because we had this mattress upstairs last winter and Henry wanted to sleep with us because the floor was cold. Henry? He has a gas problem. He's old, he's earned it. Henry farts and Red kicks him. Kicks him 'til he yelps, I kid you not. He yelps. Jerry?" She waggles the newspaper clipping to remind us Jerry is Squeegee. "He and I aren't even dating or messing around back then, but the next day, when we're all, you know, hanging out, doing our thing, Jerry tells Red to cut that dog-kicking shit out. Says dogs are not pets, they're our spiritual companions in this earthly realm. Who made man king of the jungle, anyhow? Tarzan? Reagan?"

She tugs at the tie-dye shirt.

"Jerry lent me his T-shirt because I was cold. You got any food?"

Ceepak pulls one more Power Bar out of his pants.

Henry hears the wrapper crinkle and lifts his head. He's interested.

Ceepak pulls a Pupperoni jerky strip out of another pocket. The guy lives the Boy Scouts motto. He is always prepared!

"Can your dog have a treat?"

"Is it all-natural?"

"I'm not certain. It's what they call a Pupperoni."

Henry is licking his chops.

"Pupperoni?"

"Yes, ma'am."

"Fine. But if he farts? It's your fucking fault."

Ceepak bends down and lets Henry eat out of his palm.

"Here you go . . . good boy. . . ."

The bag lady is staring at the Power Bar.

"Jesus. You got like a veggie sandwich or something? Maybe tomato-mozzarella on a baguette with some pesto or something?"

"I could check another pocket." Ceepak is trying to make a little joke.

The lady does not know this. She waits.

So he checks another pocket.

"Sorry."

"Jesus." She settles for the Power Bar. "What the hell is in this thing? Chemicals and chalk?"

"Yes, ma'am. I believe so."

"Fucking yuppie food. Next time, bring me that sandwich."

"Roger that."

"And grab some chips. Taro chips. Snapple, too. But none of that NutraSweet shit. That's a plot. A conspiracy. All about mind control. The fucking Republicans. . . ."

"Will do."

"You're a cop, right?"

"Yes, ma'am. I work with the Sea Haven Police."

"No shit, Sherlock. How's Scooter Boy?"

"You know Officer Kiger?"

"Don't get me started. That kid Kiger wakes us up all the time. Comes along on that goddamn scooter. 'Wake up, wake up, you sleepyheads. Get up, get up, get out of bed.' Kicks us off the beach before the rich people show up. Fascist fuzz. . . ." She stops to fan the air in front of her face. "Whoo! Thank you Mr. Pupperoni."

"Ma'am—do you know where Jerry is now?"

"Why do you keep calling me 'ma'am' like that?"

"Just trying to be courteous. . . ."

"Well, knock it off. Jesus. You sound so fucking subservient. Why? No bourgeois man or woman is your better. All power rests with the people!"

She raises her fist in some kind of salute. I think she might be an intellectual when she's not stoned. Or a socialist. One of those.

"So, just so we're all clear here," she says, "Jerry didn't do it."

"Didn't do what?"

"What the papers say he did." She waves the newspaper in Ceepak's face. "Murder? Kidnapping? Lies and bullshit. Just because it's in the paper doesn't make it true. It's just propaganda—paper and ink and lies and bullshit. Republican bullshit."

"If that's the case, Mr. Shapiro has nothing to fear from me."

"Bullshit. You're the fucking fuzz. Can't trust the fuzz."

"You can trust me," he tells her.

"Really? How come? What makes you so super-special?"

"I give you my word."

"Your word? Like your solemn vow?"

"Yes, ma'am."

"Wow. That's some heavy, serious shit. You give me your word? Wow. Just like Nixon? He gave us his word. 'I am not a crook.' So did Clinton. 'I didn't have sex with that woman.' Bush. 'Saddam has nukes.' Fucking Republicans."

She's staring at Ceepak, trying to figure out who he might really be.

"You can trust him," I say.

"What?"

"He cannot tell a lie."

She stares some more at him.

"Really? Who is he? George Fucking Washington?"

"Officer Ceepak doesn't know how to be dishonest," I say.

Now she's studying his eyes.

"What's the matter? Your parents never taught you how?"

"They tried," he says. "However, they failed."

"Is that so?"

"Yes, ma'am."

"Uh-uh-uh. You did that damn ma'am thing again."

"Sorry. Do you know where Jerry is?"

"Maybe."

"I'd like to talk to him."

"You won't hurt him?"

"I give you my word."

"When I was cold? He gave me his shirt. His favorite fucking shirt."

"I will not hurt him."

The bag lady bends down to rub the dog's head.

"Upstairs," she says. "Room 215."

"Thank you. Danny?"

"Yes, sir?"

"Stay here with. . . ."

"Gladys," she says.

"Yes, sir."

Ceepak holds out his hand to me.

"I need the keys to the car."

THIRTY-ONE

Gladys is sitting on the floor in front of me, petting her dog. Her legs are splayed out and Henry is nuzzling against her knee.

"He likes it when you scratch under his ears."

"Unh-hunh."

Behind her, I see Ceepak out front where we parked the Ford. He's unlocking the hatchback. Opening it. Pulling out his rifle.

"Ah, Jesus. I think he has a tick."

I glance down to see Gladys pinching something buried in Henry's fur.

"Got it."

Whatever she got, she flings across the dark lobby like I might flick a wad of earwax when no one's watching.

I look out front again and see Ceepak toting his sniper weapon system around the side of the car and heading to what I can only guess is some kind of alternate entrance. Maybe where the fire steps exit into the parking lot.

He probably doesn't want to deal with climbing up the same staircase we recently scrambled down.

He probably doesn't want Gladys to see him going upstairs with a sniper rifle.

"You have a dog, kid?"

"No, ma'am."

"Jesus. What's with you fucking fuzz? Ma'am, ma'am, ma'am."

"Sorry."

"Your partner? Slezak?"

"Ceepak."

"Yeah. Ceepak. He seems like a good man. Decent."

"Yes. He does."

He sure seems that way.

You ever talk to a bag lady for fifteen minutes? It's totally random. A barrel of laughs.

Gladys tells me all about Karl Marx and the redistribution of wealth and how Henry will always have the Milkbones he needs provided he contributes to society to the best of his ability.

Then she gets into some guy named Friedrich Nietzsche and says his tendency to seek explanations for commonly accepted values in the less-elevated realms of animal instinct was crucial to Sigmund Freud's development of psychoanalysis.

I nod and say "Is that so?" a lot.

All the time, I keep waiting to hear the rifle shot, the snap-pop report, but I guess I won't because Ceepak screwed on that silencer.

He's been up in Room 215 a long time.

I'm sure he's interrogating Squeegee, pumping him for information about Ashley. If he gets what he needs, will he still pump a bullet into the guy? I hope not. But I keep thinking about a certain pedophile chaplain in Germany who, as far as I know, nobody ever heard from again.

And why does Ceepak need a sniper rifle?

If his animal instinct is telling him Jerry Shapiro, a.k.a. Squeegee, needs to die, why doesn't he just use his pistol? The rifle with the sniper scope seems kind of dramatic. Seems like overkill. But maybe he forgot to pack a silencer for the pistol. Maybe a pistol silencer is the one thing he doesn't have in his cargo-pants pockets.

"Danny?"

Ceepak is on the staircase behind me. He's holding the rifle at his side.

I sniff the air, searching for "transient evidence," just like he taught me to. The air reeks of gunpowder.

"Jesus!"

Gladys sees the rifle.

"What did you fucking do?'

"Ma'am, you need to leave here. Now."

"What did you fucking do, you fucking liar?"

"You need to take your dog, find any of your friends who may be habitating here with you in the hotel, you need to find them and tell them all to leave. You have ten minutes."

"Where's Jerry?" She lurches toward the staircase. Ceepak holds up his hand and stops her.

"Ma'am, you do not want to go upstairs. You want to vacate these premises."

"You motherfucking . . ."

"Ma'am, like I said—you need to take your dog, find your friends, and evacuate this location. You need to do so immediately."

Ceepak checks his watch.

"You now have nine minutes and thirty seconds."

Gladys is crying. I can see the tears clearing a white path down her dirty cheeks.

"You lied to me . . . gave me your fucking word. . . ."

Ceepak doesn't say anything.

"You goddamn motherfucking son-of-a-bitch liar!"

Gladys tugs her twine leash and Henry stands up.

Her shoulders are shaking as she drags Henry toward the front. When she steps outside, she hesitates, thinks about coming back in to drag her friend's dead body out of the room upstairs.

"You have nine minutes," Ceepak shouts.

"Motherfucking fuzz!"

Henry snarls.

The two of them run and disappear into the darkness.

I turn to Ceepak.

"Did you?"

"Danny? Don't make me say things I'd rather not say."

I've never seen Ceepak look so intense. Veins pop out of his arms. His eyes dilate. It's as if he's possessed of some unnatural energy.

Guess killing a man gives a guy a rush.

"Don't force me to tell you a lie," he says.

"You mean another one?"

Ceepak just lets it hang there.

He steps off the staircase and leans the rifle against the railing and pulls out his pistol. He checks the clip, slides off the safety.

He points it to the floor and fires.

The explosion rings in my ears.

"Listen up!" Ceepak shouts. "If you can hear me, you need to leave here immediately. It is not safe for you to remain in this location. Repeat—it is not safe to remain here! You have eight minutes!"

He puts his gun back in his holster.

"We need to leave."

"Yes, sir."

I am so quitting this job.

It sucks.

Ceepak sucks.

"Danny?"

"What?"

Now there's some kind of sadness in his eyes. Like he wants to explain something but he can't.

"Do you know where the old train depot is?"

"Yeah."

"We need to go there. Immediately. To release Ashley."

"He confessed?"

"He told me where we could find Ashley."

Ceepak stalks across the lobby. I follow him because, at the moment, I don't know what else to do.

We negotiate our way across the crumbling parking lot and climb into the Ford. I feel like creamed shit on toast. My muscles ache, my joints creak, I feel like I'm somebody's grandmother with arthritis. I need a beer.

Ceepak takes the walkie-talkie off his belt and motions for me to drive away from the hotel.

"We need to relocate to a more secure position or we run the risk of becoming collateral damage," he says. He's in that cold, military-speak mode. Sort of numbs you to the horror of what you're actually doing if you use big words to describe it.

Ceepak radios headquarters.

"This is Ceepak for Cosgrove."

I start up the engine. Ceepak points to the abandoned Ship John lighthouse, like I should drive over there. I'm on autopilot, so I head in that direction.

"Ceepak for Cosgrove. Ceepak for Cosgrove."

"This is Cosgrove, go."

"Implement the mobilization plan."

"You found her?"

"We have high-probability intelligence on her location."

"Where? Where did the bastard stash her?"

"The old Pennsylvania Depot up here at the north end. She is detained in the baggage room. Request an ambulance and all available backup."

"Do you have the perp in custody?"

The Ford rocks. I hear something bang the rear window like a sonic boom from a low-flying 747. I check my mirror.

The Palace Hotel has just exploded.

"Repeat—did you apprehend the perpetrator?"

"Negative. We encountered an unanticipated snag."

A snag?

"It seems the hotel was wired to blow."

"What?"

"Implosion. I suspect Mendez. Demolition and arson are his areas of expertise. I sense he went overboard. C-4 plastic explosives coupled with strategically placed petrol canisters. Like dropping a stick of dynamite down a gas pump. The hotel has collapsed and is on fire. Request immediate fire department support."

"Are you guys okay? You and Boyle?"

"Affirmative. We were able to vacate the building two steps ahead of the fire."

"So Squeegee is dead?"

Ceepak waits a second before he responds.

"I did not see him exit the building. Copy?"

"Roger. Copy."

I figure he's got a plan. This is how you hide the bullet when you gun down your suspect instead of arresting him. You set off the C-4 and gasoline you were lucky to find all wired and ready to blow. You burn down the whole building so everything melts. You cremate the body in a towering inferno, which then turns into a pile of rubble. It's messy, but it works.

"Grab the girl!" the chief growls. "We'll meet you up at the depot!"

"Roger that. And chief?"

"Yeah?"

"Alert Ashley's mother to our situation. Be best if you did so immediately. Her daughter is safe. It's all good."

"Will do. I'll tell her you kept your word!"

There are some more explosions behind us. The fire must've found extra gas cans.

"Request second alarm on fire department response. . . ."

"Will do. Ceepak?"

"Yes sir?"

"Good job."

"10-4."

Ceepak snaps off his radio.

"Let's go get Ashley."

We're the first unit on the scene, of course.

The old train depot is really more like a covered platform with a small hut attached. On one side of the hut is the arched window where they used to sell tickets. On the other is the baggage room where they stored suitcases and packages.

It's not so dark any more. The fire from the hotel, about a half-mile farther north, is lighting up the sky pretty good.

"Careful," Ceepak says as we walk across the weedy railroad bed. There's no rails, just the rotting, tarry ties and some compacted gravel.

As pissed-off as I am, I realize he's right. We need to be careful. There might be armed guards keeping watch over Ashley. Mendez's men could be inside with their own sniper weapon systems or shotguns or whatever you use to guard a kidnapped kid.

"Should we wait for backup?" I ask.

"I don't anticipate that will be necessary. But try to remain quiet."

Ceepak tiptoes ahead and climbs up on an old rusty barrel so he can peek in a window to the baggage room. He sees something because he holds up his hand to tell me to stay still, not make a sound. He watches for a second, then slowly slips down and motions for me to follow.

We move around to the back of the depot. I see the door to the baggage room. There's a locker-room-size padlock through a hasp on the door.

"Ashley?" Ceepak calls out.

"Yes?" It's her voice. It's weak and trembling, but I recognize it.

"This is Officer John Ceepak. I am here with my partner Danny Boyle. The two of us are coming in, okay?"

"Okay."

"We may have to kick down the door."

"Hurry! Please! Before he comes back! Hurry!"

Ceepak walks to the door.

But he isn't hurrying.

THIRTY-TWO

I think every vehicle in the county with any kind of flashing light bar on its roof is parked in a circle around the train depot.

Ashley is covered with a thick wool blanket and sitting in the back of an open ambulance while a doctor and nurse check her out. Her mom is with her on the little bed, hugging her. The kid was in pretty good shape when we kicked down the door and rescued her: She was sitting on an old steamer trunk with her hands tied behind her back and her ankles handcuffed together so she couldn't run. Fortunately, Squeegee didn't tie the knots too tight, so Ashley didn't have rope burn on her wrists. The handcuffs securing her legs were pretty loose, too. They didn't pinch into her ankles at all.

Ashley was, however, still wearing the skimpy outfit she'd been forced to put on for the Polaroid. It's why she's wrapped up in the blanket now.

The chief had some of the guys set up a perimeter so the reporters who raced up here behind all the police cars and fire trucks could be held at bay. The TV klieg lights are making it feel like high noon, even though it's closer to midnight.

I see Ceepak over near a black sedan, talking to Morgan. They're

CHRIS GRABENSTEIN

nodding at each other. I guess the FBI agent understands—sometimes you have to shoot a guy in order to stop him from molesting more kids.

The chief looks happier than I've ever seen him. Completely free of acid indigestion. He's bouncing around, shaking hands with everybody he bumps into. He struts over to the reporters and TV cameras to make a statement, looking like the football coach who just won the big game. Mayor Sinclair is beside him.

"Ladies and gentlemen," the chief says, "I am pleased to report that, thanks to the diligent efforts of some very brave Sea Haven police officers and the FBI's Critical Incident Response Group, Ashley Hart is going home. She's safe. Unharmed. She's doing great."

"Do you have the kidnapper?"

"Did he shoot Ashley's father?"

"Did he confess? To the murder of Reginald Hart?"

The chief holds up his beefy right paw to calm the crowd.

"We do not have all the answers. Unfortunately, the kidnapper died in tonight's fire and explosion at the old Palace Hotel. . . ."

"How'd the fire start?"

"We're not certain, but we suspect arson," the chief says.

"Are the crimes related? The arson, the kidnapping, the murder?"

"I really can't speculate about that at this time. . . ."

"Was it just a coincidence? That the kidnapper happened to be in the hotel when an arsonist burned it down?"

"As I said, I am not in a position to speculate on those matters at this time. An investigation is ongoing. The fire department is on the scene, working the hotel. State arson investigators are on their way as well. We hope to have more answers for you folks ASAP. But right now—well, I'm just damn glad we got Ashley! She's safe, folks! She's going home!"

"And," the mayor steps up to the microphones, "tomorrow is Monday! A sunderful new week begins here in Sea Haven. We're thinking of throwing a big beach party to celebrate Ashley's homecoming! Free refreshments. . . ."

The reporters ignore him.

"Chief? When can we see Ashley? Can we talk to her? How's her mother holding up?"

"Guys? Come on. Give the kid a break. . . ."

"There she goes!"

One reporter points and all the cameras swing to see what he's pointing at.

Ashley, covered in the blanket, walks with her mother to their Mercedes sedan, surrounded by a crowd of state and local police. Looks like they'll be traveling home in their very own motorcade.

Ashley's in such good shape, I guess she doesn't need to go to the hospital.

She just needs to go home.

I walk over to where somebody has set up a folding table with food and drinks.

Hey, what's a successful end to a manhunt without a few snacks and cold beverages?

Unfortunately, there's no beer in the Igloo cooler, just Pepsi. I looked.

"Boyle?"

It's the chief.

"Yes, sir?"

"Good work."

"Thanks."

"What's wrong, son?"

"Nothing."

"Bullshit. You look like somebody just shot your dog."

Nope. No dogs were harmed in this evening's activities. Just this one homeless guy. Jerry, a.k.a. Squeegee. A guy who gave his girlfriend his favorite shirt because she was cold.

"Listen, son—Ceepak did what he had to do. He did what needed to be done."

"Do you know what he did, sir?"

"No. And I don't need to know any details. The end justifies whatever means he deemed necessary, understand?"

No. Not really.

"Yes, sir. Of course."

"You want to be a cop, you have to come to peace with this sort of thing. The greater good, Boyle. The greater good." He's actually wagging his finger at me. "The Greater Good."

"Yes, sir."

"How's Ceepak holding up?"

"Okay, I guess. Considering."

"Yeah," the chief sucks in a chestful of night air. "Rough duty whenever you bring a man down. There will be an investigation. They'll want to ask *you* a bunch of questions. How did the fire get started? What happened to your suspect? Why didn't you apprehend him prior to the conflagration? That sort of thing. They might even recover the bullet . . . provided they find the body."

"Yes, sir."

"You think you can handle it, son?"

"I hope so."

"You just need to give the right answers. It's actually pretty easy to do. Tell you what, when you're ready to go over your story, work up the details of what you remember, come see me, okay?"

"Thank you, sir."

Great. I never had a Code or anything but, on the other hand, I've never intentionally lied about something this big before, either.

Now, it seems like lying is going to become part of my job.

I go looking for Ceepak.

Hey, I'm still on the company dime and it's my job to drive the guy home.

Tomorrow?

I'll probably start the sunny, funderful new week by quitting. Or at least asking for a new assignment. I've decided I don't want to be the hitman's chauffeur any longer. And I hope the department can whitewash their internal investigation without me, because if they ask me any questions, I will tell them no lies.

"You seen Ceepak?" I ask this state cop standing guard outside the baggage hut.

"Inside."

I walk in and find him on his hands and knees studying the floor-boards.

"You ready to head home?"

"In a second."

"Still looking for evidence?"

"Roger that."

"I thought the case was closed."

Ceepak doesn't respond.

"Was he wearing boots?"

"Excuse me?"

"Squeegee. Was he wearing boots?"

"Of course. Timberlands."

"Unh-hunh. Find anything interesting in here?"

Ceepak stands up and walks to a dark corner.

"Ice chest."

He squeaks off the styrofoam lid.

"Filled with Milky Ways, water bottles, a turkey-and-brie sand-wich. . . ."

"Squeegee treated her pretty good."

"Danny, your friend Joey T.? The guy who sweeps the beach. Do you know where we might find him?"

"Tonight?"

"Is that doable?"

"He's probably sleeping. His shift starts at like five or six in the morning."

"I see. Did he work today?"

"No. They usually get Sundays off."

"Come again?"

"They usually get Sundays off."

"They don't rake the sand on Sundays?"

How many times are we both going to say the same damn thing?

"They used to. Then there were these budget cuts. Joey does a major sweep on Saturday, gets Sundays off, hits the beach again first thing Monday morning. . . ."

"Awesome! Do you know when he empties the hopper?"

"The what?"

"The bin where the surf-rake stows its trash. When does he typically empty it? Pre-sweep or post-shift?"

"How the hell would I know that?"

"Right. I just thought. . . ."

"Do you want to go wake up Joey T.? Ask him when he dumps his load?"

"No. I'll catch him at 0500. Does he park his gear at the municipal garage?"

"Yeah."

"Terrific. You up for some O.T., Danny? I'd like to check in with your friend before first light . . . before he sweeps the beach again."

"I'm feeling kind of bummed, you know what I mean?"

"Sure."

"I've never actually been that close to an actual execution. Never been in the building when a man was gunned down by the firing squad. So tonight? I think I need to get shit-faced. I think I need to stay up drinking 'til three or four in the morning and get drunker than I've ever been before. Who knows? Maybe I'll even go home and slap some snot-nosed brats around in the basement or something."

I hope it sounds as nasty as I mean it to.

Ceepak's eyes show that hurt again.

Good.

"We'll touch base tomorrow," he says.

"Whatever. You want me to drop you at the house?"

"That'd be great. Thanks, Danny."

We leave the baggage room, walk back across the ancient railbed, and climb into the Explorer.

"Seat belts," Ceepak says.

I refuse to put mine on. I just start up the car.

"Chief talk to you yet?" Ceepak asks.

"He sure as shit did."

"Good. You tell him what happened?"

"I confirmed what he already knew. How the ends justify the means. The greater good. That kind of shit. . . ."

"Good."

Ceepak keeps nodding, like everything is hunky-dory and peachy-keen.

If he says "It's all good," like he says about five hundred times every day, I might have to shoot him—even if I don't have a gun. I'll borrow one of his.

"We'll regroup tomorrow. 0730? Pancake Palace?"

"Yeah. Sure. Whatever."

He turns to look at me but I won't look at him.

"It's going to be okay, Danny," Ceepak whispers.

"What?"

"I give you my word."

THIRTY-THREE

You ever polish off a six-pack in under an hour? Me neither. Until last night.

This morning, I'm still wearing the same clothes I had on when I fell asleep in my lumpy TV chair.

Must be why no one wants to sit near me at The Pancake Palace.

The waitress brings me a mug of coffee and a plastic carafe so I can continue to pour my own and self-medicate. I rip open a little plastic packet of Tylenol I picked up at the 7-Eleven. It's my second pack of the morning and I chew the tablets like they're Flintstones vitamins. Sure the stuff is bitter, but hell—so am I.

It's 7:40. My partner's late. Highly un-Ceepakesque behavior. There are no syrup-stained rugrats stealing tips this morning. In fact, The Palace is even emptier than it was on Saturday. I guess things will pick up tomorrow—when the world celebrates the safe return of Ashley Hart with a mad dash back to the beach. I'll bet you the Tilt-A-Whirl, the train depot, the burnt-down hotel—they'll all become brand-new tourist traps. "This is where they shot him! This is where they found her!"

I'm thinking I could come up with a catchy, kidnap-themed T-shirt

or sell "write-your-own-ransom-note" refrigerator magnets, make a
million bucks and retire.

I need more coffee.

I pour another cup and try to read the newspaper. The headlines are
all kind of blurry, but I think it's my eyes that are fuzzy, not the ink.
Pictures of Ashley and her mother cover the front page. The chief, too.
Everybody looks all huggy and happy. I find my name buried in the
continuation of the front-page story on the sixth page.

> Officer John Ceepak and his partner Daniel Boyle were the
> first to find the kidnapped little girl inside the abandoned rail-
> road terminus.

What's a terminus? Sounds like the train had a bad disease.

Anyhow, I'm an official hero. The newspaper has declared it so.

Here comes Ceepak.

He takes off his cap and smiles at the ancient cashier who's smiling
at him, her hero. His eyes sweep the restaurant to make sure I'm in
the window seat where we always sit. He smiles again when he sees
I'm where I'm supposed to be.

"Morning, Danny."

I grunt.

"You hungry?"

"Not really."

"I'm famished." He waves to the waitress.

"Good morning," she says, probably hoping for another huge tip
like the one he came back to give her on Saturday. "Hey—congratu-
lations. Thanks for finding the little girl!"

"Just doing our job."

"All set?"

"Yes, ma'am."

"Fruit and cereal?"

"No. This morning I'd like to try your Lumberjack Special."

"Really?"

"Yes, ma'am. I figure it's time I ventured over to the second page of your marvelous menu."

Damn, he's chipper.

"All righty. How would you like those eggs?"

"Sunnyside up, of course." Ceepak winks at her.

The waitress writes up the order and walks away with a cute little bounce in her step. Damn. Everybody's got their sunny side up this morning. Everybody except me.

"Your buddy Joey T. is quite disciplined," Ceepak says while he mindlessly shuffles the sugar and Sweet 'n' Low and Equal packages into orderly, color-coded stacks in the table tray.

"Really?"

"It's not every young man who's willing to start work at five in the morning."

I slurp my coffee to let him know he's absolutely right on that one.

"I believe Mr. Thalken is a Virgo. He possesses tremendous organizational skills and, as I said, self-discipline."

"Right."

"Seems he cleans out the hopper each morning prior to sweeping the beach. He says he is better able to concentrate on the task at hand if he's not pre-occupied with racing back to the municipal yard to unload at the end of his shift."

"I see. So?"

"Saturday's sweep? The debris was still in the hopper. You see, to achieve a well-manicured beach, the Surf Rake's moldboard levels uneven areas while stainless steel tines on a moving conveyor belt rake debris toward an adjustable deflector plate. . . ."

Jesus.

Sounds like Joey T. and Ceepak really hit it off. They discussed this crap before the sun was even up.

Ceepak keeps going.

"The non-sand objects are then transported to a hopper which can be hydraulically dumped."

"Wow. Great. What'd you do? Climb in and go on a treasure hunt?"

"In fact, that is correct."

"Find anything interesting?"

The waitress brings a platter loaded down with eggs, pancakes, sausage, bacon, and butter tubs.

"This'll work," Ceepak says. He rubs his knife against his fork tines and looks over to me. "You sure you're not hungry?"

"No, thanks."

In fact, the smell is causing the remains of the six beers in my belly to slide down to my intestines where they can make loud, rumbling noises.

Ceepak checks his watch.

We must be on a schedule, even though I figure our big case closed around midnight last night.

He digs in, letting the egg yolk ooze across the pancakes with the melting butter and warm syrup.

I think he's purposely trying to make me hurl.

And he never says whether he found anything—because it's not polite to talk with a mouth full of eggs.

Ceepak devours his Lumberjack Special and downs several quick cups of coffee. He hasn't actually been to bed since I dropped him off at the police station last night.

He says he was "working on a few things" while I was home drinking and passing out. Now he's raring to go.

We walk to the car.

"Standard patrol, sir?"

"No, Danny. Let's swing down to Beach Crest Heights. I'd like to talk to Betty Bell."

"Why? The case is closed."

"Loose ends." Ceepak says. Then he starts humming because, of course, Springsteen has this whole song called "Loose Ends" and Ceepak can't resist.

"They have returned to the city," the butler says.

"Do you work for Miss Bell?" Ceepak asks.

"I am attached to the house in a management capacity."

I think that means he's like a live-in maid with attitude.

"I see," Ceepak says. "So you also worked for Mr. Hart? Whenever he came out here?"

"Certainly. However, he was rarely in residence."

"Mind if we come in?"

The butler does a sniff that lets us know he does mind but he steps to the side and gestures for us to come in if we must.

I have no idea what the hell we're doing here, but we walk into the sunroom.

"I need to ask you a few questions."

"Me?" The butler does a good shocked. He even flutters his hand near his heart like he might faint. "I thought the unfortunate situation had been resolved."

"Indeed. The kidnapping? That's done. When did Ashley and her mother head back to the city?"

"Before dawn."

"Well, we're just tying up some loose ends. Investigating the arson up at The Palace Hotel."

We are? Why?

The butler scrunches his face. "Nasty business, that. I understand the kidnapper, this Squeegee fellow, I understand he perished in the blaze?"

"So it seems," Ceepak says. "Did you know that Mr. Hart owned that hotel?"

"No. I am not often privy to the details of Mr. Hart's real-estate holdings."

"Of course not. Ms. Stone, however, was?"

"I wouldn't know."

"When she stayed here with him, was it all business?"

"How do you mean?"

"Was there anything romantic? Between Ms. Stone and Mr. Hart?"

"However would I know? I was not their confidante."

"They didn't sleep together?" Ceepak presses him.

"Of course not. Ms. Stone stayed in the guest cottage. Out beyond the pool."

"Is that where she spent Thursday and Friday night?"

"Yes."

"Are you certain?"

"It's where all her things were. When Ms. Bell told me to remove Ms. Stone's luggage, I went into the cottage to retrieve it. I had to pick up a few loose articles of clothing off the floor. I suppose Ms. Stone assumed she would be returning here on Saturday."

"Was there a great deal of lingerie?"

"No. None. I believe she slept in very long T-shirts."

"Really?"

The butler blushes, realizing that maybe he knows a little too much about Ms. Stone's sleeping attire.

"I found one such nightshirt hanging on a hook in the bathroom. It featured a large canary on the front."

"Tweety?" I say.

"Perhaps." The butler doesn't know from Tweety Bird.

"Tell me," Ceepak says, "in your opinion, were your employer and her daughter close?"

"Oh, yes. Extremely so. Inseparable, I'd say. Certainly, Mrs. Hart could be a stern disciplinarian, something of a perfectionist, but she and Ashley were, as you say, quite close. Quite close indeed."

"Glad to hear it," Ceepak says. "Not always the case with teenage girls and their mothers."

"Yes."

"Especially when the child has so much money."

"Pardon?"

"Ashley now owns everything Mr. Hart used to own. His houses. His corporation. His casinos. She inherited it all. She's probably one of the wealthiest little girls in the whole world."

The butler actually smiles. Maybe he thinks Ashley's a soft touch. Maybe he thinks he's overdue for a raise. Maybe a promotion. Maybe he always wanted to be a casino manager when he grew up.

"Oh, drat," Ceepak says.

"Problem?"

"Well, I wanted to call Ashley . . . talk to her about all this . . . but I don't have her cell phone number."

"Allow me. . . ."

I guess the butler figures Ceepak is going to put in a good word for him. Tell Ashley how helpful the guy's been. He writes down a cell phone number on the back of a cream-colored note card and hands it to Ceepak.

"That is the number."

"Thanks." Ceepak tucks the card into his shirt pocket. "Hey, Danny? You got a cigarette?"

I look at Ceepak like he's nuts. I don't smoke. Neither does he.

"Sorry," I say with a shrug. "Fresh out."

Ceepak eyes the sandstone box on the glass coffee table.

"Do you mind?"

"Please," the butler says. "Help yourself."

Ceepak lifts the lid and grabs a cigarette.

The butler reaches for the clunky lighter but Ceepak waves him off.

"I'll save it. For later."

He sniffs the cigarette.

"Clove?"

"Yes. Actually, they're called kretek. Djarum Black. Imported from Jakarta. Indonesia? Very hard to find. I have to special-order them over the Internet."

"Wow. You don't see many cigarettes wrapped in black paper like this, do you? I guess you can't just run down to the 7-Eleven for a pack?"

"Hardly."

"You sure you don't mind me taking one?"

"Not at all. Enjoy."

"Thanks. Well, we need to be going. Thank you again for your time and assistance."

"My pleasure. Have a pleasant day, gentlemen." The butler ushers us to the front door. "Give my best to young Miss Ashley."

"Will do."

When we're back inside the Ford, Ceepak pulls out one of his evidence bags and places the fresh cigarette carefully inside it.

"I suspect it will match," he says.

"Match what?"

Ceepak unsnaps a pants pocket and pulls out a rolled-up bag. He opens the top so I can see the evidence inside.

A stubbed-out black cigarette butt covered with gray, gritty sand. There's a thin gold band wrapping around the filter, just like on the one he snagged off the coffee table.

When the bag is under my nose, I get a good whiff.

Burnt clove.

He smiles.

"Don't you just hate it when smokers treat the beach like it's their ashtray?"

THIRTY-FOUR

We're driving back to town.

Ceepak is on his phone with Morgan from the FBI. He rattles off Ashley's cell number from the cream-colored card.

"It syncs up with what you said earlier," he tells Morgan. "Your theory on the note. . . ."

I'm trying to remember what Morgan said. Something about how our ransom note was a copy of the Jon Benet Ramsey note. That our kidnapper had never kidnapped before, so he had to cheat to make it sound like he knew what he was doing.

I still don't know what Ceepak's doing. I thought this thing ended last night.

And why aren't we telling the chief where we are?

Ceepak shuts his flip phone.

"Let's go visit Ms. Stone."

"At Chesterfield's?"

"Roger that."

I hope she's in a better mood than the last time we all got together there. Like yesterday, when we tried to bust her.

✿   ✿   ✿

"I was attempting to rescind Mr. Hart's order," Ms. Stone explains.

We're in the dining room at Chesterfield's. Ceepak's nibbling on a blueberry muffin. She has a scone going, which is like a sideways biscuit you eat with jam instead of jelly. I'm helping myself to the breadbasket and lots of expensive butter—it's cut into patties shaped like seashells.

"Mendez had been hired to bring down The Palace Hotel?" Ceepak asks.

"Yes. I'm afraid so. Mr. Hart was reverting to the tactics he employed earlier in his career. The hotel had been declared an historic landmark and there was no economical way he could complete the modifications deemed necessary to make it commercially viable."

"So Hart decided to destroy it instead?"

"Yes. It was certainly one way to skirt the restrictions imposed by the landmark laws."

"You advised against it?"

"Strongly. It was a lovely old building. Almost like a castle. I believe we could have restored it."

"But Mendez and his crew—they had it wired?"

"They'd been in town for about a week. Setting things up, placing charges in strategic positions. Timers. Their implosion plan was quite impressive."

"You saw it?"

"Mendez told us what he and his team had worked up at a luncheon meeting on Friday."

"Where?"

She flips open her daybook. I notice the pages are filled with tiny writing, like she records what she does every day in fifteen-minute intervals—probably so she can charge people all the billable hours she's due.

"The Lobster Trap."

"Danny?"

"It's up near Locust Street."

"We'll check it out."

"Please do. It's the same meeting you found listed in Mr. Hart's computer diary."

"The one you told us was cancelled?"

"Yes. Sorry. My mistake."

"Don't worry," I say and gesture toward Ceepak. "His pencil has an eraser."

Ms. Stone stares at me. She doesn't get it. I grab another chunk of raisin roll.

"Why were the timers set for Sunday night?"

"Mr. Hart planned to leave town Sunday morning, after our final breakfast meeting concerning the implosion plan. Mendez, himself, was scheduled to depart Sunday afternoon, after one last check of the wiring."

"So you'd all be long gone when the deed went down?"

"Yes." Ms. Stone sounds ashamed. "When Mr. Hart was . . . murdered . . . I contacted Mr. Mendez. Offered to sell him the hotel property."

"Why?"

"Pending probate, I had Mr. Hart's irrevocable power of attorney. I hoped to persuade Mr. Mendez to remove his incendiary devices. Thought if he owned it, he wouldn't be so quick to knock it down. I gave him some brochure mock-ups I had commissioned in a final attempt to convince Mr. Hart to develop the hotel into time-share units, not destroy it. Mendez agreed to meet with me here Sunday morning to discuss my ideas further. . . ."

"Really?" Ceepak finds Ms. Stone's love of the grand old structure a little hard to swallow. Me too. I heard those rats scampering around in the walls. I might have been in the Hart-Mendez camp. Knock the sucker down!

"Why are you so interested in this particular building?" Ceepak asks.

"Stone, McCain and Whitby."

"Excuse me?"

"My great-grandfather. Josiah Stone. He and his architectural

partners designed the original hotel. It was their grandest achieve-
ment. When I first went to work for Mr. Hart, I encouraged him to
pursue the property. I convinced him that we could restore it to its
former glory. Mr. Hart was more impressed by the business possibilities. As you know, the hotel is situated on a prime piece of shoreline
real estate. The whole north end of the island is a gold mine, waiting
for the right person to come along and rescue it from decades of neg-
lect. But refurbishing the landmarked hotel would prove prohibitively
expensive to most. . . ."

"But not Reginald Hart."

"It would have been stupendous! We were going to put trendy shops
in the lobby, gourmet restaurants and wine bars along a restored pier. . . ."

"Mr. Hart became impatient?"

"He wanted a clean slate. An empty patch of ground where he
could build something new and flashy. Maybe even a casino. He was
confident he could push an 'urban renewal' gambling referendum
through the local legislature. So he hired Mendez to bring the old
building down. But when Mr. Hart died. . . ."

"You went to work on Mendez?"

"Yes. Mendez could pull the plug, stop the demolition."

"Until we locked him up in jail."

"Yes. By then, I was afraid to tell you what I knew. . . ."

"Understandable."

"I wish now I had behaved differently. My silence destroyed my
great-grandfather's legacy. I will always regret my inaction. . . ."

"When was the last time you saw Mr. Hart alive?" Ceepak asks.

"Saturday morning. I drove him and Ashley into town."

Ah-hah. So that's how they got all the way from Beach Crest
Heights to Sunnyside Playland.

"What time?"

"We left the house before 6:30."

"Mr. Hart was an early riser?"

"No. He said Ashley 'dragged him out of bed.' He was very sleepy
when we climbed into the car."

"Why did you want Mr. Hart to change his will?"

"It made no sense. How is a thirteen-year-old child going to run a multinational corporation? I suggested we set up a trust fund for Ashley but cede corporate control to the board. . . ."

"And?"

"He told me, in no uncertain terms, to 'mind my own business.'"

"Why?"

"He never said."

"Any theories?"

"None I wish to discuss. It would only be conjecture on my part, and I refuse to engage in idle speculation."

Wow. Guess Ms. Stone has a Code, too.

Wonder if she's ever broken it.

"Why didn't Hart just drive himself into town Saturday morning?"

"I'm not sure. I think Ashley had him flustered. He told me to hurry and fetch the car. I felt like a chauffeur. I was up front, driving. They were in the back seat. Giggling. In truth, I was rather embarrassed to see this man I've always admired acting so childishly. I dropped them off and went looking for a cup of coffee."

"Can I ask you a personal question?"

"Depends."

"Your perfume. Do you purchase it at Victoria's Secret?"

"No."

"It's not a Victoria's Secret fragrance?"

"That wasn't your question."

Oh, boy. She's being a lawyer. Only answering the exact question asked.

"You asked me if I *purchased* it at Victoria's Secret. I did not. It was gift. From Mr. Hart. I don't particularly like the scent. He, however, does. I'm no fool, nor am I averse to a little brown-nosing to advance my cause, so I wore it this weekend."

"Clever."

"Didn't work. He still wanted to knock down the hotel."

"One last thing," Ceepak says. "How did Mr. Hart and his ex-wife get along?"

"*Which* ex-wife?"

He smiles. I think he kind of likes her today.

"Number three. Ashley's mother."

"Well," she pauses to think how to best phrase what's coming next, "she was the mother of his only child. . . ."

"But?"

"I don't think he trusted her."

"What makes you say that?"

"He asked me to make inquiries regarding a private investigator."

"Why?"

"The usual. He suspected she had a new lover. Someone who might prove a bad influence on Ashley. Someone who could cause trouble."

Ms. Stone pauses again, like she heard what she just said.

"Perhaps," she says, "Mr. Hart was correct."

THIRTY-FIVE

"**L**et's take a walk."

We're on the sandy concrete sidewalk outside Chesterfield's. The sun is already so hot and bright that the pavement sizzles and any gum you step on is going to be gooey and stretchy like pizza cheese.

Ceepak heads toward the end of the street where pressure-treated planks lead up to the boardwalk paralleling the beach.

"Where we going?" I ask, trying to catch up. The man does not walk at a leisurely pace

"Tilt-A-Whirl."

"Are you planning on telling me what the hell is going on sometime today?"

"I did. We're walking over to the Tilt-A-Whirl."

Ceepak is acting like the asshole big brother I never actually had. The one who thinks he's so clever, doing some kind of Three Stooges "nyuck-nyuck-nyuck" hand wave in your face. Some seagulls caw and chitter. *They* think Ceepak is fucking hilarious.

"That's not what I mean," I say as we hustle down the boardwalk. All sorts of interesting walkers and joggers come at us, pass us, move up and down the wonderfully level span overlooking the sand and surf. I feel totally out of shape. First, Ceepak walks too damn fast. Second, all these other people look healthy and fit as they speed-walk or run past in their color-coordinated exercise outfits. Third, I drank six beers in sixty minutes flat only about seven hours ago and, like I said, the sun is bright and hot and my armpits bring to mind a cheap brewery.

Ceepak dashes down a short set of stairs and onto the sand. He takes the steps two at a time, swinging from the handrails like a giddy kid. I follow him, trying not to trip, stumble, or fall.

"'This train?'" Ceepak shouts over his shoulder. "'Faith will be rewarded!'"

He's quoting another Springsteen song. "Land of Hope and Dreams." It's not really on any studio album, but Bruce sings it live all the time.

I still have no idea where the hell any of this is leading except, of course, to the chain-link fence surrounding the Tilt-A-Whirl.

Ceepak points to the bushes where I first found the needles and other drug paraphernalia.

"Maybe Squeegee was here. Maybe he came here all the time, especially when it was raining, to shoot up his drugs. Heroin, mostly. He could have been in those bushes, sleeping it off. Then, all of a sudden, he hears a gun go off. Seven, eight, nine shots. Lot of noise. Only Squeegee doesn't pop up right away. He's groggy. Did some heavy-duty smack the night before. He's half-awake, half-asleep when he hears the fence rattling."

Ceepak kicks the bottom of the fence. It shimmies and rattles and pings against its poles. It'd get me out of bed.

"Maybe he finally sits up. He looks toward the beach, expecting to see the cop who gives him his wake-up call most mornings. Only this particular morning, he sees a lady wearing sunglasses and a scarf and smoking a cigarette. A sweet-smelling cigarette. The sea breeze? It blows that fragrant smoke right up at him and he thinks it smells like something he made for his mother once, for her to hang in the closet. A clove pomander."

What do you know—Squeegee and I have at least one thing in common—we both made stinky gifts for our moms.

Ceepak points to people and things that aren't there, but I start to see them. He walks over to the trapdoor buried in the sand.

"Maybe he sees this same lady bend down and pull a pistol out of this hole. A pistol just like this one."

Ceepak pulls out his Smith & Wesson.

"Maybe the next time Mr. Jerry Shapiro, a.k.a. Squeegee, is shown such a weapon he says, 'Yeah, that's like what she had.' And, he says the lady was wearing white gloves."

Ceepak snaps open his pants pocket and pulls out a pair of those lint-free evidence gloves.

"'Like these?' I ask. 'Yeah. Like those,' he says."

No wonder he was up in Room 215 so long last night. He and Squeegee had quite the conversation.

"The lady's smart. She's not leaving any fingerprints on the murder weapon. Then our witness? He hears the lady whisper something. 'We need to talk!'"

"Is the lady whispering this to Squeegee?"

"No. He thought so at first. Apparently, some of his recreational drugs increase his sense of paranoia. However, he soon realizes—the lady tucking the gun into her beach bag is talking to somebody else. Somebody up in the Tilt-A-Whirl."

"Okay." This is getting creepy.

"Now, let's pretend you're a heroin addict. A junkie. You've just been rudely awoken. You've seen a woman with a gun, whispering to someone you can't see. What do you do?"

"Freak out?"

"Good answer. You see the gun lady run away. Maybe you get up and run through the mud over there where that broken sprinkler head soaked the ground. You run out from behind the Sunnyside Clyde sign and see a bloody body slumped in one of the Turtles. You freak out even more, pace around and leave your bootprints all over the platform. Then you realize, if you stick around? Everybody is going to say you did it, they'll say the murder was a robbery gone bad. So you decide to get the hell out of there before . . . before? Danny? Before what?"

"Uhm . . . uh. . . ." I didn't know this was going to be one of those audience-participation game shows.

"Focus, Danny. You're the junkie. You're a tramp who gets busted for sleeping on the beach or in the bushes or under the boardwalk or up in the Tilt-A-Whirl all the time."

"So you know everybody's schedule?"

"Awesome! So what do you do?"

"Get the hell out of here before the cop on the scooter shows up?"

"Good answer. But—you realize. That cop usually comes here earlier. Adam Kiger typically swings by when the sun's barely up. In fact, you realize, even though you don't have a watch or an alarm clock, you got to sleep in a little later than usual this Saturday morning. You can tell by how high the sun is over the ocean. But you hear noise. In the distance. A tractor."

"Joey T.?"

"The Sand Rake sweeps this sector of the beach between 0725 and 0730. As I indicated earlier, your friend keeps a very rigid schedule. Squeegee can hear him coming."

"So the junkie . . . he crawls out of the hole and high-tails it . . . wherever."

Ceepak nods.

"Did Joey see him?"

"No," Ceepak says. "He was up the beach, facing north, about to double back and rake south. Like mowing a lawn—he does the beach in overlapping lines."

"I see."

"So our junkie friend? He gets extremely lucky. He scurries through the hole and runs up the beach. A few minutes later, Joey T. comes along and covers up his tracks for him. The lady's too. But Jerry saw the lady stub out her cigarette. . . ."

"Which Joey swept up?"

"Check."

"Which ended up in the Sand Rake's hopper?"

"Double check."

"Which is now in your pants pocket?"

"Checkmate."

"So—why didn't Squeegee see Ashley?"

"Firstly, he's, as you say, 'freaking out' so he's not seeing much of anything except Mr. Hart's bloody body. Secondly, Ashley was hiding behind the turtle. Remember her footprint path? How it went around to the back?"

Ceepak pulls out his little notebook.

"I asked her, 'Which way did he go?' She answered, 'I'm not sure. I went behind the Turtle to hide.' I believe she was telling the truth. About hearing Squeegee in the bushes, maybe even catching a glimpse of him stumble-bumming around. She was scared and hid until she was sure he was gone. Probably heard the fence rattle again when he crawled under it."

"You think she lied about everything? To protect her mother?"

"They're very close. The butler said so. We've observed it ourselves."

"And the kidnapping?"

"An excellent means of expediting the whole probate process. To ensure no one contested the will and Ashley immediately inherited everything—billions and billions of dollars. Surely, the richest girl in the world would share some of her newfound wealth with her mother. I believe Betty Bell Hart cooked up the kidnapping scheme early Saturday afternoon, when she realized Ms. Stone was in a position of power and able to dispose of assets. . . ."

"So all of a sudden, you think she did it? Did everything all by herself?"

"Not all of a sudden, Danny."

I'm remembering our walk from the bank.

"And," Ceepak adds, "not all by herself."

"But how would Ashley know to tell us about the crazy man with the buggy eyes?"

"I believe Ashley and Mom had a quick little chit-chat. After the murder, after the junkie was gone. Miss Bell most probably ran off the beach . . . around there . . . to the side . . . somewhere where they couldn't be seen. Maybe behind another Sunnyside Clyde sign. I suspect she coached her daughter on exactly what to say . . . and Ashley was scared . . . covered with blood . . . horrified . . . but mom calmed her down . . . talked her through it. . . ."

"That would take some time. . . ."

"Yes," Ceepak says. "At least fifteen, twenty minutes. But Betty was very clever. She didn't overload her daughter with too much information. Just enough. About a crazy man with googly eyes. I suspect they talked and rehearsed from 0725 to 0745."

"Which is when we saw Ashley in the street!"

"A full half hour after her father died. I never stopped to ponder that lag in the timeline until I talked to Squeegee."

"Squeegee gave you a lot of information."

"He's our first eyewitness. His testimony, however, would be vigorously contested in any court of law, given his vagrant background and history of drug abuse. . . ."

"So why'd you shoot him?"

"Who?"

"Squeegee."

"Danny, did I ever say I shot anybody?"

"No but . . . I assumed. . . ."

Oh, Jesus. My dad was right. I made an ass "out of u and me." I drank all that beer last night without just cause.

"But. . . ."

"Danny, I could not ask you to lie for me when the chief, as I knew he would, asked you what I did inside the hotel. Furthermore, telling everyone the suspected kidnapper was alive might have endangered Squeegee before I had a chance to see if he was telling me the truth."

"But—you fired your rifle! I smelled it."

"As I knew you would."

"I see. So you sort of set me up?"

"I allowed you to jump to a conclusion. Yes. Sorry."

"It's all good." I actually say his catch phrase back at him because I am totally relieved. "So—who did you shoot at?"

"No one. I took a little target practice. You know that lighthouse? Where the red paint meets the white?"

"Yeah?"

"I think I nailed it. Right on the line. Split it down the middle. We should run by and check it out . . . later."

"And the hotel burned down because?"

"I couldn't deactivate the timers."

"But you knew when the building would blow?"

"I used the sniper rifle's telescopic sight to read the digital output on the timers secured high in the rafters of one of the turrets. It's why I encouraged evacuation of the premises in such a dramatic fashion."

"You mean firing your pistol into the floor like that?"

"Affirmative."

I feel all warm and fuzzy. The Code lives on. So apparently, does Squeegee.

Ceepak crouches down near the sand-covered trapdoor.

"Now then—we never actually checked the bottom of this fence for fibers. If Betty crawled out, perhaps. . . ."

"Don't touch that fence!"

A skinny old lady in shorts and a cowboy hat is limping up the beach, yelling at Ceepak.

"Do not touch it!"

THIRTY-SIX

"**Y**ou Ceepak?"
       "Yes, ma'am."
       "Where are your gloves?"
"In my pocket."
"Not doing us much good in there now, are they?"
"No, ma'am."

The old lady is wearing khaki shorts and a Hawaiian shirt and one of those Australian cowboy hats with the flap buttoned up on one side. She's squinting and crinkling her pixie nose because she really should have worn sunglasses. She has Irish eyes and fair, freckled Irish skin, neither of which does particularly well in the sun. The Irish were designed for mist, fog, and bogs—not sand, surf, and sun.

Ceepak pulls on his evidence gloves.

The lady nods her approval.

I think she should have reconsidered her choice on the shorts. She has these white, Bic-Stic ballpoint pen kind of legs with carbuncled knees like Popeye's girlfriend, only this lady's are wrinkled.

Ceepak is studying her face.

"Dr. McDaniels?"

"That's right. Call me Sandy. Like the inside of my shoes. Come here."

Ceepak moves closer so the little lady can lean against him with one hand and use her other to shake out the sand in her tennis shoe. She has short-cut white hair that might've been red once and blue eyes that twinkle, like she just told herself a dirty joke.

"You work out?" she asks Ceepak while she's balancing against his bicep.

"Some."

"I could tell. You do more curls than anything else." She slips the shoe back on her foot. "So what we got?"

"First, Dr. McDaniels, I want to thank you for coming out so early. . . ."

"Save it. I'm just sorry I was on vacation Saturday. I hear Slobbinsky royally screwed the pooch."

"Not too badly. Fortunately, the rest of your team did a fantastic job. . . ."

"They always do. Slobbinsky sat next to the dead guy and ate a greasy sandwich, hunh? Figures. With him, a sandwich is not a sandwich unless big globs of grease drip out from between the bread slices. I can always tell what he's had for lunch by studying his tie. Soup. Chili. Chicken fingers with honey mustard sauce. . . ."

I put two and two together. This is the fabled Dr. Sandra McDaniels. The legendary Crime Scene Investigator.

"So you talked to Chris Morgan?" Ceepak asks.

McDaniels nods. "He's good people. For a Fed. We've worked together before."

"He mentioned our peculiar situation?"

"Yep. Nobody knows I'm here. Hell, *I* think I'm still on vacation. My plane lands sometime around noon. Unless, of course, I caught an earlier flight because an old FBI pal called me late last night. . . ."

"Thank you."

"Yeah, yeah. Don't get all mushy on me." She knuckle-punches Ceepak in the arm. "So, find anything interesting in the garbage this morning?"

"Yes, ma'am."

Ceepak pulls out two evidence envelopes.

"This was swept off the beach Saturday morning."

McDaniels looks at the clove cigarette butt.

"Ah, Djarum Black Kretek," she says. "An Indonesian import. It is widely believed that the name Kretek derives from the crackling sound that cloves make when burned—'keretek-keretek.' As you see, I share Sherlock Holmes's fascination with tobacco products."

"Indeed," Ceepak says.

Man, I can so see these two nerding out in front of the TV with milk and cookies, thrilling to *Forensic Files*.

"This," he tells her, holding up the second evidence bag, "comes from the suspect's home."

McDaniels peeks in the bag.

"Looks like a perfect match. We'll run it through the lab. How'd you secure it?"

"I asked politely."

"Oh. You're a sneaky one, hunh?"

"Yes, ma'am."

McDaniels puts the envelopes in her cargo pockets. I guess that explains the shorts: lots of pockets. Not as many as Ceepak, but almost.

"Can I borrow your magnifying glass?" she asks him, just assuming the big guy lugs one around with him at all times—which, of course, he does.

"Thanks."

She grunts as she bends down to study the twisted tips at the bottom of the fence.

"Oh, yeah. This fence is like a cat brush."

She pulls out her own tweezers and a stack of evidence bags and starts plucking fibers I can't see.

"So," she says, "this is where it all went down?"

"Yes, ma'am. That car there. . . ."

Ceepak points to the Tilt-A-Whirl.

"Second turtle from the left," she says without looking. "I know. Morgan E-mailed me the whole file. Of course, the skinny guy? This homeless bum with the goatee? You know he didn't do the kidnap."

"Yes, ma'am. I know."

"You do?" I'm sort of startled here.

Dr. McDaniels chuckles.

"Officer Ceepak—please explain to the class how you know what you know." She looks up at me. "I love to torture my students."

"We know Squeegee was not the kidnapper," Ceepak says, "from examining the boot impressions left in the sand behind the Hart beach house."

"Go on."

"The tread marks matched those we found on the Tilt-A-Whirl. . . ."

"But?" Dr. McDaniels arches an eyebrow.

"But the boot prints on the beach were deeper."

"Ergo?"

Now she's using Latin like Batman sometimes did on that old TV show.

"Therefore," Ceepak says, "the kidnapper weighed more than the man who walked across the Tilt-A-Whirl platform."

"How much?"

"Excuse me?"

"How much did the kidnapper weigh?"

Ceepak drops his eyes like he forgot to study that chapter.

"Sorry. I didn't calculate the exact weight."

"273 pounds," she says. "Big guy. A big galoot of a guy."

"How can you be certain?" I ask, impressed.

"Hey—I wrote the book. Besides, my guys took your plaster cast back to the lab and made some measurements."

"So it was kind of a trick question?" I ask.

"Yeah. That's my favorite kind. So, you know—watch your back, kid." This time, she knuckle-punches my shoulder. It stings.

My partner's smiling. He likes this feisty lady.

"I need another number," he says.

"Shoot."

"More precise time of death."

Dr. McDaniels shakes her head and sighs.

"I'll re-check his eye jelly numbers, but you know we can't be precise. There is no way to nail it . . . not with one hundred percent certainty."

Okay—I have to ask.

"Eye jelly?"

"Officer Ceepak?" the professor once again calls on the smartest kid in the class to explain.

"The vitreous humor is a transparent jelly that fills the eyeball," he says. "Potassium levels are low in the vitreous humor of a living eye, but rise at a known rate after death. If we measure that potassium level, we can calibrate a more exact T.O.D."

"It's the best I can do," Dr. McDaniels says, staring up into the crime scene, slowing turning her head, scanning it all in like she's one of those disposable cameras that gives you the panoramic view. "We can't pinpoint a precise time, but I'll give you my tightest interval of confidence."

"Appreciate that."

"Okay," she says. "I always like to see the crime scene. Photographs only tell you so much. Now that I've seen it, I need to leave. Even though I was never actually here."

"Roger that."

"If you need me? I won't be in my office."

I think that means she will be. She walks up the beach toward the access road, stopping once to lean against the fence and shake more sand out of her shoe.

"Oh, Ceepak?" she hollers back.

"Yes, ma'am?"

"You need more evidence to nail these bastards."

"I know."

"So solve the first crime to solve the second."

"Solve the murder to solve the kidnapping?"

"No, dummy—the *first* crime. Capisce?"

Ceepak gets it. I don't know what *it* is, but he's nodding his head.

"Will do. Thanks for the tip."

"What tip?" she says over her shoulder as she walks away. "I wasn't even here, remember?"

He smiles like he's just met his favorite movie star.

"Come on, Danny," he says when she's gone.

"Where to?"

"Boardwalk Books. I promised Squeegee I'd pick him up a compilation of Ginsberg poems. I believe the bookstore also has a fax machine."

"So I've heard."

We're riding up Ocean Avenue.

The tourists are coming back. Traffic is snarled and slow and I see lines outside some of the better Monday brunch places. People go to brunch on Monday down here because they're on vacation and they can go to brunch all week long if they want to.

Ceepak's staring out his window and rubbing the top of his head, thinking. His hand makes a raspy sound when it scrapes over the short stuff on the back of his neck. He lets go with a big, gaping-mouth yawn. I don't think he's had any sleep in days.

Too bad. I have more questions.

"Why the Tilt-A-Whirl?" I ask when we hit a red light.

"I suspect Betty told Ashley to take her father there. Gave her precise time coordinates. That would explain why Ashley was rushing everyone out of the house on Saturday morning."

"Did Ashley know what her mother was up to?"

"I hope not. I think Ashley did whatever her mother, the 'stern disciplinarian,' told her to do."

"And mom went to the ATM because?"

"She'd seen enough television news coverage of fugitives on the lam to know that ATMs photograph and time-stamp every user. Giving her a rock-solid alibi for 7 A.M."

"So," I say, putting three and three together this time, "you're hoping Dr. McDaniels does her eye-jelly magic and pegs the time of death closer to 7:20?"

"Well done, Danny. We need to account for that stroll from the bank to the beach."

"Gotcha." This is pretty cool. Like working a math problem or jigsaw puzzle or the Jumble in the morning paper, which I only do if somebody else starts it for me. I mean, it's cool if you forget you saw Reginald Hart's body with all those bullet holes in it. If you remember that? The coolness sort of goes all lukewarm on you.

"As Dr. McDaniels indicated, we need more hard evidence. I'm basing too much on conjecture. . . ."

"So we ask at the bookstore? We flash the clerk Betty's mug shot?"

"Roger that."

"When do we tell the chief what we know?"

Ceepak turns to look at me.

"The chief?" he says. "That big galoot?"

Oh, Jesus.

Time to put four and four together.

"How much would you estimate Chief Cosgrove weighs, Danny?"

My mouth goes kind of dry.

"Oh, I dunno," I croak. "273 pounds?"

"Yeah. That's what I'd figure, give or take a pound. 273."

THIRTY-SEVEN

I used to go to Boardwalk Books when I was a kid, to buy comics and sneak a peek at the artsy-fartsy photography books that usually have a picture or two of naked women sprawled across their glossy pages.

I'm hoping they have a fresh batch of nudie books for me to flip through today. Might help take my mind off the fact that my boss, the chief of police for Sea Haven Township, is probably moonlighting as a co-conspirator in a grisly murder/kidnap scheme.

The bulk of the books for sale in the small shop are paperbacks— fiction of the airport variety, my favorite genre. I learned that word from a college girl I took to the movies. "Genre." It means you're watching a film, not a movie. I prefer movies. We only went on that one date. It was a film. An old one in black and white about a foreign guy playing chess with Death, a guy who wore a creepy black robe and spoke Swedish.

Boardwalk Books also sells a lot of road maps and navigational charts, which are like road maps for the ocean because they tell you how deep the water is, which way the current flows, where you might bonk into a buoy, stuff like that. I never knew the ocean had maps until one day, on my lunch break, the chief showed me on a chart where he was going fishing that weekend.

In his boat.

Suddenly, I'm feeling queasy again and, this time, beer has nothing to do with it.

The boat that pirated Ashley away from her mansion? I have a funny feeling Chief Cosgrove was the skipper.

I'd tell Ceepak what I think but I believe he is, at least, two or three pages ahead of me.

"Has she ever been in here?"

Ceepak places a photograph of Betty Bell Hart on the glass counter in front of the droopy-eyed clerk. The guy looks like he reads too much. I know when I read, I always get sleepy. He's wearing a T-shirt showing Shakespeare in swim trunks holding a small beach ball in one hand, rubbing his chin with the other. It's the Boardwalk Books logo.

The clerk rubs his chin and studies the snapshot.

"Yeah . . . the old weather girl . . . she's in here all the time."

The clerk sips coffee from a mug with a different Boardwalk Books logo printed on it. This time, I think it's Charles Dickens in the swim trunks. He's building two sand castles.

"She lives in that glass McMansion down on the south beach? Right?"

"Right," Ceepak says. "She come in here often?"

"Sure. She loves books. You wouldn't think it to look at her, would you? I mean she's still pretty hot and all."

"What kind of material does she read?" Ceepak asks.

"Harlequin romances. True crime. Those Motley Fool investment guides."

"Was she here on Sunday?"

"Sorry, I didn't work this weekend. Duane did. You want me to call Duane? He's the manager."

"She ever use the fax machine?"

The guy thinks about it for a second, tilting his head sideways.

"Nope."

Ceepak looks disappointed.

"Wait a minute. . . ."

Bingo.

"She did use it this one time. I had to help her. This was a couple weeks ago. Yeah. I remember thinking she was acting so totally blonde, you know what I mean?"

Ceepak nods.

"I mean, it's pretty simple. Just like a copy machine. You lay your paper down, lower the lid, punch a few buttons on the keypad, and bam—you're done. It's why it's totally self-serve. But she kept asking questions. Made me show her how to do it, over and over, like a hundred times."

"Guess she wanted to make sure she got it right."

"Yeah," the guy chuckles. "In case she ever had like, you know, a fax emergency."

Or if she was ever in a hurry to fax a note spelling out the details of where to deliver ten million dollars in ransom money.

"Where to next?"

We're sitting in the Explorer out front of Boardwalk Books. I can tell Ceepak has a list of spots he wants to hit before he busts the bad guys. He checks his watch.

"Remember that tricycle theft?'

"No."

"Saturday morning? Adam Kiger caught the call?"

"Yeah. Okay. . . ."

"We never did solve that crime, did we?"

"No. We've been kind of busy."

Ceepak nods.

"Still," he says, "that trike owner is a tax-paying citizen. Well, his parents probably are. They're entitled to a full and proper criminal investigation."

"They are?"

"It's our sworn duty, Danny."

"Oh-kay. . . ."

"Besides—it was the first crime of the day."

Solve the first crime, solve the second.

Advice from Dr. McDaniels. Okay. Got it.

Maybe it was no coincidence Officer Kiger wasn't on the beach Saturday morning to give Squeegee his wakeup call, wasn't there to see folks crawling in and out under the fence, shooting people on the Tilt-A-Whirl.

Maybe he was taken out of the game a half hour before kickoff.

They sent him to answer a call on Rosewood Street.

The mayor's sister's house. The kind of summons you usually can't refuse, especially if you want to keep your job.

We're in the bushes near the front porch steps. Rose bushes. Thorns, wild tangles. I guess if your street is called "Rosewood," you're officially obligated to grow the prickly buggers.

Ceepak has his magnifying glass out, looking for fibers, I bet. The trike thief could have snagged his shorts on the thorns. I know I just did.

"Excuse me. What are you gentlemen doing in my bushes?"

I think it's the mayor's sister. She's very tan. And very stacked.

"Good morning, ma'am." Ceepak is, of course, friendly, courteous, and kind. "We're investigating your report of a stolen vehicle."

"You work for my brother?" she asks Ceepak.

"We work for Sea Haven Township."

"Like I said . . . you work for my brother?"

"Yes, ma'am. I suppose we do."

"I'll have to commend him on his new hiring policies."

Ceepak steps back from the bushes and onto the lawn.

"Sorry to bother you like this, ma'am."

"Oh, it's no bother."

"We have a few questions."

"So do I. Are you married?"

Ceepak actually blushes.

"Was the tricycle situated here on the porch?" he asks.

"The tricycle?"

"Yes, ma'am. Was it on the porch?"

"Are you really investigating a missing tricycle?"

"Yes, ma'am."

"What a waste of *man*power." Now she's arching her back, like she's yawning, like maybe she needs to go back to bed and maybe somebody should go with her.

"Miss?" I say. "We're kind of in a hurry."

"Who are you?"

Figures. When you're with Ceepak, women don't even notice you.

"What is this? Take A Stupid Kid To Work Day?"

The mayor's sister? She has this nasty side. And when it comes out is when she squinches up her nose and glares at you. Then you notice where the plastic surgeon didn't do such a hot job.

"Where exactly did you go to cop school?" she asks me. "Some doughnut shop?"

I'm no Boy Scout, so I don't have to do the courteous bit.

"Where'd you get that tan?" I say. "Sears, or Costco?"

"Oh, I see. You're the comedian cop?"

"He's part-time," Ceepak says.

"He's going to be no-time after I call my brother."

"No need to bother your brother," Ceepak says, whipping out his little notebook. "I'll take care of it." He jots something down.

"What're you doing? You writing him up?"

"Yes, ma'am."

"Hah! Good."

"Now if you could . . . could you please tell us what happened?"

"Of course." She acts like she's composing herself, smoothing out any crinkles in her shorts, front and back. She spends more time smoothing out the back than the front. "My son left his tricycle on the porch steps like he always does, even though I tell him not to. Maybe if his father were still living with us, maybe if I was still married—which, incidentally, I'm not—maybe things would be different. . . ."

"When did you first notice it was stolen?" Ceepak asks.

"When he was stealing it! The thief made so much noise! He banged the thing against my screen door!"

"Did you see him?"

"No. I called the police right away. I was all alone . . . I didn't dare confront him. . . ."

Now she's doing a damsel-in-distress thing that makes it look like she's a ship flashing Morse Code because her eyelids are painted baby blue and every time she blinks we get a dot or dash of bright light.

"You must have been terrified," Ceepak says.

"Oh, I was. He was right here. And my bedroom? It's right there. . . ."

She points dramatically to a window. I can make out chintzy pink curtains on the other side and one of those hurricane table lamps catalogs say add a touch of romance to almost any room.

What all this means is that the trike bandit banged it against the door just to make certain anybody inside knew he was out here stealing something.

The thief wanted her to call the cops.

"He even kicked over one of my potted plants."

"We'll write it up . . . additional damage . . . for your insurance claim. . . ."

Ceepak jots down another note in his pocket pad.

"And, look down there. . . ." She points to the other side of the porch. "He crushed my Fairy. My beautiful pink Fairy."

"Your Fairy rosebush?"

Oh. Ceepak knows horticulture, too.

"Yes! See?"

"Yes, ma'am. What a shame."

"I'll say."

"Fairies are prolific climbers," Ceepak says.

"I'm impressed. You know your roses. . . ." She's leaning on the porch railing again.

"A little," Ceepak says, looking down at the shrubbery instead of up at the mountains. "I'm no expert. Not like you. You did an excellent job mulching these flower beds."

"Moi?" She gives Ceepak a coy, "silly boy" look. "Hardly. I hire a man to do it for me. He says mulch is the only way to retain moisture in our sandy soil. It's so *hot* down here."

She says "hot" like she said "man" earlier.

Ceepak studies the trampled rosebush.

"What a shame. He crushed it under his boot," he says.

I look down and see where the moist, mulched soil has retained a print.

"His Timberland boot?" I ask.

Ceepak nods.

"Only kind he ever wears."

We're back in the car. Working Ceepak's punch list. Off to dig up more evidence.

"So," I say, "the chief sent the first ransom fax? Because of the boot prints, right? Outside the hotel room? On that patio there?"

"Solid analysis, Danny. I may need to write you up in my little blue book again."

"Are you really going to give me a reprimand for mouthing off?"

"Negative. I said I was writing you up. I was contemplating penning a letter of commendation to place in your personnel file."

"Excellent. It'd be like my first, I think."

"Perhaps. But I doubt it will be your last."

I glance over. Ceepak has the proud-big-brother smile on his face again.

It's all good.

"The way I see it," Ceepak says, "Chief Cosgrove wore his Timberland boots whenever he wanted us to think Squeegee had been somewhere. I speculate that Cosgrove had met Mr. Shapiro and knew of the man's fondness for thermal boots, even in the summer months. In fact, it's highly probable that, once the chief and Miss Bell selected

Mr. Shapiro, a.k.a. Squeegee, as their scapegoat, they paid keen attention to such telling details. It's why they chose the Tilt-A-Whirl. They knew we'd find evidence linking the location to Squeegee, even if he wasn't sleeping in the bushes Saturday morning. They knew we'd find his blood sample in the hypodermics, his muddy footprints on the platform. . . ."

"Why'd the chief wear his boots to the mayor's sister's house?"

"Simple."

"What?"

"He made a mistake. Most criminals usually do. It's how we catch them. He never anticipated we'd investigate a tricycle theft."

"Hell, you wanted to do it first thing Saturday morning!" I'm feeling kind of jazzed, like you do after chugging two cans of Red Bull and snarfing down some Hostess Ding-Dongs. "Remember? Before any of this other shit even went down. You wanted to 'swing by and check it out.' Remember?"

"Did I?"

"Hell, yeah. Fuckin' A!"

"Yes, now that you mention it, I do recall expressing an interest. And Danny?"

"Yes, sir?"

"Swearing is the sign of a limited vocabulary."

"Yes, sir."

Next stop is The Smuggler's Cove Motel, where Ceepak suspects our suspects "had their trysts." I think that means they went there to have sex on a regular basis.

"She stayed there Friday night because she knew, as she stated later, 'they're very discreet.'"

Ceepak is flipping through his notebook again. You tell this guy something? He writes it down or memorizes it.

"Remember how the chief acted when she told us that?" I remember stuff, too. "He was so totally ticked off."

"Roger that. I suspect he would have preferred that his accomplice make some other choice of accommodations so we wouldn't ask questions that might warrant unwanted answers."

"So the chief's, like, cheating on his wife?"

"So it would seem. In fact, I wouldn't be surprised if we were to discover that Chief Cosgrove has made an arrangement with the motel's management allowing them to operate in their unseemly fashion in exchange for their discretion as called for. The pornography. The inherent probability of prostitution. . . ."

"Doesn't really fit with the whole Sea Haven 'family fun' image, does it?"

Ceepak just shakes his head.

I think he's very disappointed in his fellow soldier. His brother in arms. Chief Cosgrove knows The Code, but chose not to follow it because, frankly, he didn't feel like it. I guess that's what a lot of guys do.

We're at Ocean Avenue and Locust Lane.

The Smuggler's Cove is about three blocks up and two over.

I see flashing lights in my rearview mirror.

A cop car requesting that I, another cop car, pull over.

"Pull over, Danny." Ceepak sees them too. His eyes are glued to the side mirror.

I ease to a stop in front of Santa's Sea Shanty.

Some of the women hauling Sailor Santa Nutcrackers out of the year-round holiday store stop to gawk as Ceepak and I climb out of the Ford.

Two cops step out of the other cruiser.

Malloy and Santucci. Two of the chief's favorites.

"Hey, guys," Ceepak says. "What's up?"

"You need to come with us," Santucci says, giving his chewing gum a sharp snap.

"We're on a run—"

"It can wait. The chief needs you in his office. Now."

"That'll work," Ceepak says. "We'll follow you guys in."

Santucci takes another step forward. He even does the lean-on-his-gun-belt thing I've seen Ceepak do.

"It'd be best if you rode with us," he says. "Both of you."

THIRTY-EIGHT

"**J**esus! What the hell did you guys freaking do?"

Gus Davis greets us from the desk as we enter headquarters. Santucci and Malloy are flanking us as they escort us into the building like we're on a perp walk.

If our theories are correct, if the chief is capable of helping his girlfriend bump off her ex-husband and then masterminding a kidnapping hoax with cold-hearted, military precision, I'm sure he's worked out some clever way of taking care of Ceepak and anybody else who might stand in his way on the road to riches. People like me.

"Ceepak? Boyle? Get your asses in here."

The chief stands behind his desk. His face is flushed, redder than raw meat.

"Move it! Now! Move!"

I pick up my pace.

Ceepak takes his time.

"You need us, boss?" Santucci asks.

"Wait outside."

"Yes, sir." Santucci and Malloy leave.

"Would you like me to close the door?" Ceepak asks pleasantly.

"Yes! Close the goddamn door! Now!"

When Ceepak pushes the door shut, I see Gladys, the bag lady from the hotel.

Ceepak sees her too.

"Good to see you again. I take it you safely evacuated the hotel?"

"Fuck you, fuzz!"

Gladys has not mellowed much in the hours since last we met. She hasn't bathed either. I can still see those white streaks on her cheeks where the tears trickled down.

"What am I going to do with you, John?" the chief says.

"Sir?"

"I gave you this job to help you recover from what you've been through. To take you away from the horrors of war. The senseless loss of lives. . . ."

"You're a war criminal," Gladys shouts. "A baby killer! I heard what you did! How you gunned down that taxi driver's family! Baby killer!"

Guess the chief shared some stuff with Gladys he might've kept confidential if he lived by a different kind of Code.

"I thought I could bring you home," the chief says, all hushed and earnest. "Thought I could give you a chance to put it all behind you. Instead, you go all gung-ho? Become some sort of vigilante? You hunted down and killed your suspect?"

I'm going to keep my mouth shut.

Not because I'm afraid, even though I totally am, but because I have a hunch Ceepak doesn't want me saving his butt by blurting out the truth about Squeegee. Otherwise, he wouldn't have hidden it from me last night at the hotel.

"Goddammit, John." The chief shakes his head in disbelief. "You took a sniper rifle upstairs to execute Squeegee?"

"His name is Jerry!" Gladys screeches. "Jerry Fucking Shapiro!"

The chief raises his hand, cueing the radical socialist bag lady to put a lid on it.

"You shot him like a dog?"

"He did!" She's spitting with rage. "I was there when it went down, man. I'll fucking tell the world what you fucking did, you fucking motherfucker!"

"I'm sorry, sir," Ceepak says. "What is it I'm supposed to have done?"

"You fucker!"

"Miss? I'll handle this." The chief rivets his gaze on Ceepak.

Ceepak doesn't flinch. In fact, he smiles and raises his eyebrows as if he's eager to hear what the chief has to say.

"Last night, you tracked down your suspect, this woman's fiancé. . . ."

They're engaged? I'll have to find out where they're registered.

The chief checks his legal pad.

"Mr. Gerald Shapiro, a.k.a. Squeegee. You tracked him down and proceeded into the old Palace Hotel with an M-24 sniper rifle. . . ."

"Awesome weapon system, sir. But, of course, you already know that. You're the one who gave it to me."

The chief ignores that shot across his bow.

"You then went upstairs and, instead of apprehending the suspect for further questioning, you shot him. . . ."

"Negative. I did not shoot Mr. Shapiro."

"John, John, John." The chief kind of chuckles, one for each John. "I will not lie nor tolerate those who do. Remember our Code? You shot this man because you suspected him of being a child molester. You took the law into your own hands."

"No, sir. I did not. However, I'm certain that was your intention."

"Come again?"

"Was this the final phase of your plan? To dispose of me via these false accusations?"

The chief puts down his notepad.

"What plan?"

"You brought me here to Sea Haven, sir, not, as you claim, for rest and relaxation, but to kill whomever you and Miss Bell decided to blame for your own nefarious actions."

"What's he talking about?" Gladys asks. I think the word "nefarious" got her attention.

Ceepak turns to her.

"I did not complete my mission as envisioned by Chief Cosgrove here. Your fiancé? He's safe."

"What?" The chief is even redder.

"In fact—if you walk to the top of the Ship John Lighthouse, I believe you will find Mr. Jerry Shapiro up there enjoying the view, perhaps taking a well-earned nap. I did ask him to not indulge in hallucinogenic drugs while sequestered there. It wouldn't be prudent. The steps inside are quite steep."

"Jerry's alive?"

"Yes, ma'am."

"You didn't kill him?" the chief looks like he was just sucker-punched.

"No, sir. I know you wanted me to. In fact, I know gunning Squeegee down was the sole reason you invited me to join your police force. Why you said 'you don't even have to drive. . . .'"

"You're nuts, Ceepak. You know that?"

"Can I go now?" Gladys has forgotten her righteous wrath. A reunion is what's on her mind, and she's in a hurry.

"Get the hell out of here!" the chief screams at her.

"Fuck you." Gladys bolts.

When she swings open the door, I notice we've attracted quite a crowd in the hallway.

"Go back to work!" the chief yells. "All of you!"

Nobody moves.

I suspect folks have been eavesdropping.

"Now! Move! Go! Boyle? The door?"

"Yes, sir." I swing the door shut. When he does that coach-yell at me? I do as I'm told. Reflexes.

"You two? You're fired. Both of you."

"Earlier today, I did some research," Ceepak says, moving closer to his old friend's desk. "Asked Gus. Adam Kiger. Even your pals Santucci and Malloy. Nobody has ever heard of one Jennifer D'Angelo, the young victim of a rape perpetrated by a homeless man underneath the boardwalk. . . ."

"We kept it quiet!"

"No, sir. You made it up."

"Bullshit."

"It was really quite clever."

Oh, boy. Ceepak's addressing me. Like I'm the jury box or something.

"You see, Danny—because of our past friendship, our time spent together in Germany, the personal and sometimes painful stories we told each other over a few beers. . . ."

Of course. The chief knows about Ceepak's drunk father. His brother. The dead kids in Iraq.

". . . because the chief thought he knew me, he orchestrated what he thought would be the perfect scenario to turn me into his personal killing machine. Why do you think Ashley was instructed to lure her father to the Tilt-A-Whirl Saturday morning? Because the chief knew *we* would be in The Pancake Palace at precisely 0730. That, being a creature of habit, I would be sitting up front . . . in the window seat. They staged the whole scene to draw me in."

I hear the chief's chair squeak. He's leaning back.

"You get any sleep the last couple days, Ceepak? I gotta tell you—you're sounding kind of goofy. Squeegee lend you some of his wacky tobacky?"

"You had a good plan, chief. Thought of every angle. Hart was killed when you knew Dr. McDaniels would be out of town and Slominsky would catch the call."

"How much you been drinking? I heard you were down at The Frosty Mug the other night bending your elbow. Some buddies of mine said you were soused, all tears-in-your-beers about Iraq. Hell, maybe you can't hold it . . . maybe being a lousy drunk runs in your family. . . ."

"Remember those evidence gloves I brought in?"

"How could anybody forget? We all laughed about them for weeks."

"The box is empty. You took them all."

"Bullshit."

"No, sir. I have a witness who saw Miss Bell wearing a pair. Oh, she had Gus's gun, too."

"Who told you this crap? That junkie?"

"Yes, sir. Did you know Mr. Shapiro is a former member of Mensa? He has something of a photographic memory. . . ."

"No one would believe him. His word against Betty's? Besides— Betty was at the bank when Hart was murdered, so you have diddly."

"Don't do it, sir."

"Do what?"

"Make me shoot you. You know I will. I'm a lean, mean killing machine. Remember?"

Ceepak suddenly has his pistol pointed at the chief's forehead.

"Kindly place your hands on top of your desk."

I move a half step to my left.

Oh, Jesus.

I see what Ceepak must've heard. The chief's hand is on the handle of his top desk drawer. He's slid it an inch open.

Must be where he keeps one of his other guns.

"Get out. We're done here. You're fired. Santucci?"

He yells at the door.

"Santucci? Malloy? Get your asses in here! Now!"

The door opens.

It's not Santucci or Malloy. It's Christopher Morgan from the FBI. He's wearing evidence gloves and carrying a pair of Timberland boots.

"They were in your Expedition, chief," he says. He reaches into his suitcoat and pulls out a document. "Oh, by the way—here's the search warrant."

"You sons of bitches. . . ."

The chief must be sending some blue blood up to his red face because it's turning purple.

"Oh," Morgan says, "almost forgot. Ran that cell phone number by Verizon." He pulls another sheaf of papers out of his pocket.

"Find anything interesting?"

Ceepak and Morgan are acting like the chief isn't even in the room—except, of course, for Ceepak aiming his gun at the chief's head. That's still going on.

"After she was kidnapped? Ashley called her mom."

"That was thoughtful," Ceepak says.

"Oh, yeah," Morgan cracks. "Very considerate. Then, this one." He sort of shoves the paper in the chief's face. "That's your number, right? That incoming call there? Sunday night? Guess you had to let Ashley know Ceepak was on his way. Give her time to handcuff her ankles and slip the rope back over her wrists."

"Danny and I almost interrupted your conversation," Ceepak says. "I had to wait for her to hide her phone."

"Which," Morgan says, "we found underneath the floorboards, just like you said."

"You guys think you're so fucking clever," the chief manages to snarl. "You don't know jack shit."

Ceepak lowers his weapon and strolls to the door.

"Gus? Can you join us in here?"

"*Now* what?" the chief is shaking his head in disbelief. I'm keeping my eyes on that top desk drawer and his hands. So is Morgan, thank God, because I still don't have a gun. Everybody else seems to have at least two.

"What's Gus got to do with any of this?" The chief clasps his meaty paws behind his head.

Gus toddles into the room.

"Yes, sir?" he says it to the chief.

"Gus?"

"Oh, hey, Ceepak. Heard all about . . . you know. Sorry it went down that way, but I'm glad you did what needed to be done, you know what I'm saying?"

"Gus, please escort the chief to a holding cell."

"What?"

"Arrest him."

"You can't arrest me!"

Morgan pulls out another sheet of paper. The guy must have pockets in that suit coat like Ceepak has pockets in his pants.

"I, however, can," he says. "Federal bench warrant. For the kidnapping of Harriet Ashley Hart. Which, as you know, is a federal offense—"

"Bullshit!"

"He kidnapped the little girl?"

"He also stole your gun," Ceepak says.

"He did what?" Gus starts to steam pink like boiled shrimp.

"That day in March when you said you lost it? The chief took it. He saw you were without a weapon when he first bumped into you at the Surf City Shopping Center, but he didn't mention it," Ceepak explains. "Instead, he told you to go get your muddy car washed, to make it plausible that Squeegee stole your weapon. You then ran into the chief a second time . . . outside the florist shop. . . ."

"Yeah."

"That's when he boosted your gun. While you were inside buying flowers. He'd been tailing you all day."

"Bullshit!" the chief says. "Ceepak's a liar."

Gus looks at Ceepak. Looks at the chief.

"No, chief. Ceepak never lies. He's a freaking Boy Scout, remember?"

The chief rolls his eyes.

"You have the right to remain silent," Gus says.

"Ceepak, you don't know shit!"

"Shut up!" Gus yells. "Remain freaking silent and give me your goddamn gun."

I can see the folks in the hall staring. Gus neglected to close the door when he came in.

"You just wait, Ceepak. You ever find out the real truth? You'll do like your faggot brother. You'll blow your fucking brains out."

Morgan's cell phone rings.

"Morgan." He covers the mouthpiece. "It's McDaniels."

The call Ceepak's been waiting for.

"What you got? Excellent. I'll tell Ceepak. She's tightened up the time of death."

We wait some more, but not long.

"Yeah. She says death took place sometime between 6:57 A.M. and 7:02."

"Not 7:20? 7:25?"

"No."

"She's certain?"

"As certain as she can be."

"See?" the chief gloats. "You boys don't know shit."

THIRTY-NINE

Gus locks the chief in one of the two windowless holding pens we have in the house.

Mendez is in the other one.

"Yo!" he yells at Ceepak. "You burn down my condo complex? I thought you wanted a time-share. . . ."

"*I* didn't burn it down," Ceepak says. "I just couldn't reach the alarm clock you rigged for the trigger."

The chief interrupts.

"I want to call a lawyer! Now! Move! Get me a phone!"

"Maybe later, chief." Ceepak says. "After we visit your girlfriend."

"Trust me, Ceepak—you don't want to do that."

I don't think Ceepak's trusted the chief ever since he "lied a little" to nail Mendez. He motions for me to follow him out of the cellblock.

"The truth can really ruin your fucking day, Ceepak. You'll see! You fucking Mary Poppins!"

Ceepak doesn't stop to listen, so neither do I.

We walk out the door.

Like Springsteen says:

I'll walk like a man
And I'll keep on walkin'.

Ceepak is stalling on letting the chief make his one phone call because
he knows Cosgrove wouldn't call his lawyer.

He'd call his girlfriend.

So we need to drive up to the city before she figures out we're
coming.

We climb into the Explorer.

"The FBI has her apartment under surveillance," Ceepak says,
handing me a map of the city with the block circled with wax pencil.
"You know the way?"

"Yes, sir."

We pull out of the parking lot and the radio starts squawking.

"All units, 10-34, Playland Arcade. Repeat. 10-34. Playland Video
Arcade. Suspect is considered armed and dangerous. . . ."

Ceepak snatches the radio mike.

"This is Ceepak. We're on it. Roll, Danny. Playland."

"Sirens?"

"And lights. Come on. Roll!"

I flip the switches. The light bar spins, the siren wails. We squeal
tires.

"You know what a 10-34 is, Danny?"

Great. A drive-by pop quiz.

Fortunately, while I race through a red light and cut the tires hard
to the left, Ceepak answers his own question.

"It's a 10-24 still in progress. An assault with a deadly weapon."

Got it.

There's a guy with a deadly weapon inside the Arcade at Playland
and the assault is still going on.

I step on the gas, push the pedal all the way to the floor and make
my engine roar.

Springsteen would be proud.

❉ ❉ ❉

We're the first unit on the scene.

Poor Playland. They were closed all weekend on account of the Tilt-A-Whirl murder. Now they've got somebody with a weapon terrorizing people who'd rather be dropping quarters into coin slots. If this kind of action keeps up, the Family Fun Park may have to change its name to Slayland.

The video arcade building is a vast, open space—like a giant warehouse with Astro-turf green carpet and enough evenly spaced red poles to hold up the roof. Usually, there are all sorts of bells and whistles and ray guns going off the second you step inside the front doors. Today, all I hear is about a hundred kids screaming.

"What's the situation?" Ceepak asks a guy in a red tunic with huge pockets up front sagging with quarters.

He points to the far side of the arcade.

"Some guy's got a pistol!"

"Where?" Ceepak asks, his eyes surveying the situation.

"Dodge City!"

"Where?"

He is obviously a first-time visitor to The Playland Arcade. I, however, know where everything is because this is where much of my youth was misspent. Most of my quarters, too.

"This way," I say.

Dodge City is this corny shooting gallery that's been in the far corner of the building ever since sometime in 1962. It's this life-size barroom where you shoot a six-gun at a piano player, Black Bart and his gang at the poker table, whiskey bottles—that sort of stuff. When you hit the targets, the mannequins move and say stuff like, "Dang! You shot me, sheriff." You ring enough bells, shoot enough bad guys, you win a tin star you can pin on your girlfriend's chest.

I wish it were still that easy.

People are panicking, hiding under pool tables, clustered behind Skee Ball targets.

Once again, Ceepak shows no fear.

His gun is out in front, sweeping left, searching right.

"Over there!" a girl screeches from beneath the Alpine Racer. "It's Ben!"

Guess she knows the guy with the gun.

"Follow me." Ceepak uses pinball machines and giant gumball dispensers for cover. When we get to the Crab Claw, this crane you move around to snag stuffed animals, we see the kid with the gun.

He looks like he's drunk.

"She's a hoochie-mama!"

Sounds like he's drunk too—not making much sense, jabbering gobbledegook.

"Chicken head, hoochie-mama!"

Guess he and his girlfriend had a spat this morning. Or, he caught her cheating and has decided to take it out on the world, including me. He points his gun in my general direction and I hit the deck, crawling to safety under a fake Formula One Racecar.

The kid looks to be sixteen or seventeen. Preppy clothes with brown, blotchy stains down the front of his shirt. Preppy puke. Something about him looks familiar, like I should know who he is, like he's one of my buds' kid brothers or something. He twirls, almost topples, then spins around to point his pistol at Ceepak who is standing right in front of him, holstering his own gun.

The spinning makes the kid even dizzier. He waves his pistol in circles over his head like he wants to be a Dallas Cowgirl cheerleader when he grows up.

"Put that down, son," Ceepak says.

The kid tries to stand still.

"Snap. You smell bacon? Here come 5.0."

He is what we call a wigga: a rich white boy who wants you to think he's ghetto. He must've bought a Gangsta Slangsta dictionary last time he was at the mall. Bacon and 5.0? They both mean the same thing: cops.

"Wassup, braw?"

Ceepak doesn't understand a word.

"Hand me your weapon, son."

"Ease up, braw!"

"Put it down. On the floor. Now."

The gun hand rushes up to cover his mouth. Up chucks some more puke. Beer and whisky? Mighty risky.

"Son?" Ceepak towers over the boy who's looking down and wiping vomit all over his shirt. The kid is also what we call a sloppy drunk. Maybe he should stick to doing Jell-O shots.

That's why I recognize him.

Saturday night. The Sand Bar. He's the underage asshole I wanted to bust.

"Mr. Sinclair?" Ceepak knows the kid, too. "We met Saturday night, remember?"

"Wassup, braw?"

The kid's eyeballs swim around, trying to find something in the room that isn't gyrating.

"I'm Officer John Ceepak. We talked when your girlfriend Ashley was kidnapped?"

"Hoochie-mama!"

"Hand me the pistol, Ben."

Ben waves the pistol like a wet flag.

"Man, if you don't stop buggin', I'm going to open a can on you!"

"Which machine did you tear it off?"

"I'll pop a cap, braw . . ."

"Not with that gun. It's plastic. A toy."

The kid looks down at his weapon. People peek out. Some laugh—the ones close enough to see Ceepak is right: The kid's deadly weapon was ripped off a video game. I see a cable curling out of the pistol grip.

"You'll find that most lethal weapons are made of metal," Ceepak says. "Plastic has a tendency to melt in high temperature situations such as that created when bullets exit a gun barrel. Friction."

The kid looks dumbfounded. Or maybe just dumb.

"Oh. Yeah," he says, flashing back to his prep school physics class. "Friction."

He drops his gun on the floor and, now that I hear it clatter, I know for certain it's a toy.

Ceepak figured it out earlier.

Back when it was dangerous to be wrong.

Ben Sinclair is our honorable mayor's son. This makes the Playland manager nervous. Not Ceepak.

Thirty minutes later, we're in the Arcade office with the six other cops who responded to the 10-34.

"We see no need to press charges," the manager says. He's about thirty years old and wears a tie tucked under the floppy collar of a short-sleeve polo shirt, which, if you ask me, never really looks all that classy. A metal change dispenser is clipped to the front of his belt.

"No harm done." The guy is studying the plastic pistol with the wire pigtailing out its butt. "We can repair the machine."

Somebody brings Ben a Sprite to help settle his stomach. It'll probably be another day before the smell of food, especially curly fries or funnel cakes, doesn't make him sick.

"When was the last time you talked with Ashley?" Ceepak asks Ben.

"This morning. After she bounced out of town."

"Where is she going?"

"I dunno. Someplace with her mom."

"And that upset you?"

"Naw. Take notes, fellas—I'm the pimp-daddy playa."

"Danny?"

I translate: "He has lots of girlfriends."

"So why the scene with the gun?" Ceepak asks. "You're the mayor's son. Surely you know better than to scare all these innocent people. . . ."

The way Ben Sinclair smirks? I think what he knows is that the *best* part of being the mayor's son is you get to roll around town doing whatever the hell you damn well feel like doing.

"That Ashley is wacked, dogg. Got all up in my face and punked me when I was representin' what be in my heart."

Ceepak just looks at me this time.

"She made fun of him when he tried being romantic. I think."

"She laughed, braw! Dat's cold. So I went out and got housed. Totally licked."

"After your telephone conversation with Ashley, you started drinking?" Ceepak says, now getting the hang of it.

"Yeah. I drank me some. I'll tell you true, braw. I'm gonna miss Ashley. Hottie like that don't come along every day."

"Like what?"

"You know. A hoochie."

Ceepak just stares. The kid can do his own damn translation.

"A sexy shawty."

Ceepak's still staring.

"A loose chick. You know—a girl who'll do anything you want. She'll let you get all up in it with her."

"You're saying Ashley Hart is promiscuous?"

"Fo' real, dogg. Girl is one hoochie-mama. That night she got kidnapped? She was all ready to get busy with me. . . ."

"Saturday? After her father was murdered, Ashley wanted to have sexual relations with you?"

"Fo' real, dogg. And she know how the deed be done, because she already stickin' it with some old dude. Told me so herself this one time. . . ."

Ceepak looks at the manager.

"You should leave."

"I can hang around. In case you guys need anything else. Maybe some more soft drinks?" The manager wants to hear the good stuff, the teenage girl having sex with older men stuff.

"Thank you for your assistance, but your customers need you more than we do."

"Not really. We have change-making machines on the floor. . . ."

"Adam?"

"On it. Sir?"

Adam Kiger, who's pretty big, gestures for the manager to get off his butt and head out the door. The doofus finally takes the hint.

"You want we should leave, too?" another one of our guys asks.

"Yeah. Thanks for the backup, guys. We're all good here."

"You two need anything, holler."

The Sea Haven cops? They dig Ceepak. I think they're hip to The Code. I think it's why they signed on to do what they do every day instead of becoming, oh, I don't know, video arcade managers.

Now it's just me and Ceepak and Ben.

Ceepak sits down.

"Who?"

"What?"

"You say Ashley admitted to having sexual relations with an older man?"

"Fo' real. She might just been jawsin', selling me woof tickets—"

"Lying," I translate before being asked.

"Fourth of July? Me and my peeps was kicking it on the beach and Ashley got all heavy, like she wanted to confide some down low secret. She axed me what I think if she be getting it on with somebody even older than my old man. Whoa, I say. I don't need to be hearin' that kind of nasty-ass detail. I mean, Ashley got a nice booty and all, but I don't need to get all up in her Kool-Aid, you know what I'm saying?"

I do. Ben liked making out with Ashley, feeling her up on the beach, getting his rocks off. But getting to know her? Listening to her problems? That required far too much effort.

"I told Ashley to ease up, dogg. W.T.M.I. Way too much information."

"So you don't know who the older man is?"

"Naw. But I know who the newer man was gonna be."

"Who?"

"Me, braw. She invited me on over to her crib for some, y'know, oral action. Saturday night. But then—she got kidnapped and all like that. . . ."

"I find it hard to believe that a girl like Ashley—."

"Ceepak?" I say.

"Yes?"

"Saturday night? I was at The Sand Bar. This guy was in there too. Doing Jell-O shots."

"Go on."

"He received a call on his cell phone."

"That's right. . . ." The kid finally has enough brain cells functioning to remember stuff.

"I heard him tell his friends he was, and I quote, 'late for a blow job.'"

Ceepak winces.

"That was Ashley! Why do you think I left my boys at the bar and raced all the way down to her place? I thought I was finally gonna get me a little somethin'-somethin'. She's a real chicken-head, braw."

Ceepak looks to me to translate one more time.

I wish I didn't know what the kid was saying.

"He's suggesting that Ashley enjoys performing oral sex acts."

The chief was right.

Sometimes the truth really can ruin your day.

FORTY

Ceepak radios for Jane Bright to join us at The Playland Arcade.

Jane spent a good deal of time with Ashley on Saturday morning. Ceepak wants Jane to ride into the city with us. He thinks when we get there, Ashley may need to talk to someone like Jane.

"Bring the photos," he tells her. "Right. Ashley in the sundress. From when we found her in the street. Thank you."

Ben Sinclair is nursing another Sprite, replenishing his fluids in an attempt to stop his brain from banging against the insides of his skull. I hope it doesn't work.

Mayor Sinclair is on his way over to, once again, rescue his son from the long arm of the law.

Ceepak looks at Sinclair and shakes his head.

"Wha—?" Ben asks, seeing the headshake.

I can tell he's had enough Ben Sinclair to last months. The kid disgusts him.

"Come on, Danny."

We head for the door.

"Hey, she's laughing at you too, you know." All of a sudden, Ben's dropped the whole gangsta act. He's just a whining, spoiled brat.

"Excuse me?" Ceepak says, one hand on the doorknob.

"This morning? On the phone? When she dumped me? She was all giggly and goofy and did like this nursery rhyme making fun of you guys, you pigs."

"You mean us 'bacon'?" Ceepak's a quick study. "What'd she say?"

"I dunno."

"Tell me. I'm extremely interested."

"Tough titty, po-po."

Ceepak slams the door shut, rattling the glass in all the windows — and this office has a whole wall of windows.

"*What the hell did she say?*"

I think he'll probably tell us what Ashley said now.

He probably won't call us pigs or po-po again, either.

"It was that Gingerbread Man deal . . . you know: 'run, run, fast as you can,' this is so lame. . . ."

"Finish it."

Ben shrugs.

"'Cops can't catch me, I'm with the I-I-A, man!'"

"What's the IIA?" Ceepak asks.

"I dunno." Ben sips his drink. "She's just wack."

"Think harder," Ceepak says. Ben looks at me.

"Time Crisis Three," I say. "The International Intelligence Agency. IIA."

"What's that?"

"It's a video game. I play it all the time. They have one here."

"Show me."

The first time I played Time Crisis Three was in the lobby of a multiplex movie theater while we were waiting for The Stupid Lame Comedy of the Week to start.

The game is huge. It has two video screens, both about as wide as a car door, set up inside these hulking black boxes. Two people can play at once. You get to pretend you're these good-guy super agents with the IIA, the International Intelligence Agency, and your job is to basically shoot as many of the bad guys as you can. The bad guys are these thugs who pop up all over the place—behind rocks and cargo crates, out of gopher holes and jeeps and this helicopter-type airplane—and you have to make them go boom before they do the same to you.

It's extremely cool.

And extremely violent.

We leave the manager's office and go to where two kids are blasting away at the doublewide screens. They're knocking down the enemy, racing through a clip of ammo strung across the screen in a bar graph of bullets.

Their time runs out.

The one on the left must've done pretty good. He gets to enter his initials in the game's flashing list of top scorers.

He'll be number ten.

Another high scorer occupies spots one through nine: H-A-H.

"Harriet," Ceepak says. "Ashley is her middle name. Harriet Ashley Hart."

Seeing the letters stacked on top of each other, running down the screen in a list (HAH, HAH, HAH), I can hear Ashley laughing at us.

Ceepak turns his back on the machine.

"This must be where they sent her for target practice."

I'm a little slow to follow, and my face shows it. He explains.

"Ashley is our shooter. This was her pistol range."

FORTY-ONE

We're driving up to the city.

Ceepak's riding shotgun, studying the Polaroids of Ashley in her blood-spattered sundress.

Jane Bright is in the back seat, gazing out the window.

I'm up front, wondering what kind of kid kills her own father.

We're on cruise control, doing 85 up the parkway. No sirens or lights, but no state trooper's going to pull over a speeding cop car, even if it is painted turquoise and pink.

I have plenty of time to wonder about the old guy messing around with Ashley. Who was it? Who would do that kind of stuff with a girl her age? I mean, is she even thirteen? Was it the chief? Did he have some kind of mommy–daughter three-way deal going on?

I look up into the rearview mirror and catch Jane's gaze.

"Officer Bright? Can I ask you a question?"

"Sure."

"If some old man was really forcing himself on Ashley, would she even be interested in doing anything with boys like Ben?"

"You mean would she be 'loose' like he claims? A hoochie-mama?"

"Yeah. Wouldn't she be sick of sex? Or even anybody, you know—touching her?"

"Many sexually abused children become promiscuous. It's how they've been taught to seek attention. If the abuse has been ongoing, it might be the only way the child knows to earn someone's love."

Anybody who does this kind of sick stuff to children? I'm starting to think Ceepak *should* be allowed to shoot them in dark hotel rooms with his sniper weapon system.

"It's why there were no palm prints on her side of the safety bar," Ceepak says to the stack of photos in his lap.

"Hunh?"

"At the Tilt-A-Whirl. There were no bloody prints on the safety bar. Remember the splatter pattern?"

"No" is probably the wrong answer, so I choose to remain silent.

"Like a flicked paint brush? But only on the bar in front of Mr. Hart. Nothing on Ashley's side."

Oh, yeah. That. Forgot about that.

All I really remember is the bucket of blood dripping down Ashley's face and dress.

"It's why she was so soaked," Ceepak says, reading my mind.

I glance over and see that he is re-enacting the shooting as best he can while riding in the front seat of a car. He puts his hands together and aims an imaginary pistol at the windshield.

"She was covered with blood because she stood in front of her father and fired a full clip. If she had been sitting next to him, as we initially chose to believe, only one side of her dress would have picked up the spray. The other side? It would have remained relatively clean."

He, of course, is right.

It's why the side panels next to the urinals in The Pancake Palace show rust marks spreading out like a cheese wedge. The pee hits the pot, some splashes out sideways, hits the metal wall like radiating sunbeams. If everyone turned around and peed directly against the divider, the floor would be wet and the whole wall would be rusty.

"And the time frame. . . ." Ceepak is shaking his head in the way that means he's kicking himself for not seeing something sooner. I'm starting to know his headshakes.

"I concentrated on how her mother was able to walk from the bank to the Tilt-A-Whirl so quickly. The question I should have asked? What took so long? Why did it take over half an hour for Ashley to run into the road seeking assistance?"

"She was waiting for something," Jane says from the back seat. "Or someone. Someone to tell her what to do next."

"It's a possibility," Ceepak says, tucking the photos back into their envelope. "She was also waiting for us. To be in position at The Pancake Palace. And then, we helped her destroy the most incriminating evidence."

"I cleaned up her face and hands," I say. "In the fudge shop. I grabbed towels and wiped away any trace of gunpowder with all that hydrogen peroxide."

"I bought her a new dress," Jane adds. "Threw the bloody one away. Helped her in the shower. . . ."

"I fell for it," Ceepak says, summing up the offense I guess we're all most guilty of.

399 Third Avenue. Pretty swanky address. Not the nicest apartment building in the city, but none too shabby. It looks sort of new, so it's probably wired for high-speed Internet, but the apartments will be cramped white boxes with tiny bedrooms and very few closets.

I see a plumbing van parked across the street. I figure that's the FBI. They just radioed us: Betty and Ashley are upstairs. The feds have been extremely decent about jurisdiction and turf wars. I think Morgan wants Ceepak to bust the bad guys because he saw how the bad guys tried to bust Ceepak.

We enter the lobby of the high-rise and show the doorman our badges. He lets us in without buzzing the tenants upstairs first, because that's what Ceepak tells him to do.

We take the elevator. My ears pop.

Usually I'm totally psyched when I visit the city. Usually we come to have some fun.

Not today.

"Officer Ceepak. What a pleasant surprise."

Betty Bell Hart greets us at the front door. I forgot what a good actress she is. She's dressed in a soft, bright yellow jogging suit—the kind nobody ever sweats in.

"We need to talk to you," Ceepak says. "You and Ashley."

"I really wish you would've telephoned first. We're rather busy at the moment. . . ."

"Packing?"

"No. We're planning a funeral. Reginald's family is flying in on Wednesday."

Ceepak moves into the living room.

"Let me call Chief Cosgrove," says Betty.

"You can't. He's been detained."

"Really? This wrongful death business? Isn't that *your* problem, Officer Ceepak?"

"The chief's caught up in it too."

"I see."

The apartment feels sunny. Betty, the retired meteorologist, has happy-face suns—clay, plastic, porcelain, Mexican—sitting on top of everything. The walls are cluttered with framed photos of her shaking hands with all the celebrities who waltzed through the Channel Five newsroom while she was Queen of the Small Screen, which is what the local *TV Times* magazine called her on its cover once. It's framed, hanging right next to the one of Betty hugging an astronaut—or somebody famous with really short hair.

There are no pictures of Ashley anywhere.

"Where's Ashley?" Ceepak asks. He's not looking for photos. He wants to see the girl he now knows shot Reginald Hart.

"In her room."

"This way?" Ceepak starts down the central hall.

"Yes, but Mr. Ceepak. . . ."

"I want to see *her* collection," Ceepak says.

"What collection?"

"The turtles? Remember?"

Betty looks like a newscaster who can't read her cue cards in the middle of a live broadcast. I see her mental wheels spinning, the gears grinding.

"Oh," she says, "we got rid of those."

"Really?" Ceepak is sticking his head into doors, looking at orange towels on the bathroom floor and dirty yellow dishes in the kitchen sink. "When'd you do that?"

"Last month."

"Who'd you give them to?"

"I'm not certain. Some charitable organization. Salvation Army. Goodwill. One of those. The doorman arranged it. . . ."

Ceepak digs his notebook out of his front pants pocket. "How about that turtle wallpaper?"

"Excuse me?"

"The wallpaper you had 'custom-made in Milan'?" he says, reading from his notes. "Did you rip that down and donate it, too?"

"No, of course not," she says, cool as a cucumber somebody popped in the freezer. "We painted over the wallpaper last fall."

"Uhm-hmmm."

Ceepak sees a door with a sparkly gold star surrounded by stickers of unicorns and cats and Disney princesses.

No turtles.

"She really isn't feeling well," Betty says. "This whole ordeal has finally taken its toll. . . ."

Ceepak knocks.

"Really, Officer Ceepak. . . ."

Ashley opens the door.

She's wearing the same bright yellow jogging suit her mother has on, only smaller.

She smiles, like she's delighted to see an old friend.

"Hello, Mr. Ceepak."

"Hello, Ashley."

"Thank you for doing your duty. Thank you for shooting Squeegee for us."

FORTY-TWO

"**A**shley? Be still!"

"Yes, Mother."

Ashley's hands instinctively go up to her head to block the blows that don't come. Not this time.

Ashley retreats to her bed, afraid to look anybody in the eye.

"I'm sorry, Mommy."

"Be quiet."

Ceepak pivots so he's facing Betty Bell Hart.

"I wonder if you'd leave us alone for a few minutes."

The woman rubs her hands together nervously like she's washing them with air.

"Chief Cosgrove told me you shot the homeless man. That you killed him."

When Ceepak does not reply, she takes this as an admission of guilt.

"Shall I call Robert? See how that's going for you? I'm sure you acted in self-defense. . . ."

"As I stated earlier, the chief has been unexpectedly detained."

"Is it the FBI? Are they involved?"

"Yes, ma'am. I guess you could say they are."

"I'm so sorry. For you. Your reputation. Your family. . . ." She shakes her head, as if in sad sympathy.

"I need to speak with Ashley," Ceepak says. "Alone."

This seems to irritate Betty.

"I don't mind, Mommy. . . ."

Betty puts a rigid finger to her lips. A silent warning.

"But I like Mr. Ceepak."

"No!" Betty's neck tightens. She glares at her daughter.

"He's nice, Mommy. . . ."

And Betty's nice and mad. In fact, all of a sudden, she's trembling mad. Her pancake makeup is cracking. Near her eyes I can see jagged lines that look like those high-pressure systems she used to draw on weather maps.

"Ma'am. . . ." Ceepak begins.

Betty cuts him off.

"What do you want? No. Don't tell me. I see it in your eyes. You men all want the same thing. You can't wait to be *alone* with my beautiful little girl, can you? Alone in her bedroom."

"Miss Bell, I assure you. . . ."

"Well, I won't let you. I am Ashley's guardian!"

"I know that, ma'am."

"But do you know what that means? I have to protect her. From men. Men like you!" Her voice is shrill, like steel wheels screeching to a stop.

Ceepak moves a step closer. He practically whispers.

"Ma'am—is someone molesting your daughter?"

She stares into Ceepak's eyes.

Then she smiles.

"Not anymore. We took care of that. The same way you took care of Squeegee."

Now she winks.

I'm not sure I follow but it looks like Ceepak does. I see sadness seeping into his eyes again.

Betty drifts toward the bed.

"I'm a good guardian, aren't I, Ashley?"

"Yes, Mommy. The best."

"Tell them."

"Mommy is my guardian angel."

"When Ashley was little? She called me her 'gardening' angel. Didn't you, dear?"

"Yes, Mommy."

Betty sits on the bed and lightly taps the mattress, commanding her daughter to come sit next to her. She hits us with her high beams. Her blazing weather girl smile.

"Isn't my daughter sweet? Pretty, too."

Ashley squirms. Betty pats Ashley's knee.

"That's why her father would not be denied," Betty says. "Oh no. There was absolutely no denying Mr. Reginald Hart. Not when he wanted something. But we could negotiate terms. Couldn't we, dear?"

"Yes, Mommy."

Oh man. I should've seen it. The older guy? It's her father.

Betty takes Ashley's hand and squeezes it tight. Too tight.

"Mommy?"

"Quiet!"

"Let go of her hand, ma'am."

"Of course, Officer Ceepak. Of course." She sniffs the air. "Do you like Ashley's perfume? Reginald certainly did. Drove him wild. I picked it out myself. At Victoria's Secret? Are you familiar with the scent?"

"I've smelled it before," says Ceepak.

"Smell triggers memory faster than any of our senses. Did you know that?"

"Yes, ma'am."

"Then you know if that bag lady, I believe her name is Gladys, yes, if Gladys were to ever smell a recently discharged sniper rifle, perhaps in court, why she'd remember everything she saw and heard at that hotel, wouldn't she?"

"I'm sure she would."

"So, Officer Ceepak—you and I are eternally linked. Tangled together in our twisted webs of vengeance."

"I can understand why you might think that."

"Would you like to know how and when when it started?"

"Mommy? We're never supposed to tell anybody."

"Oh, we can tell Officer Ceepak. He's on our side, now. He has to be after what he did. And these others? They're in it with him." Now she's smiling at Jane and me. "Destroying evidence? Helping Officer Ceepak hunt down an innocent man? Shame on you two. You're both part of a big, fat conspiracy and cover-up, aren't you? Well, you'll keep quiet. You have to. Don't they, Johnny?"

Ceepak doesn't say a word.

"Ashley, of course, acted in self-defense. Your friend Ceepak understands. He would have done the same thing. Officer Ceepak doesn't like men who fornicate with small children. No. Not after what that priest did to his little brother. That's why he killed Squeegee."

Ashley smiles prettily up at Ceepak.

"Thank you," she tells him again.

"Miss Bell? Why don't you explain it to Danny? Everything. I'm sure he'd like to know, to understand."

"Hmmm. Very clever. I see what you're up to, Johnny. Dragging your partner and this policewoman in deeper. Making them full accomplices. Smart. Very smart. Let's see . . . I should give you a little background. Would that be helpful young man?"

She's asking me. Smiling. Her teeth have all been capped. I can see metal rims. But that's not the only reason her grin reminds me of a mechanical witch from The Haunted Castle over on the boardwalk.

I say nothing, but I don't need to. She hesitates a moment then flashes a look to the guy she figures is her big-time co-conspirator: Ceepak.

Still beaming, still bright and sunny, Betty totally focuses on me.

"It all started when Ashley was three. . . ."

Great. Ceepak has pried open the door but all the sick-o stuff is going to come tumbling out on top of me.

"Reginald would crawl into Ashley's bed and start tickling her. Tickle Bug he called it. Then he'd rub up against her soft pajamaed bottom with his erection. Do you know what he said the first time I caught him? That he was having a dream. A dream that he was with me, not Ashley. I, of course, believed him. I believed him for far too long."

Yeah. I'd say so.

"Later, when I found the photographs—"

"He took photographs?" Jane is incredulous.

"Yes. Indeed. Of him and Ashley having intercourse. Ashley was four or five at the time. . . ."

"Four, Mommy. My birthday, remember?"

"Hush, honey. Mommy's talking. Yes. That's right. It was right after the party with all her little friends . . . I suppose the event aroused Reginald. . . ."

Ashley bows her head and stares at her hands.

"Why didn't you alert the proper authorities?" Jane asks.

Betty Bell stares at her like she's the silliest woman on earth.

"And whom might these proper authorities be? Someone Reginald did not already own? Some judge? Some police officer beyond his financial reach?"

"Yes, ma'am."

"Oh, grow up. Reggie knows people. The kind who burn down buildings. Who kill people. No. I could not alert anybody. I could, however, negotiate a deal. He and I would divorce and, if he wanted . . . certain visitation privileges. . . ."

Holy shit. She pimped her daughter.

". . . well, those would cost extra. Maybe a beach house and butler? A trip to Paris? If we wanted to ski in Vail? Why, Reggie could purchase an extra weekend with Ashley. And the will. I was insistent about his will. Ashley must receive everything he owned. Reginald agreed. It was only fair." She pats her daughter on the knee. "We were looking out for her future."

"Thank you, Mommy."

"Who am I?"

"You are my guardian angel."

The two sunny blondes beam at each other on the bed.

"If you and Mr. Hart had it all worked out," Ceepak says, "why'd you need to kill him?"

"Now *that* was not my fault. No, sir. You can blame that little matter on that bitch with the briefcase. She was the one — encouraging Reggie to re-write his will. Been nagging him about it for months. 'Oh, certainly,' she told him, 'leave your daughter something. But not *everything*.' As if a few million dollars would be adequate compensation. No. We couldn't let Ms. Stone do that to us. We simply could not."

"So you had Ashley shoot him."

"That's right."

Ashley tugs her mother's sleeve.

"Can we tell them how we did it, Mommy?"

"Of course, sweetheart. We're all in this together."

She looks at me this time.

"Aren't we, Danny?"

It dawns on me: I was another part of the chief's plan. I was the one who'd make sure Ceepak was always where they needed him to be.

"Yeah," I say. "I guess so."

We're all in this shit together pretty damn deep.

FORTY-THREE

"**D**id you actually believe Reginald Hart would be caught dead sitting in the Tilt-A-Whirl at a cheap seaside amusement park?" Betty says. "Oh. I guess he was. He was *caught dead*."

They giggle like sisters sharing a secret joke.

"That's funny, Mommy."

Betty loves having an audience hanging on her every word, even if those words are, basically, a murder confession.

"The two of them didn't go there because Reggie liked bending the rules! Or because Ashley had a turtle named Stinky!"

"Stinky!" Ashley giggles some more. "That's such a silly name for a turtle!"

"The whole Tilt-A-Whirl scenario was preposterous! But Chief Cosgrove knew the comings and goings of certain vagrants who frequented the spot and would provide us with a convenient scapegoat. Someone for Officer Ceepak to go shoot, thereby curtailing any investigation that might eventually lead to us."

"Mr. Ceepak?" Ashley's eyes look so innocent staring at her hero. "I'm sorry I lied to you."

"You did not lie!" Betty says sweetly. "Officer Ceepak simply chose to believe what you told him." She winks at him. "Bob told me you had a soft spot for children—especially children in any sort of danger."

Ceepak turns to Ashley.

"Tell me what happened that morning at the Tilt-A-Whirl."

"Can I, Mommy?"

"Yes dear. They need to know so they can help us keep it secret."

"Okay." Ashley smoothes out her pants like I've seen her mother smooth out a skirt. "I told Daddy that the Tilt-A-Whirl was where all the really cool kids went nowadays to make out. I told him I wouldn't do any of the stuff he wanted me to do, not in the beach house, anyway. Not with Ms. Stone staying in the guest cottage and all."

"Then what?"

"Let's see. We had to get up real, real early Saturday morning because we had to do everything before the beach got crowded and while you two were still eating pancakes. Ms. Stone dropped us off and we ran around to the beach and snuck in under the fence. I had my beach bag. . . ."

The bag we found with the cartoon monkey on it.

". . . 'cause that's where I had the gun. Uncle Bob got it for me."

"Chief Robert Cosgrove is Uncle Bob?" Ceepak asks.

"Yes. He and Mommy are dating. . . ."

"Ashley, sweetie, that's not correct. I've told you: We're simply two adults who enjoy each other's company."

"Anyway," Ashley moves on, "Mommy was late."

"Only a few minutes."

"She was supposed to pick up the gun from the little tunnel under the fence right after seven. . . ."

"But I had to be at the bank at seven . . . the time we scheduled for the actual shooting."

"Then she needed a ciggy-boo."

"Ashley?"

"You did!"

"Dear. Please."

"Sorry."

"Are you finished?"

"Yes, Mommy."

"I can tell my story?"

"I'm sorry."

Betty beams at us.

"Suffice it to say—I missed my cue . . . ever so slightly. . . ."

And dropped your ciggy-boo butt on the beach.

"But I got there, didn't I, sweetheart?"

"Yes, Mommy."

"It was my job to take the gun. If Ashley had a pistol tucked in her panties, why even *you* might have figured something was awry. Where are my cigarettes now, honey?"

"In the other room?"

"Be a sweetie. Fetch them for Mommy."

Ashley stands up. Ceepak motions for her to sit back down.

"Later."

"I'd really like a cigarette. . . ."

"Just finish walking us through it."

"Fine." She sighs. Smiles. She can flip a scowl into "say cheese" faster than anybody I've ever met.

"Ashley climbed over the chain-link fence at the entrance— something we practiced at the playground—ran up Ocean Avenue, and put on the performance of her life!"

"I'm a very good actress, aren't I?"

Ceepak nods. "One of the best I've ever seen."

"And this was way harder than *Our Town!* I had like so much stuff to memorize. . . ."

"Ashley? Why don't you give them a brief encore?"

Ashley stands up, takes a deep breath.

"My fa . . . fa . . . fa . . . ther! He killed my father! The crazy man. The crazy man!"

"She's good, isn't she? All right, dear. Sit back down. Thank you.

You, of course, can see why she won the drama competition at her school two years running!"

"You know what my favorite part was?" Ashley says, looking right at me. "The free fudge at Pudgy's!"

Mom shoots her a look.

"Fudge? No wonder you're so fat. Have you seen how big her bottom has become? Anyway, where were we? Oh, yes—Bob picked Ashley up in his chief's car and reminded her what Squeegee looked like. Showed her some photographs we had taken of the man. . . ."

"Later, I forgot about the beard," Ashley says. "About what kind it was. Uncle Bob helped me!"

"So did I. When I brought you down to the beach house. . . ."

Ceepak's had enough of the Betty Bell show. He wants to change the channel.

"Tell me about the kidnapping, Ashley."

"Can I, Mommy?"

"Yes, dear."

I can tell Betty hates sharing the spotlight. But ever the good Weather Gal, she realizes it's time to toss things over to the Sports Guy.

"Okay. Let's see. I climbed out of my window and all to make it look like, you know, I really was sneaking out to see Ben. I had to be real quiet. Uncle Bob was on the beach with his boat . . . but he was wearing these hiking boots with his swimsuit and that made him look so silly. I called Ben on my cell from the rowboat. . . ."

"What happened after the boat ride?" Ceepak asks.

"Uncle Bob took me to the train depot and I stayed in my room like Mommy told me to do."

"The baggage room?"

"Yes, sir."

"You stayed there all Saturday night and Sunday?"

"Yes, sir. It was kind of scary and I couldn't leave or make any noise or I'd ruin everything. I peed in my pants."

"Ashley? Really. Do we need to know that?"

"Sorry, Mommy."

"Must've been hard," Ceepak says. "Up there all alone."

"It was."

"We all made sacrifices," says her mother the martyr.

"Can I have my bracelets back?" Ashley asks shyly.

"The ones we found?"

"Yes. Uncle Bob made me drop them so you would find clues and stuff. Can I have those back? My daddy bought them for me. . . ."

"She doesn't want them," Betty says. "Throw them away. Burn them."

"Mommy?"

"We'll buy new bracelets. We're very rich now, remember?"

Ashley drops her head again.

"By the way. . . ." Betty lowers her voice. "Did Chief Cosgrove offer you three people any of our money? I don't really think you've done enough to warrant payment; however, if Bob made certain promises. . . ."

"What'd you do while you waited in the baggage room?" Ceepak asks Ashley.

"Nothing," Ashley mumbles.

"She ate candy bars and drank soda pop!" Her mother sounds very disappointed in her.

I hear the apartment door open.

I look down the hall and see Morgan and a couple of his guys.

Betty is watching me. "Who's that?"

"I think it's the cavalry."

She ignores me and goes to the door.

"Oh, god. Did they follow you here? Hush, Ashley!" Betty hisses. "Not another word."

"Yes, Mommy."

Ceepak calls out to Morgan.

"Hey!"

"Hey," the FBI agent answers. "We'll wait out here, in the foyer."

"Thanks."

"Officer Ceepak?" Betty is puzzled.

"Yes?"

"Do they know about you and Squeegee?"

"Yes, ma'am. They know I didn't shoot him."

"What?"

"I did not shoot Squeegee. By the way—his real name? It's Jerry Shapiro."

"You didn't shoot him?"

"No, ma'am. You see, I gave my word that I would not."

"So . . . ?"

"We're not in this together."

All of a sudden, there's this squeal of feedback.

"Sorry about that," Morgan calls from the foyer, adjusting the volume on the walkie-talkie clipped to his belt.

"No," Ceepak says. "My fault. I forgot to turn mine off."

I see a red light glowing on the walkie-talkie clipped to the back of Ceepak's belt.

So does Betty.

She understands now that Morgan and the FBI have heard everything.

"You son of a bitch. I'm going to call Cosgrove—"

"Chief Cosgrove can't help you any more," says Ceepak. "He's in jail."

"You goddamn son of a bitch!"

Ceepak ignores Betty. "Ashley, remember when I gave you my word? Said I would protect you?"

"Yes."

"I meant that. I'm going to take you away from your mother now—"

"No!"

"We'll take you someplace safe, okay, sweetie?"

"Get away!"

"Jane?" Ceepak says calmly. "Please take Ashley out of here."

Betty stretches her arms to her daughter, but Ceepak restrains her.

"Come on, honey," Jane encourages.

"No! I need to stay with Mommy. Stop!" Ashley kicks at Ceepak.

"Leave her alone!"

Jane reaches for Ashley.

"Come on, honey!" she repeats.

"No!" Ashley screams like I hope I never hear anybody ever scream again. "No! I want my mommy! I want her now!" Ashley is kicking and blubbering, her whole body shaking.

Ceepak loosens his grip. Betty loses her balance and falls to the bed. Ashley immediately curls up against her, her thumb in her mouth.

Betty is wailing into the bedspread.

Ashley twists her head back to face us, just as Morgan and his men enter from the hallway.

"Leave my mother alone," she hisses at Ceepak, "or I'll kill you, you son of a bitch! I'll kill you!"

He steps back.

Ashley grabs a stuffed animal. A pink lamb. She squeezes her hand tight around its neck and glares at Ceepak, then Jane, then Morgan, then me.

"I'll kill you all, you goddamn bastards!"

I think we just lost another child.

EPILOGUE

I'm not a lawyer, but I hope Ashley gets a good one. She needs to be locked up in a loony bin, not a juvenile detention center or whatever. But like I said, I'm not a lawyer.

The chief and Miss Betty Bell?

They're in custody and need very good lawyers.

Me? I'm thinking about becoming a cop full-time. Not that I'll ever be as good as Ceepak, but I think the world could use a few more guys trying to be half that decent.

Ceepak?

They rocked his world. Rocked it hard.

Defend the defenseless, do your sworn duty, look for the good in everything, and then boom—he turns over this rock and sees nothing underneath but worms.

But he's still on the job.

At least today.

We meet at The Pancake Palace at 8 A.M. Tuesday. Ceepak decided we've both earned an extra half hour of sleep.

Everybody in the place is pretty glum, barely pushing their pancakes around their plates, glued to their newspapers, reading how a little girl and her mother and the Sea Haven chief of police tried to dupe us all. Sent us for a ride on our own little Tilt-A-Whirl. You can hear a lot of stainless steel scraping against plates this morning. Not much else.

Ceepak's back to fruit and cereal.

I order the same thing. Figure I should at least try it. At least this once. We eat in silence.

Every now and then, the waitress comes over to pour us more coffee and that sloshing is the loudest sound in the dining room.

Maybe tomorrow will be better.

Maybe Springsteen is right.

Maybe faith will be rewarded.

Maybe tomorrow.

"You ready to roll?" Ceepak says when half his cereal is gone. Guess he's not so hungry this morning. Me neither.

"Yeah. Where to?"

"Wherever."

He's right. We are currently without a boss, since there's no chief of police on the job in Sea Haven. We can make up our own duty roster.

"How about we cruise up Beach Lane? It's busy this time of day...."

"That'll work."

We pay and head to the parking lot.

I wonder if Ceepak will stay in Sea Haven.

After all, he was sort of lured down here under false pretenses. It's not like he grew up here or has family here. His one friend? His old Army buddy? You know what they say about friends like that— they're total assholes.

We cruise up the road fronting the beach. I see people lugging all sorts of gear across the street and down to the sand.

"Pull 'em over."

I don't know who Ceepak is talking about.

"Pull 'em over."

He points to these two kids riding bicycles behind their father in the bike lane with the other bikers and joggers and early morning fast-walkers. The kids don't appear to be doing anything terribly illegal.

But I do as I'm told.

I whoop the siren once and give the lights up top a twirl.

The father looks over his shoulder and motions to his kids to stop.

I pull the Ford over to the curb.

The family straddles their bikes. Other people stop what they're doing to rubberneck. Ceepak and I climb out of the Explorer.

"Good morning," Ceepak says.

"Morning," the father says. "Is there some problem?"

"No, sir. It's all good."

He bends down to talk to a boy on a blue bike.

"What's your name?"

"Sam. Sam Morkal-Williams."

"And who are you, young lady?"

"Meghan Morkal-Williams."

"Do you like riding your bikes?"

"Yes . . ." the boy says, kind of quietly.

"How about you Meghan?"

"I love it!" She sort of shouts.

"Good," says Ceepak. "That's awesome. I see you're both wearing your helmets."

"Yes, sir," the boy says.

"We always wear them when we ride our bikes," the girl adds.

The father just sort of smiles, leans back on his bike seat, and raises up both hands as if to say, "Hey, they're my kids, of course they're perfect." He has on his helmet, too.

"Does your daddy wear his helmet all the time?"

"Yes, sir."

"Awesome. Well, then. Here you go."

Ceepak reaches into one of his many pockets and pulls out two slips of paper.

"These are for free ice cream cones. Because you know the law and you chose to obey it and that makes my job a whole lot easier. So this morning? I just wanted to say 'Thank you.'"

He hands them the ice-cream coupons. I wonder when he had time to buy them.

"Mister?"

"Yes, Sam?"

"Does dad get one? He's wearing his helmet, too."

"You're absolutely right. Fair's fair. Here you go, sir."

"That's okay," the father says.

"Sir, it is my pleasure."

The dad smiles and takes the ice-cream coupon. The people watching? They applaud.

"Danny?"

"Yes, sir."

We head back to the car.

"Know any good sandwich shops?" Ceepak asks when we open our doors.

"We just ate breakfast."

"Roger that. But I promised Mr. Jerry Shapiro I would bring him and Gladys a tomato, mozzarella, and basil on a baguette. One for each of them. And chips. He requested taro chips. Know any good vegetarian establishments?"

"There's The Good Earth, this veggie place on Ocean Avenue."

"Sounds like it'll work." He checks his watch. "Let's roll. I gave him my word."

"Yes, sir."

"Danny?"

"Yeah?"

"If you don't mind—let's switch sides. I feel like driving today."

"Roger that."

We do a quick Chinese Fire Drill routine around the Ford and change seats.

Ceepak drives okay. A little slow, but okay.

Watching him behind the wheel, I'm reminded of that song

Springsteen wrote for the New York City Fire Fighters after 9/11, the guys who went "Into the Fire" because they knew it was the right thing to do.

> May your strength give us strength
> May your faith give us faith
> May your hope give us hope
> May your love give us love

Like I said, some guys have a code they live by, some guys don't.

John Ceepak? He has a code.

Me?

I'm working on it.

BONUS CHAPTER

Don't miss **Mad Mouse**, the second book in the
John Ceepak series.

ONE

August 30th is National Toasted Marshmallow Day, so, naturally, we're celebrating.

Sure there's some debate: Is National Toasted Marshmallow Day August 14th or August 30th? We go with the 30th because it's closer to Labor Day. Besides, if you dig a little deeper, you'll discover that August 14th is also National Creamsicle Day, and we firmly believe Creamsicles deserve their own separate day of national recognition.

Five of my longtime buds and I are driving out to Tangerine Beach. Here in Sea Haven, New Jersey, the beaches get named after the streets they're closest to. On the way, we pass Buccaneer Bob's Bagels, Sea Shanty Shoes, and Moby Moo's Ice Cream Cove. In case you can't tell by the waterlogged names, this is your basic down-the-shore resort town: We live for July and August because our visitors go home in September and take their wallets with them.

I'm a part-time summer cop with the Sea Haven Police. That means I wear a navy blue cop cap and help elderly pedestrians navigate the crosswalks. This year I might go full time when summer's over, which is, basically, next week. They usually offer one part-timer a job at the end of the season. The chief gets to pick. We have a new one. We'll see. Anyhow, I put in my application.

Riding up front with me, twiddling her sparkly toes on the dashboard, is Katie Landry. She's a friend who I hope will soon become a "friend." Like the Molson billboard says: "Friends come over for dinner. *Friends* stay for breakfast." So far, Katie and me? We're just doing takeout. Mostly Burger King or Quiznos.

In the second row are Jess Garrett and Olivia Chibbs—a sleepy-eyed surfer dude and an African-American beauty queen slash brainiac. Jess and Olivia are already buttering toast and squeezing orange juice together. She comes home from college every summer to make money to cover the stuff her med school scholarships don't. Jess lives here full time. He paints houses when he's not busy goofing off.

Then there's Becca Adkinson and Harley Mook. Becca's folks run the Mussel Beach Motel, she helps. Mook (we all call him Mook) is short and tubby and loud. He's in the wayback, popping open a bag of Cheetos like it's a balloon. He's just in town for a week or two, which is fine. You can only take so much Mook. He's in grad school, working on his MBA.

According to Jess, that means "Me Big Asshole."

"Hey, Danny . . ." Mook hollers. "What's the biggest crime down here these days? Taffy snatching? Overinflated volleyballs?"

Mook's not funny but he's right: People typically come to our eighteen-mile strip of sand for old-fashioned fun in the sun. It's not the South Bronx. It's not even Newark. But Sea Haven *is* where I saw my first bullet-riddled body sprawled out on a Tilt-A-Whirl over at Sunnyside Playland. I remember that morning. It wasn't much fun.

"Traffic!" Becca says. "That's the worst!"

I'm driving because my current vehicle is a minivan with plenty of room for beer and gear. I bought the van "preowned," my mother being the previous owner. She sold it to me when she and my dad moved out to Arizona. It's a dry heat.

I'd say half the vehicles in front of me are also minivans, all loaded down with beach stuff. Bike racks off the backs, cargo carriers up top.

You can't see inside anybody's rear windows because the folding chairs and inflatable hippopotami are stacked too high. I have plenty of time to make these observations because our main drag, Ocean Avenue, is currently a four-lane parking lot.

"Take Kipper!" This from Mook. Now he's chugging out of a two-liter bottle of grape soda.

"Hello? He can't," says Becca. She points to the big No Left Turn sign.

"Chill, okay?" Katie teaches kindergarten so she knows how to talk to guys like Mook.

"For the love of God, man, take Kipper!" Now Mook's kneeling on the floor, begging me to hang a Louie. For the first time all day, he's actually kind of funny, so I go ahead and make the illegal left.

Oh—the streets in this part of town? They're named after fish. In alphabetical order. Only they couldn't find a fish that starts with a Q so Red Snapper comes right after Prawn.

As soon as I make the turn, a cop steps into the street and raises his palm.

And, of course, it's my partner. John Ceepak. He signals for me to pull over.

There's another cop with him. Buzz Baines. Our brand-new chief of police. Some people thought Ceepak should've taken the top job after what happened here in July. Ceepak wasn't one of them.

I'm not sure if Buzz is Baines's real name or if it's just what everybody calls him because he's really an Arnold or a Clarence or something. Anyhow, Buzz is the guy I hope will give me a full-time job next Tuesday. Today he's going to give me a ticket.

"Danny?" Ceepak is startled to see me behaving in such a criminal fashion.

"Hey."

Ceepak is a cop 24/7. He's 6'2" and a former MP. He still does jumping jacks and pushups—what he calls PT—every morning, like he's still in the army. He also has this code he lives by: "I will not lie, cheat or steal nor tolerate those who do." An illegal left turn? That's cheating. No question, I'm busted.

"Hey, Ceepak!" Becca sticks her head over my shoulder. She loves his muscles. Maybe this is why Becca and I don't date anymore: Where Ceepak's beefcake, I'm kind of angel food.

"Who we got here, John?" Baines hasn't recognized me yet.

"Auxiliary Officer Boyle."

I hear Becca sigh. Ceepak? He's handsome. Buzz Baines? He's handsomer, if that's a word. Sort of like a TV anchorman. You know what I mean, chiseled features with a lantern jaw and this little mustache over a toothpaste-commercial smile.

"Of course. Boyle. You and John cracked the Tilt-A-Whirl case."

"Roger that," says Ceepak. "Officer Boyle played a vital role in that investigation."

"Keep up the good work." Chief Baines winks at me. "And don't break any more laws."

"Yes, sir."

"Call me Buzz."

"Yes, sir. Buzz."

I hear Ceepak rip a citation sheet off his pad. It's all filled in.

"You're writing him up?" Baines asks.

"Yes, sir. The law is the law. It should be applied fairly, without fear or favoritism."

Baines nods.

"John, when you're right, you're right. Sorry, Danny. If you need help with the fifty bucks, come see me. We'll work out a payment schedule."

"Drive safely," says Ceepak.

"Right. See you tomorrow."

"No. Thursday's my day off."

"Oh, yeah. Mine, too."

Ceepak eyes our beer coolers. Marshmallows aren't the only things that get toasted at our annual beach party.

"Then have a cold one for me, partner."

"Roger that."

"But pace yourself. It takes a full hour for the effect of each beer to dissipate."

"Right. See you Friday."

"That'll work." Ceepak smiles. No hard feelings. He even snaps me a crisp "catch you later" salute.

I pull away from the curb, real, real slow. I can't see any signs but I assume 10 m.p.h. is below the posted speed limit.

I can't afford two fifty-dollar tickets in one day.

The late-night guy on the radio is saluting "The Summer of '96," reminding us what idiots we were back then.

"Tickle Me Elmo *was under every Christmas tree and Boyz II Men were climbing the charts with Mariah Carey . . .*"

Great.

He's going to make us listen to her warble like a bird that just sucked helium.

It's almost midnight. We're the only ones on the beach. Most of the houses beyond the dunes are dark because they're rented to families with kids who wake up at six A.M., watch a couple of cartoons, and are ready for their water wings and boogie boards around six fifteen. The parents need to go to bed early. They probably also need vodka.

I like the beach at night. The black sky blends in with the black ocean and the only way to tell the two apart is to remember that the one on top has the stars and the one below has the white lines of foam that look like soap suds leaking out from underneath a laundry room door.

Katie's sitting with the other girls around our tiny campfire, smooshing marshmallows and gooey Hershey bars between graham crackers. I bet she's the kind of kindergarten teacher who'd let you have s'mores in class on your birthday. She's that sweet, even though she grew up faster than any of us. Her parents died eight or nine years ago. Car wreck.

I need another beer.

I slog up the sand to the cooler. Mook and Jess are hanging there, probably talking baseball, about the only thing they still have in common. Mook wears this floppy old-man bucket hat he thinks makes him look cool. He has one hand jammed in the pocket of his shorts, the other wrapped around a long-neck bottle of Bud, his thumb acting like a bottle cap. The world is his frat house.

"Hey, Danny . . ." Mook shakes the Bud bottle. "Think fast."

He lifts his thumb and sprays me with beer. Now it looks like I just pissed my pants.

Mook's belly jiggles like a Jell-O shot, he's laughing so hard.

"Jesus, Mook." Jess says it for me.

I forgot about Mook's classic spray-you-in-the-crotch gag. One of his favorites. He also used to buy plastic dog poop at the Joke Joint on the boardwalk and stuff it in your hamburger bun when you weren't looking.

"Very mature, Mook." I wipe off my shorts.

"You're not going to arrest me, are you, Detective Danny?"

"No. I'll let you off with a warning. This time."

"You want a beer, Danny?" Jess fishes a long-neck out of the watery ice.

I check my watch.

"What's with the watch?" Mook saw me. "You're actually waiting an hour between brewskis? What a weenie! Your cop pal is a hardass. And that haircut! Who does he think he is? GI Joe?"

If Mook knew Ceepak like I do he'd realize: GI Joe probably plays with a Ceepak Action Figure. The guy's that good. I shake my head, ignore Mook, and mosey away with my beer.

Becca, Olivia, and Katie are sitting in short beach chairs, the kind that put your butt about two inches above the sand. I plop down with them.

"Someone please remind me why we hang out with Mook," I say.

Becca shrugs. "Because we always have?"

I guess that nails it.

On the radio, the deejay's yammering about *"Sea Haven's gigantic Labor Day Beach Party and Boogaloo BBQ. MTV will be broadcasting live. So will we . . ."*

They've been hyping this Labor Day deal all month. Come Monday, the beach will be so crowded, you'll be lucky to find enough sand to spread out a hand towel, maybe a washcloth.

"Here's another hot hit from the sizzling summer of '96!"

The radio throbs with "C'mon 'N Ride It (The Train)"--a bass-thumping dance tune from the Quad City DJs, the same people who gave the world "Whoot, There It Is." The choo-choo song was big in 1996, the summer The Marshmallow Crew first got together and somebody said, "You know what? We should do this again next summer!"

"Hey, let's dance!" Katie pops up, like she's ready to teach us all the hokey-pokey—the adults-only version.

The girls fling off flip-flops, kick up sand. Becca cranks up the volume on the radio, shimmies her blonde hair like she's in a shampoo commercial. I attempt to get my groove thing going. Basically, when I dance, I stand still and sway my hips back and forth. Tonight, I also "move my arm up and down" as the singer suggests. Lyrics like that are extremely helpful for those of us who are dance impaired.

"Hey, isn't dancing on the beach against the law?" Mook brays like an annoying ass. Actually, the herky-jerky moves he is currently making should be ruled illegal. "You gonna haul us off to jail, Danny? Get your picture in the paper again?"

Ceepak and I got some press back in July. The wire services and magazines picked up the Tilt-A-Whirl story. I was semifamous for about a week. On top of being obnoxious, Mook sounds jealous.

Fortunately, any thoughts of Harley Mook drift away when Katie sashays over to dance with me instead of the whole group. She opens up her arms, swings her hips, invites me to move closer.

Then I hear these pops.

Pop! Pop! Pop!

Like someone stomping on Dixie cups up on the street.

I'm hit.

My chest explodes in a big splotch of fluorescent yellow.

Katie's hands drop down and fly behind her. She must be hit, too.

Pop!

A paintball hits the radio and sends it backwards. The batteries tumble out. The music dies.

Pop! Snap! Pop!

We're all hit—splattered with this eerie yellow-green paint that shines like a cracked glow stick. My sternum stings where the paintball whacked me.

"Danny?" It's Becca. She sounds hurt. "Danny?"

She sinks to her knees and brings a hand up to cover her eye.

It's fluorescent yellow and red.

The paint is mixing with her blood.